COUNTDOWN

BOOKS BY SARA DRISCOLL

Echoes of Memory
Shadow Play

FBI K-9s

Lone Wolf
Before It's Too Late
Storm Rising
No Man's Land
Leave No Trace
Under Pressure
Still Waters
That Others May Live
Summit's Edge
Deadly Trade

NYPD Negotiators

Exit Strategy
Shot Caller
Lockdown
Terminal Impasse

COUNTDOWN

An NYPD Negotiators Novel

Sara Driscoll

kensingtonbooks.com

KENSINGTON BOOKS are published by

Kensington Publishing Corp.
900 Third Avenue
New York, NY 10022

All Kensington titles, imprints, and distributed lines are available at special quantity discounts for bulk purchases for sales promotion, premiums, fundraising, educational, or institutional use. Special book excerpts or customized printings can also be created to fit specific needs. For details, write or phone the office of the Kensington Sales Manager: Attn.: Sales Department. Kensington Publishing Corp., 900 Third Avenue, New York, NY 10022. Phone: 1-800-221-2647.

The K with book logo Reg. U.S. Pat. & TM Off

ISBN-13: 978-1-4967-5831-6 (ebook)
ISBN: 978-1-4967-5832-3

First Kensington Paperback Edition: May 2026

10 9 8 7 6 5 4 3 2 1

Printed in the United States of America

The authorized representative in the EU for product safety and compliance
Is eucomply OU, Parnu mnt 139b-14, Apt 123
Tallinn, Berlin 11317, hello@eucompliancepartner.com

To Olivia,

Welcome to the world, dearest one. Your family was beyond excited to meet you, and we very much look forward to sharing your adventures as you grow. Love you!

CHAPTER 1

GEMMA CAPELLO STEPPED OUT OF the biting winter wind and into the vestibule of the shuttered restaurant, expelling a relieved breath as warm air flowed over cheeks stung by the cold. She pulled off her gloves, folding them in half and tucking them into the pocket of her full-length coat, then paused, her hand on the long wood handle of the inner door as her heart rapped against her sternum.

She was back.

Was she ready?

You're ready. Get it together. One note of hesitation, and Garcia will kick your ass back to scribe, exactly where it belongs if you're second-guessing yourself. He gave you time to settle in. You're settled.

She took a deep breath, squared her shoulders, opened the door, and strode through the gap like she owned the place.

No one owned the place now.

Once a busy restaurant, the deserted space in front of her easily spanned two hundred feet. A long, burnished oak bar stretched down the middle of the room, its smooth run intermittently interrupted briefly by long, slender panels of electric-blue and bloodred stained glass inset into a decoratively capped panel of dark wood. Under the 150-year-old beam ceiling, a line of steampunk-style metal tubes and gauges ran the length of the bar. Metal barstools with blue leather cushions lined both sides, as if waiting for the next patron to pull up to the rail.

But the bottles were gone, the shelves and racks that once held glasses stood empty, and the wide-screen TVs hanging from the ceiling, which once likely displayed the menu or the latest sports match, were dark.

Abandoned.

Abandoned worked for the Hostage Negotiation Team as they needed a location close to their newest emergency. Since being on a boat in New York Harbor wasn't feasible or necessary, the historic Victorian structure on Pier A, which reached hundreds of feet into the harbor, worked perfectly. It was close, and, just as importantly, it was big enough to work as HNT incident headquarters, as well as a staging area out of the frigid winter weather for the NYPD's Apprehension Tactical Team—or A-Team—officers she knew would be arriving shortly.

Would Logan be among them?

It had only been a few weeks since she and Detective Sean Logan, out on their first official date on a rare joint night off, had the bad timing to pass through Grand Central Terminal in Midtown at the moment gunmen had taken control of the space, and had been held as part of a hostage group of fourteen individuals. Having watched two MTA cops in the Main Concourse die in the initial assault, Gemma and Logan had fiercely protected their real identities, knowing their lives would be immediately forfeit if they were discovered to be NYPD. Instead, Gemma had posed as a business negotiator and had offered herself to negotiate for the group with her own HNT colleagues, even as Logan's fellow A-Team officers had filled the windows around them.

She would have died that night three weeks ago had Logan not been willing to sacrifice himself to get to her. In fact, for a few minutes, she thought she'd lost him forever when she watched him fall under a hail of bullets. However, the vest he'd stolen from one of the other hostage takers had saved his life, so he could then save hers.

It had been a traumatic experience, but one that brought them closer together as a couple. They'd taken advantage of their department-stipulated recovery time immediately following the incident to do what they hadn't done fifteen years earlier: During their time at the academy, they'd briefly succumbed to their attraction for each other in one unforgettable night in

Logan's bed, but this time they purposely put their physical relationship on hold to get to know each other better.

For weeks they'd talked—over dinner, after a movie, while ice-skating in Bryant Park, or while strolling hand in hand through the Columbus Circle Winter Market—sharing details of their current lives, their families, their future hopes. They'd much too casually walked away from their feelings for each other as they left the academy to pursue their careers; now they were determined to explore whether they actually had a basis upon which to build a solid relationship.

If Logan was one of the A-Team members working this incident, it would be their first true test to show their superiors their personal relationship was entirely independent of their working relationship. Their relationship was known to the NYPD brass going straight through to Gemma's father, Tony Capello, chief of Special Operations, but was allowed because neither was in a command position over the other. In fact, they were at the same level, working side by side in separate capacities during an incident.

They'd proved in the past that their connection allowed them to work together on a different level from most negotiator-tactical pairings—they could shortcut directions to each other in a crisis, and read each other's moves ahead of time, allowing them to work seamlessly. Their teamwork had saved multiple lives in the past. In Gemma's opinion, their new connection would only allow them to work even better. And if his or her lieutenant didn't like any plan of action, they could order a change.

Gemma had been back at work for two weeks, but Garcia had been playing it safe with her, starting her in the scribe position, then moving her to coach. Finally, tonight was the first time since Grand Central Terminal she'd be sitting as primary, the negotiator whose role was to talk the hostage taker down. She understood his gradual reintegration—the primary held the lives of both the hostage taker and the hostages in their hands. Anything that might interfere with being attuned to the hostage taker and the active listening process required to deal with them—such as PTSD from being in the hostage position only a few weeks earlier—couldn't be allowed for fear of a hostage paying the ultimate price of a negotiator being off their game.

Her attention was attracted by a figure stepping into the open stretch of flooring that ran roughly east to west for the length of the massive restaurant. Seeing her, the man waved an arm over his head.

"Capello! Down here!"

Trevor McFarland—her closest colleague at the HNT, though one she hadn't worked with since Grand Central Terminal. He'd been the team member she'd "negotiated" with that night. He was also the one who always had her back and would give her the most confidence tonight.

Thanks, Garcia.

"Coming!" she called.

She strode to the other end of the restaurant, passing tables with benches or stools that lined the windows overlooking the night-darkened harbor. Once past the bar, glossy electric-blue tiles bordered the curving windows on her right, revealing the deserted kitchen beyond. Near the end of the restaurant, she reached a secondary bar area, located directly across from a small, glassed-in room of empty wine racks, the words *Private Wine Cellar* stenciled on one of the panels.

McFarland had selected a heavy wooden table next to the wine cellar that looked out through a large eight-paned window to the harbor beyond. He'd arranged four farmhouse spindle-back chairs around it.

"McFarland, good to see you."

Short and wiry, with dirty-blond hair and wearing a smudge-brown suit that surprisingly looked like it might actually fit him—a rarity—McFarland looked up from the equipment he was organizing at one end of the table and grinned. "Back at you." His gaze slid up to her forehead.

Gemma knew he was checking her only outward injury from that night three weeks before—a gash a little over an inch long at her hairline above her right eye, caused by exploding glass when a hostage lunged for an automatic weapon. But it was now healed—only the lightest line still showed, and she'd been assured that, given enough time, it would disappear entirely.

His gaze slipped down to meet hers. "You up for this?"

"Yes." Her tone held no hesitation.

McFarland gave her a single sharp nod. "Told Garcia you'd be fine."

"It's time."

"Told him that, too. Also told him I could step in if needed, but it wasn't going to be."

"No." Gemma paused for a moment, her gaze flicking to the equipment and then back up again. "Though it's good to know, just in case."

"Anytime."

"What's going on? All I got from Garcia was there's a hostage situation out on a boat in the harbor and to meet here."

"Details have been rolling in, but they're still a little scanty. Starting with their location." He turned and faced the window. "They're out there somewhere, but that's all we have so far."

Gemma turned to follow his gaze. It was a cold and windy night, but the sky was clear of clouds, with a few stars showing through the combined glow of the five boroughs. Atypically for this time on a winter night, the harbor was busy, with white, green, and red lights bobbing on the choppy water. "Are there usually this many boats out on New Year's Eve?"

"From what I understand, yes. Especially on a clear night like this. While it's breezy, it's not so bad it's going to make anyone seasick. But the harbor is one of the best places to see the fireworks they set off from the barge in front of Liberty Island."

"Totally unobstructed view."

"Yeah. Let me give you the rundown of what we know. Garcia knew I'd get here first, so he's had all info channeled to me to share with the group. Chen and Ramos are incoming, and we'll bring them up to speed as soon as they get here." McFarland sat down and opened the laptop he brought to every negotiation, woke it, then scrolled to the top of a document. "A call came through to 911 at 8:12 PM. A college kid..." His gaze scanned his document. "Noah Swift reported he was hidden belowdecks on a luxury yacht in the harbor. His aunt, Rae Swift, is the steward on the boat and runs the interior crew. They're throwing a big, glitzy party tonight and had to bring on extra crew to cover some of the shifts—servers, bartender, et cetera. He's a starving college student home for the Christmas break, so she had him come in to help the chef on the q.t. to earn some extra money to give him a boost. A multicourse dinner for twenty-five was served at seven o'clock, and dessert had gone in about ten minutes before a message came through from the owner, who wanted all staff in the dining room."

"Everyone?"

"Everyone."

"What about the captain?"

"Yup."

McFarland's arched eyebrow told Gemma he'd caught the same detail. "So no one would be in control of the boat? In New York Harbor? With all that traffic?"

"It appears so. The kid said the first officer came into the kitchen to tell everyone to go into the dining room. Instead of complying, the steward sent the kid belowdecks to stay out of sight because the owner didn't know he was part of the crew and she wasn't sure how he'd feel about the nepotism of her hiring her own nephew. Apparently, he's kind of an overbearing, touchy boss. Noah went to the bottom of the stairs, just off the kitchen, so he could hear what was going on. The captain was going to meet them there once the anchor was dropped. Apparently, he'd protested leaving the controls unattended, and the owner told him to do as ordered if he wanted to remain in command of *his* yacht."

"Pretty ballsy."

"You'll see why shortly. Anyway, the captain dropped anchor for what he believed would be at most a couple of minutes, but as the situation stands now, it could be hours. And for all we know, they could be smack in the middle of the transportation lanes of the channel."

Gemma stared out the window, at the lights out on the water. "Which means our clock is ticking faster than ever. Everyone on board is potentially at risk of a collision. But it's an idiotic thing for a hostage taker to do. He's on the boat with them. He's put himself at risk as well."

"We may be dealing with someone who hasn't thought the situation through clearly," McFarland stated. "Anyway, everyone but Noah went through as requested. Then shots were fired a few minutes later, which is likely why the owner pressured the captain to leave his post. He had a literal gun to his head."

"You said shots, plural. How many?"

"At least three. The kid is rattled, and he was down one level toward the front of the boat, and the party is one deck up toward the rear. He thinks he heard all the shots, but he's not sure. They also came in quick succession, so it might have been four."

"He's on a boat—any risk of the hull being breached and them taking on water?"

"He didn't say, but it's something to consider, depending on the type of bullet and how it penetrated. A hostage situation is bad enough. Adding in the stress of a boat taking on water would definitely make it worse. If we end up with people in the water, there's the additional risk of drowning or hypothermia if we can't get them out fast enough."

"One crisis at a time. Noah doesn't know if anyone was hit, I assume?"

"No. He was brave enough to creep up the stairs, closer to the living and dining areas on the main deck. He was behind a closed door but could hear yelling from where the party was. Specifically, a male voice telling everyone to sit down and shut up. He knew he was out of his league—one guy against someone with firepower—so he crept back belowdecks, hid in the laundry room, and called 911. Had he not called 911, we'd have no idea the incident had even occurred."

Gemma latched on to the salient point. "No one's reached out with demands."

"Not so far."

"The owner may not know Noah is on board, but obviously members of the interior crew do. His aunt, the chef, likely some of the pursers or servers. If they let it slip that he's on board—"

"It wouldn't go well. The hostage taker might threaten the crew, or threaten his aunt if he finds out about the familial relationship, to get Noah to join them. It could be another pressure point where someone could be killed."

"If the crew is smart, they'll realize he's their best chance to raise the alarm to bring help. You'd think they'd work to keep his presence a secret."

McFarland's expression conveyed his lack of confidence. "You know people sometimes act against their own best interests when they're under pressure."

"Oh, yeah. We'll have to see how that plays out. Step one for us, though, is identifying which boat is the center of this crisis."

"I don't think that will be as hard as we might have feared. We've determined the overbearing boss throwing the glitzy party is Lucas Horner. His superyacht is going to be the biggest boat out there."

"*Che cavolo*." Gemma sank down into the chair next to McFarland, shaking her head in disbelief. "That puts an entirely different spin on it."

"Yeah."

Everyone in the city—hell, likely in the country—had at least heard of Lucas Horner. Brash, arrogant, larger than life in every negative way possible as far as Gemma was concerned, he was well-known for taking lucrative chances on tech companies, lately focusing primarily on those interested in developing artificial general intelligence, or better, artificial super intelligence. So far, those risks had paid off in spades, giving the billionaire a more prominent platform and more money to invest in new technologies. He was infamous for not creating anything himself but for some extremely savvy business moves, which ranked him in the top ten venture capitalists worldwide.

"Suddenly it's clear why we didn't know," Gemma said. "The hostage taker doesn't need to make demands of *us*. The person they want to make demands of is literally sitting on the boat with them."

"I've already started a deep dive on Horner. Using his own AI, SagAIcity, to do it."

"SagAIcity? What does that even mean?"

"It's a play on words. Sagacity, but with AI in the middle. Means 'wisdom,' but with added AI."

"Shouldn't have picked a ten-dollar word. A lot of people won't know what it means. But will it help us?"

"Should gain us some time as long as it's not hallucinating and making stuff up."

"Hallucinations. Awesome." Gemma rolled her eyes. "Keeping your search in mind, we need to look at who he's pissed off in his career. Who he's ruined. That might lead us to our suspect."

"He's also widely known as a womanizer, one who doesn't care about the marital or partner status of the woman he's pursuing. There could be some ill will coming from that."

Gemma considered for a moment, then shook her head. "Could be, but that doesn't ring true for me. At least not in this scenario. A betrayed spouse might shoot him on the street, but to go to this extent? To me, this is someone who wants a payout, not just revenge for a relationship humiliation. But you're right. There might be a couple of superyachts in the harbor; however, his particular yacht should be easy to identify. I've seen pictures of it in the *Times*."

"The *Salacia*. It's huge, so it will likely be the largest boat out there. The Aviation Unit will be in the air shortly and will identify its location."

"Step two will then be making contact. But how do we do that? It's not like we can use a throw phone," Gemma said, referring to the cell phone the team would occasionally provide a hostage taker so they had a way to reach out to them to start the conversation. Without that conversation, hostages could die.

"I have all our usual communications equipment." He pointed at the standard unit they used for phone negotiations—the console that recorded all conversations with connections for the teams' headsets so everyone was a part of the negotiation. Instead of being set out on the table as normal, it was jammed under the window, four headsets stacked beside it. "But because no one has reached out with their demands, we don't have a number to call."

"Sure we do. We just don't know it yet."

McFarland leaned back in his chair and crossed his arms over his chest. "Come again?"

"Horner. Even if we don't know any of his party guests' identities at this point, we know he's on the boat. Someone must have his personal cell phone number. A man like that won't be without his phone. He wouldn't pick up initially, wouldn't have the freedom to, but repeated calls to it might open a channel to him and, through him, to the hostage taker. Another option is the kid's aunt. We have his number since he called in to 911. Are we willing to risk texting him to get her number? That would be at most a single alert, as opposed to the repeated ring of a phone. Or, hopefully, he has his phone on silent. We don't know that his aunt is carrying her phone—and she may not be because she's working this party—however, it's another option to consider."

"Here's another idea. I'll take a look at Horner's social media. He's known as a show-off and may have posted pics live as the party was getting started, maybe even tagging some of the guests. You know how social types like that like to have their posts amplified by others, and that's a surefire way to do it. That could build the guest list and generate more phone numbers, because depending on a single number isn't the best idea. And if anyone has posted themselves or has shared photos, then we know they have their phones with them. There must be some way to get through. If all else fails, Garcia said the Harbor Unit is going to drop us off a VHF—very high frequency—radio to use, if needed."

"VHF is what boats use to communicate with each other? If so, won't we then be making contact with every boat in the harbor?"

"Yes and yes."

"And can anyone listen in?"

"Also, yes."

"I don't like that. What if someone else thinks they should chime in? Egg the hostage taker on? Or belittle them? Or just as disastrous, think they can be the vigilante hero and try to save the hostages, potentially becoming a casualty or another hostage?"

"It's not optimum, but we may not have another workable option." He held up a hand before she continued to protest the idea. "Let's not make any plans until we find out what our options are. We can begin on one channel and then ask them to move to another, more private channel, but anyone who hears the request could follow us there as well. Better yet, try to get them to use a cell phone after the initial contact."

"Simply communicating that number could block it from us if others listening in call it." Gemma blew out a breath. "Sounds like our options have some challenges, but we'll figure it out as we go. What about recording the negotiation? Will the equipment they give us be able to do that?"

"I was going to put together a Raspberry Pi connected to the squelch pin on the data jack of the SDR, but apparently the unit they're giving us has an SD card that can capture fifty hours of radio traffic, so we're covered."

Gemma's remaining tension fizzled away under the comforting load of McFarland's technobabble. She didn't understand ninety percent of what he'd just said, but didn't need to because she knew he did. It was a reminder that teamwork made the HNT so successful. She wouldn't stumble because the team wouldn't let her.

They were back.

"You realize you don't make any sense to normal people, right?"

"I'm a normie." McFarland tried to look affronted, but his expression cracked into a grin seconds later. "Relatively, anyway."

"It's all relative." Gemma patted him on the shoulder. "So we have no information about the hostage taker?"

"None. The kid didn't recognize the voice. Not to mention, whoever it is isn't reaching out to us, and we can't reach out ourselves, at least not yet."

"We don't even know it's only one hostage taker," she said. "Noah heard one voice, but there could be additional suspects with guns on board."

Voices attracted Gemma's attention, and she looked up to find a group of A-Team officers coming through one of the side doors off the pier about twenty feet away. They were dressed in identical Emergency Service Unit—ESU—head-to-toe black winter gear of layered tactical thermal shirt, pants, and winter jacket.

Their tactical equipment completed their uniforms—each wore a helmet with a streaming camera clipped to the brim, a loaded duty belt, and a Kevlar vest jammed with extra magazines, while carrying a rifle in their gloved hands and a Glock 19 strapped to their right thigh.

The man leading the group didn't look in her direction, but Gemma easily identified him. She'd spent so much time lately watching Logan move, checking for any signs of pain as he'd healed, she could identify him simply from the way he entered the empty restaurant.

Three weeks before, he'd taken four rounds from a submachine gun to the chest and abdomen and had needed extra time to heal from his injuries. While none of the bullets had penetrated his Kevlar vest, the extraordinary damage done had been vividly clear in the wide, brutal bruising that had turned his flesh nearly every color of the rainbow. For the first few days, he'd been restricted to basic movements and shallow breathing to escape the agony of his badly bruised ribs. But he'd healed quickly, able to cautiously laugh again by the end of the first week and to ease into the kind of physical workouts required to stay in shape for his challenging role in the NYPD shortly after.

By two weeks after the incident, he'd been champing at the bit to get back to work and had finally come on duty immediately following Christmas. But his deployments for the past week had been less physically oriented. The fact he was here tonight meant his lieutenants felt he was back up to full activity.

Logan scanned the open space, looking first to his right, then his left, quickly finding her. Their eyes locked, one corner of his mouth quirking into a smile.

You got this.

Be careful.

He sent her a quick wink, and then his face smoothed into neutral lines as his name was called.

Gemma's gaze shot past him to the far end of the restaurant, where Lieutenant Cartwright strode toward them, a folder under his arm.

She must have made a sound, because McFarland chuckled. "I hear you. Thank God it's not Sanders."

"Am I that transparent?"

"To me, yeah. Because I feel the same way." McFarland's gaze stayed locked on the A-Team officers. "Logan's up to being on duty?"

"He's been back for a week now. And yeah, he's up to it. Nothing was broken. Just badly battered."

"That man has a horseshoe hanging over his head. So many things could have gone so much worse that night."

Gemma knew it, had the nightmares to prove it. Nightmares where the bullets flew but Logan had no vest. Where he had the vest but took a fatal head shot instead. Where he was a fraction of a second later and she'd taken a fifteen-bullets-per-second stream to the gut, lying in his arms as she bled out on the upper platform in Grand Central Madison.

"That's an understatement." More movement behind Cartwright drew Gemma's gaze. "Let's finish getting set up so we're ready when the rest of the team arrives. Then we can hit the ground running."

CHAPTER 2

CARTWRIGHT STOPPED BESIDE A TABLE about thirty feet from where the HNT was setting up. "Detective Logan, your men are ready?"

"Yes, sir."

"The Harbor Unit's sending a team from the Brooklyn launch, which will be here shortly. Let's get organized." He slapped the folder down on the wooden surface. "Gather around."

Logan scanned the faces around the table, taking in the four men and one woman who'd been trusted teammates on many deployments. They were a solid team, well trained and highly skilled, and he knew their thought processes almost as well as he knew his own. They were also extremely resourceful, which was a necessity—when you worked in tactical operations, out-of-the-box thinking was required nine times out of ten because you never knew the lengths some insane perp would go to. Rolling with the punches was what he and his team did.

Tonight, Cartwright had assembled a stellar group of detectives. Wilson was one of the senior members of the team, a man who'd seen it all and would keep his head no matter the situation. Johnson was the people person, the one who could connect with victims even while his hammer fell on the suspect. Turner, the lone woman on today's team and one of only a handful in the Emergency Service Unit's roughly three hundred officers, was often a crucial olive branch, especially for female or teenage suspects. Likely because of the scarcity of women in the ESU and the guys' tendency to turn it into an old boys' club, Turner always made sure to step in front of the men to make sure her voice was heard, an alternate point of view Logan always appreciated. Sims, a team leader in his own right, would be Logan's right-hand man on this incident, a solid, dependable officer, with more courage and logical thinking than anyone could ask for. Finally, Perez, the youngest team member with the least experience but with unbeatable technical skills and an incredible team spirit. A future team leader in the making.

They were a good team, a solid and successful team. A team to bolster Gemma.

It had only been a quick glance, but it was enough to see through her facade. She looked calm and put together, her dark eyes cool, and her shoulder-length curly hair clipped into a twist to keep it out of her eyes. She wore a navy blazer over a white turtleneck, and he knew from experience her shield would be clipped to the waistband of her matching pants.

But under her calm surface, he could see the jitters she'd shared only with him. She couldn't even share them with her close-knit family because too many of them were cops—her father being her commanding officer—and she wouldn't allow herself to be pulled from this assignment unless she was truly not ready. She thought she was, but that didn't mean this first time back in the saddle wouldn't carry some nerves. Nerves weren't necessarily bad—they could keep you sharp, keep you on your game. They'd both suffered trauma from their time as hostages, but Gemma's experience had been amplified when one of the three hostage takers had used her as a human shield while he planned his escape. Logan had interrupted those plans with a well-placed bullet.

Their roles in this emergency were different, just like how their trauma might affect them. As part of the tactical unit, Logan would be walking straight into a dangerous situation, but the sheer physicality of what they were about to attempt would be an outlet for any stress he might feel in his role of coming face-to-face with the hostage taker. Whereas Gemma, as the primary negotiator, needed to get into the hostage taker's head. It was a remote but high-stress situation where she essentially held the lives of every hostage in her hands. A wrong word from her, and everyone aboard might die. If she let any of the trauma from the incident three weeks ago color her judgment or interfere with the connection she needed to forge with the hostage taker, it was game over in so many ways. This was why Garcia had eased her back into leading the negotiation.

Logan had absolute faith she could handle both herself and the incident. He'd seen her manage some of the worst crises imaginable with a deft skill and patience he could never match. However, he would use his skills and those of his team to keep the tactical aspect of the incident from being an additional stressor for her.

Cartwright flipped open the folder and pulled out a stack of folded, legal-sized pages. "This is what we know so far. We have a hostage situation on a yacht in the harbor, the *Salacia*, owned by Lucas Horner." His gaze cut ruthlessly to Wilson when he muttered a colorful epithet. "Yes, *that* Lucas Horner. He was hosting a New Year's Eve dinner party. Noah Swift, a college student working without Horner's knowledge, hid belowdecks when the crew was called to the main deck dining room. Because he stayed behind, when everyone else got caught in the hostage situation, he stayed clear of it and could call for help. We have few details on the incident so far, but it's likely a safe assumption that Horner is the intended target."

"The man has more money than God," Turner commented. "If anyone can pull together a large ransom, it's him."

"That's our thought, but it's going to be up to the HNT to make contact with the boat to confirm." Cartwright arranged the four pieces of paper in order down the table so everyone could see. "Speaking of the HNT, McFarland started doing research on Horner while he was waiting for the teams to arrive. Based on Horner's social media postings, especially when he was bragging about the yacht when he first took possession, McFarland identified the make and model of the vessel and found the blueprints for it online. It's a two-hundred-foot superyacht, designed by Weaver Industries and berthed at the Chelsea Piers Marina. With what McFarland dug up, the NYPD contacted Weaver. Luckily, they're three hours behind us in Washington State, so we caught someone still in the office. They referred us to the CEO, Henry Sullivan, who confirmed the boat model but let us know Horner made some custom changes to the base design. Most won't matter to us. One will.

"Horner purchased the boat four years ago and took possession of it earlier this year. He upgraded a lot of the interior aspects and one exterior aspect." Cartwright tapped the third blueprint in the line. "Right here on the main deck. As you can see, the original design has this exposed space at the stern for outdoor dining and a small pool that leads down to the swim deck. Horner had them glass in the aft deck right up to the pool decking to allow for a larger living and dining area on the main deck."

"Makes sense for a boat in a northern climate." Logan leaned in to study the aft area of the main deck. "Based on these specs, that has to be where the hostages are. The top two decks are too small." He paused as he searched for the proper label. "The sun deck at the top is entirely exposed to the elements. The bridge deck below is about fifty percent enclosed, but two-thirds of that is the bridge, the captain's quarters, the foyer with a curving staircase and an elevator to move between decks, and a small kitchen. The rest of the internal space, the Skylounge"—he tapped an index finger over the sketch of a small table with four chairs and the adjacent couch, double wing chairs, and coffee table arrangement—"is too small for this kind of party."

"Too much of that deck is set aside for outdoor living," Sims said. "It could be where they planned on watching the fireworks at midnight, but not where they'd hang out for long periods of time at these temps. Unless the hostages have been split up and are being held in different locations on the boat by multiple hostage takers. I bet they're not. My money's on the hostages being together inside on the main deck."

"Lots of room there. Space for dining and lounging." Johnson looked up at Cartwright from where he bent over the table. "Do we have an idea of how many hostages we have? Or who they are?"

Cartwright waggled one hand in a so-so gesture. "Swift reported it was dinner for twenty-five, so that's likely Horner and twenty-four guests. As far as who they are, we don't have a list yet. We're looking for someone not on the boat who had an invite list. But the total count is in question because we don't have a handle on the boat's crew. Swift is only there as a temp and doesn't know the normal staffing situation."

"Looking at these drawings," Turner said, "twenty-five seems reasonable if you're doing a full sit-down meal. It doesn't have to be a big party. In fact, keeping it small and exclusive could raise its profile with the social set."

Cartwright pulled a pencil out of a pocket of his cargo pants and wrote *24 guests + Horner* in the open space of the main deck lounge, writing *crew?* underneath. "From Weaver, we know the superyacht normally staffs and sleeps a crew of twelve." He opened the folder and pulled out a single piece of paper. "Sullivan said Horner told him he wanted rooms for this crew: captain, first officer, chief steward, chef, bosun, and chief engineer, as well as two deckhands and two technicians. He also has a spa therapist and a personal trainer, but that's likely for longer excursions, and it's doubtful they'd be included on this little jaunt. But Swift said they had extra staff specifically for the party, which is how Swift got on board without anyone noticing, because there were a bunch of new people."

"Any chance he'd know new people from old?" Sims asked.

"Only by uniform. Catering staff are in black pants, white shirt. Boat crew is white and white. And he doesn't know any of the catering staff personally."

"That would be the way for someone with an agenda to get on board," Logan stated. "You have to assume Horner knows all his guests—"

"Unless they brought a plus-one he hasn't met," Sims interjected.

"Point taken. He had to assume that whoever is brought on board by someone he trusts enough to sit down at a table with can also be trusted. Same with his staff. But his one-off party hires? His type would leave that job to one of his existing staff."

"That would be the job of his chief steward," Perez said. "They're in charge of managing the entire inside staff, which would include hiring on additional staff for big events." When six pairs of eyes fixed on him, he shrugged. "My girlfriend loves *Below Deck*, and I've been forced to watch an episode or two...or forty...with her."

Wilson elbowed Johnson. “Good to know we have a luxury yacht expert with us.”

Perez rolled his eyes as Johnson snickered.

Cartwright carried on, ignoring the antics. All ESU officers used humor to manage the stresses of their high-intensity jobs, so it was par for the course. “Let’s say we have twenty-five at the party, including Horner and possibly his own plus-one. Ten regular staff puts us at thirty-five.” He pinned Perez with a pointed look. “Does your viewing experience tell us how many people they’d bring on to have a party on the boat?”

“Maybe six? A sous-chef, a bartender, and then maybe four servers to supplement the existing internal crew?”

Cartwright wrote *10*, then *6* on the plans. “That makes a possible total of forty-one hostages. We’re going to take a two-pronged approach. Normally, HNT would do its thing and we’d position ourselves for a possible incursion but then wait until the time is right to take action. We don’t have that luxury this time. If things go to hell, there won’t be time to ferry you out there in time to save lives. You need to be there already. Once the Aviation Unit identifies the location of the yacht, the Harbor Unit is going to take you out. You’re going to board the vessel but then try to hold back, if possible, allowing the HNT to work on a peaceful resolution.”

“We could make it all go to hell if the hostage taker or takers figure out we’re on board,” said Turner. “Immediate threat to the hostages would be the obvious way to keep us out or get us off the boat.”

“Which is why you’re going to get on undetected.” Cartwright’s flat tone said he expected nothing less.

“What’s the Harbor Unit’s plan for getting us out there quietly?” Johnson asked. “If they can’t do that, it’s all over, then and there.”

“I spoke to Inspector Kate Egan just before coming in. She’s arranging for her team to bring in a RIB—a rigid-hulled inflatable boat. Stealth trumps speed in this case, so they’re taking the time to swap out their regular gas motor for an electric motor. They don’t have the same speed capabilities, but they’re nearly silent.”

“That boat is going to keep us low in the water.” Logan’s gaze slid to the window, to the bobbing lights out in the harbor with the Statue of

Liberty, brilliantly lit from below, standing tall over all. "Lots of traffic out there tonight as people jockey for position to watch the fireworks. They're in place early, which will give us cover. And it's not quiet out there. You can hear people partying across the water. More cover."

"Every little bit helps," Sims said.

"What's the plan to board?"

Logan studied the side-view sketch of the entire yacht. It showed the three above-water decks, starting with the smallest sun deck, then the larger bridge deck and the even larger main deck. The bow of the boat rose high in the water to the bridge deck, the anchor pulled in high near the front of the yacht, while the stern section of the main deck dropped low to near water level.

Perez tapped a small inset door in the side wall of the main deck. "This must be the normal way to board when they're tied up at the dock—a gangway up to the main deck leading into the foyer. But the other normal way to board the boat is via the swim platform at the stern."

As a group, they leaned in to study the stern of the yacht.

Logan quickly decided the swim platform, while the easiest point of entry, wouldn't work. He scanned the plans, his gaze darting from the yacht profile sketch to the main deck plan.

Maybe…

"The swim platform's a possibility," Wilson stated, breaking into Logan's thoughts, "but I don't like it. The platform is at water level, so easy access, but it's essentially a dead end unless you want to announce your presence to everyone in the living and dining area twenty feet away. The only steps lead up to the main deck proper. Once you're there, there's a hidden flight leading down to the tender garage, but that's *way* too close to the hostages. Even if they had the windows completely covered—and I'd be surprised if they didn't, or else they'd be an easy sniper shot—even as quiet as we are, they'd hear something."

"I have a better idea," Logan interjected. "I agree, the swim platform is too easy, too obvious, and potentially too exposed. If they're expecting an incursion, that's the direction they'll watch. So we go the other way." He tapped a section of the yacht in the front quarter of the ship.

"You want to board up front?" Johnson asked.

"Not exactly. Look at this profile sketch. See this cutout section? Now look down here." He indicated a section off the owner's stateroom on the main deck, a recessed section of deck, inset into the line of the hull. "That's a private balcony off Horner's bedroom. It's only about fifteen feet above the waterline, not thirty feet above, like the bow. From the RIB itself, it's likely only twelve or thirteen feet, and we can cover that distance pretty quietly with a boarding ladder. Full-height windows and a glass door lead into the stateroom; if it's locked, we can cut the glass for a silent entry. It's about forty-five feet from the living and dining area, separated by the door to the stateroom, the door to the owner's study, and then the door to the main foyer."

Logan looked up to meet Cartwright's eyes. "We go this way, and we stick to the front section of the yacht, leaving a buffer zone between us and the hostage taker, until we need to breach it. We can do that in seconds. But until we do, we have access to not only the main staircase for the guests but also the crew staircases, which lead to the area belowdecks. Where's Swift hiding?"

"Laundry room." Cartwright tapped the labeled laundry room on the hull deck twice.

Turner nodded in approval. "Smart. He probably thought if anyone came looking for him, they'd search the main mess and the sleeping areas, leaving out areas like the laundry. Plus, the laundry might give him places to hide. We need to get him out."

"We could do that while"—Logan caught himself about to say *Gem*—"Capello negotiates. Then we won't have to worry about him if everything goes to hell. He can stay out in the RIB with the Harbor boys."

"I like it," Cartwright said. "It should get you on safely, without announcing yourselves, and will let you get the kid off while you stage for a potential incursion."

"Here's something to keep in mind as well." Johnson pointed first to the bow of the boat on the main deck plan and then the stern on the hull deck plan. "This yacht is large enough to have its own smaller tender and water toys, in this case two jet skis. However the hostage taker got on the boat, he could get off via any of those smaller vessels."

"A jet ski would be a distinct advantage in these waters," Wilson said. "Cold as hell unless they have a wet suit, though they could put up with that in the short term. But a jet ski could navigate a crowded harbor much faster than even a small boat like a RIB. If the hostage taker gets to a jet ski, we could lose them."

"They'd have to figure out how to get a jet ski off the boat." Turner's tone was skeptical. "It's a fancy yacht; there will be a fancy mechanical way to do it, but if he can't work or access the controls, those slick water toys will be useless to him."

"Valid point," Cartwright said. "Here on the bridge deck, the plans include a telescoping davit, so that's the crane they'd use to move the jet skis in and out of the water. We don't know how familiar the hostage taker is with marine equipment."

"He wouldn't necessarily need to be," Logan stated. "He has the entire deck crew under threat to help him." He pulled back his cuff to reveal a black watch, large digital numbers displaying the time on its face. "We need to get moving. When do we expect the RIB?"

"Let me check with Egan and confirm they're carrying the boarding ladder. They know generally what we intend to do, even if not the exact plan, so they should have it, but I'll double-check. Get organized." Cartwright stepped ten feet away and pulled out his phone.

Logan met the expectant gazes of each of his team members. "As soon as the RIB is here, we're going to move out. We don't know what kind of window of time we have for this incident. With no call, we have to assume no window at all. Let's get our roles and equipment organized so the second it gets here, we're a go."

CHAPTER 3

GEMMA CHECKED HER WATCH FOR the third time in under five minutes. "When are we expecting the Harbor Unit?"

"Anytime." McFarland's voice was calm, but his gaze flicked toward the window again, belying his impatience. So much of their job was hurry up and wait, they were accustomed to long stretches of time when the ball was in someone else's court, but that didn't mean they liked it. "Remember, a lot of them are already patrolling the harbor. They may have had to pull in off-duty officers. It's like the Fourth of July again out there."

"If they're on the water, they may find the *Salacia* sooner than the Aviation Unit."

"If they do, they know to keep their distance. This has to be dealt with very carefully." McFarland looked down the restaurant toward the A-Team. "Here comes Logan. He might be able to fill us in."

Gemma turned to find Logan striding toward them, one gloved hand securely gripping his M4A1 rifle on a single-point sling, the barrel pointed at the floor.

"Got an update for us?" McFarland asked.

"We're in a holding pattern. As soon as the Aviation Unit nails down the yacht's location and the Harbor Unit arrives, we'll head out. We'll board the yacht using the balcony on the main deck level to enter via Horner's stateroom. That will give us access to the front half of the boat while still separated from the hostages, who we think are in the rear half of the main deck level."

"I'll see what I can do to confirm that for you," Gemma said. "Will you be able to get Noah Swift out?"

"Unless we have to move on the hostage taker, we'll get Swift out and onto the RIB first so he's out of any line of fire. It'll be cold, but cold is better than dead." Logan extended two throat mics with attached earpieces. "Cartwright will command from here and can work with the HNT, but if you need to contact me or the team directly, or if you learn something you don't want to pass along the chain because of the type of message or because of time, either of you can use the radio. I may not be able to respond with anything more than radio clicks, but you can get more complex information directly to me. It will also allow you to keep up with our operation in real time. We'll be radio silent as long as he doesn't know we're on board, but once he does, and things start to move, we'll be using the radio and you can follow along. If it goes to hell on our end, you can try to talk the hostage taker down, knowing the situation."

"Good idea, thanks." McFarland took the equipment and set it on the table.

"Are you ready to reach out?"

"Not quite. We're also waiting on the Harbor Unit as our backup," Gemma said. "Calling a known cell phone would be the best way to handle this privately, but if that's not possible, I want to take a page out of the playbook we used at Rikers Island—we'll try contacting them via the VHF radio the Harbor Unit is bringing us. That gives us the freedom to talk to them without them needing to answer a phone."

"Aren't you talking to every boat in the harbor that way?"

"That's a definite downside, but we may have to take that chance if we have no other way of making contact short of you walking into that room on the yacht. If we have to manage it via the radio, we'll work on first opening channels of communication, then bringing it down to just us via a cell phone. If we can't make contact with them in any way, we'll have no choice but incursion." Gemma met Logan's gaze head-on. "Hostages could die. You and your teammates could die. It's not the best strategy." When he started to protest, she cut him off. "I have faith in you and your team. In your skills and your smart strategy. I'm not saying you're not competent."

"Shit happens," McFarland stated.

Gemma leveled an index finger at McFarland while keeping her gaze on Logan. "That. Right there. We don't know who we're dealing with, how many hostage takers we have, and what firepower is in play. So let's keep that from happening."

"Always the goal." Logan threw a quick look over his shoulder to where the A-Team officers stood around the table, at ease, clearly still waiting. "Can I grab a quick word?"

Gemma glanced at McFarland, who pointed toward the back of the restaurant. "There's an empty space back there leading out to another set of doors," he said. "We're in a holding pattern, too, for now. Take a minute. I'm going back to my research but will yell if you're needed."

"Thanks."

McFarland gave them a nod and slid the throat mics along the table to sit in front of their chairs.

Gemma led the way past the wine cellar and toward the double glass doors that exited onto the eastward end of Pier A. She stepped toward the window just to the south, tucking them out of sight behind the bulk of the wine cellar, providing a modicum of privacy. Out the tall window, lights flickered in the darkness of the harbor beyond, testifying to the heavy boat traffic. Nearly two miles away, Lady Liberty kept watch over her harbor, a glowing green beacon of hope and welcome for almost a century and a half.

Somewhere out there, people were in trouble.

"You're ready for this." Logan kept his voice low, but his statement was backed by confidence. "You know that, right?"

She nodded. "I know what I'm doing. And McFarland is with me if I screw up, but that's not going to happen. I'm steady." She looked up and gave him a half smile as she grasped his free hand, the nylon and silicone of his tactical glove contrasting textures of smooth and grip under her touch. "This is weird."

Logan's low laugh was amused. "You and me juggling our personal and professional lives?"

"Yeah. First op together as a couple. Doesn't it feel weird?"

His grin answered before his words. "Not to me. I like it. We work well together. This should only make it stronger." The grin faded. "Remember what we talked about. We don't protect each other, because it will hold us back. As soon as this op starts for real, it's strictly work mode. Nothing changes."

"I know. We got this."

"Damn straight. One other thing I didn't say out there you can let your team know about—keep your on-shift phone handy. The kid has a cell signal out there, so that's an alternate communication system for us. If there's something I need you to know for the negotiation but I can't talk because we're still undetected, the gloves are touch screen compatible, so I'll text you. Be sure to reply, even just a '10-4' to let me know you received it. I'll do the same for Cartwright to keep him in the loop, if needed. Obviously, if things go to hell and the shooting starts, I'll be using the radio directly because there won't be any reason to stay silent. And my hands will be full."

"Understood. Before we get into work mode…I want you to be careful out there. Just getting out to the yacht in these temps in that little boat over choppy water, that's a challenge all in itself. Then once you're out there…" Logan's pointed look under raised eyebrows made Gemma grind to a halt. "See? Weird. I need to learn how to compartmentalize better."

"You. The woman who lived through being a hostage when she was ten and who voluntarily puts herself into the head of every hostage taker she negotiates with? You're the queen of compartmentalization." His lips quirked into a sly smile. "You know, it's pretty hot watching you bend a negotiation to your advantage."

She knew he was purposefully blurring the line between professional and personal to buffer his statement about her experience as a child, an experience that included her mother being murdered by one of the hostage takers right before her eyes. But his words also pushed at her growing desire to tear down the roadblocks to a physical relationship they'd set for themselves so they could explore a deeper connection. They'd already had a few moments where things nearly got away from them—once at his apartment, once at hers—but each time, one of them had stopped them from going too far. Finally, she was ready to make that move, and she suspected he felt the same way. They'd set aside the time they'd wanted to take it slow, to make sure it was more than just hormones—and trauma—pushing them together. She was now ready for the next step as long as he was. They both understood they'd only move forward when they were in agreement on the timing.

But for now, she could play along. "Then prepare to get scorched." She gave him a wink and squeezed his hand before releasing it. "We need to get back to it. The Harbor boys will be here shortly, and then we need to get in the zone." She met his gaze, held it, wanting to go up on tiptoe to kiss him, to wish him luck, to advise him to temper his tendency to be a hotshot, to have one last moment of contact with him before he led his team on a dangerous mission. But she was a detective on duty, just as he was, and it wasn't the time or place.

However, a few words, as taught to them by one of their academy instructors, would convey all that to him. And more. "Head up."

"Eyes open." His response was immediate. *Message received.*

Together, they walked into the hustle and bustle and silently separated to join their teams.

It was enough.

They'd each heard what the other hadn't said out loud.

CHAPTER 4

THE HOSTAGE NEGOTIATION TEAM WAS assembled.

Gemma sat by the window, facing west down the long run of the abandoned restaurant, allowing her to keep an eye on the personnel coming and going during the incident. Just to her right sat the large digital clock McFarland carted around with all his gear, the timepiece with large glowing red numbers that would rule their lives for the rest of this incident.

McFarland sat to her left, the telephone equipment now centered in front of him, with four sets of headphones spidering out of the boxy recording unit. Especially when they were in a location shared with other units, headphones for each member so everyone could clearly hear the phone call was a necessity, though only Gemma was mic'd.

Each member of the team had a yellow legal pad and pen, ready to make notes during the negotiations, though McFarland also had his ever-present laptop in front of him beside his pad and pen. Never one to let a research moment get away from him, he tended to research on the fly during a negotiation. A full set of blueprints for the *Salacia* was spread out in the middle of the table where everyone could see.

Each of them also had their department-issued cell phone on the table. Personal cell phone use for investigations was banned, and each NYPD officer was given a secure cell phone for access to the NYPD's systems through the department's VPN, allowing them to discuss cases virtually, email reports and images, access NYPD and State Police databases, and run specialized applications.

Gemma was the primary negotiator, but she had a dependable team around her. McFarland would take the role of coach, the member of the team who was the primary negotiator's main support, someone to make suggestions, to listen to the conversation with fresh ears and, because he wasn't spending as much attention on forming a bond with the hostage taker, sometimes to be the one to hear nuances the primary might miss. Gemma and McFarland had worked many negotiations together, in either position of primary or coach for each other, and they had a good rhythm and understanding of the other's mindset to be able to fill in some of the other's blanks. When Gemma was in the hostage group and "negotiating" for their release, their connection was why Garcia had put McFarland on the other end of the call—to read between the lines.

Currently McFarland was madly searching through Instagram, and Gemma had seen a number of party photos flash past. The yellow pad at his elbow had a short list of names, and he kept opening new tabs in his browser with each new addition. Gemma would give him another minute before pushing him to share his knowledge since it appeared he was making progress.

Across the table from Gemma sat Jimmy Chen, whose appearance was a sharp contrast to McFarland. Where McFarland consistently looked like he got dressed in the dark and didn't own a hairbrush, Chen was always neatly and conservatively dressed with his dead-straight black hair neatly trimmed. Today he wore a dark suit, white shirt, and a rich burgundy tie. Though an experienced detective, he remained one of the newest members on the HNT, but Gemma liked working with him because he had an ability to make connections with suspects, especially those who didn't fall into the classic white male stereotype. He talked the least, preferring to listen, to weigh his response, but everyone knew to pay attention when he shared an opinion about a hostage taker. Chen held the post of scribe for this negotiation, the one to record the conversation verbatim. The recording equipment would capture the negotiation, but when it came to needing to recall part of the conversation at a moment's notice, the scribe's notes could be easily scanned and used to refresh the negotiator or their team.

Beside Chen sat Ángela Ramos, wearing a soft sand-toned cowl-neck sweater under a blazer the color of red clay. Of Afro-Latino background, she kept her long, wavy dark hair, shot through with only a few strands of gray, contained in a low coil at the nape of her neck. Long past her twenty-year service requirement for retirement, she was one of the senior members of the HNT. Unlike most officers who did their twelve years of service first as a patrol officer, then a detective in other units of the NYPD before joining the HNT, Ramos had worked a full twenty-two years as part of the Special Victims Division before deciding she'd done enough reactive police work, and it was time to do some proactive work for a change. Time to stop the crime before a victim was traumatized for life or that life was ended.

Tonight, Ramos stood as the coordinator, the team member who worked with all the other involved aspects of the NYPD operation to ensure the incident progressed smoothly and the negotiator was left to concentrate on their connection to the hostage taker. She excelled at that position because she was a detail-oriented cop and could juggle all aspects of the incident brought in by different units.

McFarland picked up his throat mic, settled it into place around his neck, and slipped the earpiece into his left ear. "Put your throat mic on but leave off the earpiece and let me monitor the A-Team for now. I'll let you know if you need to tune in if you're free to do so."

"Thanks." Gemma glanced at the gathered A-Team detectives who bent over blueprints spread across the table farther down the restaurant. Knowing that team, they were committing the plans to memory to be able to cover the ship to clear it of hostage takers or any guest or crew member who might have been missed in the original collection. "Harbor's not here yet, so no traffic so far anyway." Her gaze shifted to Ramos. "Any update there?"

Ramos checked her phone. "They should be here in about ten. I get why the A-Team needs them, but what are we waiting for?"

"We don't have a phone number to call anyone directly," Gemma began.

"Yet," McFarland mumbled and jotted down another name.

"We're working on it." Gemma cocked her head in McFarland's direction. "But we need a solid plan B if that doesn't work, thus the boat radio."

"Which is different than our standard radios?"

"That's not a question for me. McFarland?"

He didn't take his eyes off his screen, but the question didn't slow him down even for a second. "We use UHF—ultra-high frequency—radios, which are better for urban settings. The signal can penetrate structures, but the trade-off is it only transmits maybe up to forty miles in perfect, unobstructed conditions. Put that radio in the downtown core, and it might be only as far as four miles, so the NYPD uses repeater towers to boost the signal with higher power. But every boat has a VHF—very high frequency—radio. That's old-school, long before cellular communications, but it's still the way boats operate because you don't lose signal when you're more than twenty-five miles away from a cell tower. VHF is line of sight but transmits to a distance of about one hundred miles. If you're in trouble out on the ocean, VHF is your only communication savior. So all boats have them."

"But how do we contact one particular boat?" Ramos asked. "And doesn't that depend on the fact that someone is standing on the bridge to hear us calling?"

"In the old days, yes. But nowadays, most boats have portable radios as well as the built-ins. In fact, Weaver—the company that custom-built Horner's boat—said the radio system they installed in the boat has a built-in command center in the bridge, but they also provided additional portable units for use by the crew for inter- or intra-ship communication. There's an intercom system on the ship, but that's not always convenient, depending on where the crew are working. If you're standing on the swim platform assisting people out of the water, you're not near an intercom, so a radio would be handy. In this case, I'd bet money on the fact the captain grabbed one before he left the bridge, especially because he was essentially forced to leave his post by his boss. The radio is his only connection to the outside world if something goes sideways while he's away from the controls."

"But will we know what channel they're on?" Chen asked. "We could be talking to everyone but that one particular captain."

McFarland opened a tab with a photo of three women in short, sparkly dresses, holding cocktail glasses and standing in front of a large picture window with the lights of Manhattan's skyline around them. Two of the three faces were tagged, and he opened a new tab from one of them. "True. However, I'm betting on the captain being concerned about an emergency." He clicked through to send a private message, and the messaging window popped up. He put his hands on the keyboard but paused. "There are fifty-seven VHF channels with distinct numbers that relate to a specific frequency. For instance, channel 9 is the normal channel for public communication out on the water. Many channels are specific to commercial shipping. Several are for port operations or strictly for the Coasties. But channel 16 is our sweet spot. Its specific use is for emergency calling only."

Chen's gaze sharpened, and he nodded in understanding. "We have a captain who's been called away from his bridge. No one is at the controls. If something goes wrong and anyone tries to contact them, it will be on channel 16. He'll have set his radio to channel 16."

"That's what I think." McFarland bent over his keyboard and started to type.

Gemma watched him for a moment, drawn by his intensity as he typed in short sentences, sending each as an individual message. Whoever was on the receiving end was being bombarded. "What are you doing?"

"Trying to keep us from having to use channel 16 as our only option." He sent two more messages, then moved his hands away from the keyboard. "If that doesn't get their attention, I'm not sure what will."

"Text bombing a stranger?"

"Sort of. Not enough to disable them, just trying to get their attention."

"Who and why? I don't think you're trying to up your Insta game in the middle of an incident. What's the plan?"

McFarland snorted. "Definitely not upping my Insta game. I'm using it as a tool. Hopefully a useful one." He spun his laptop around so everyone could see it. "I found these pictures from tonight." He switched tabs to the profile page of a stylish blond woman. The first three photos on her page showed her paired with different people. McFarland clicked to enlarge a photo showing her in a knee-length jet-black wrap coat that Gemma would bet a whole paycheck was some kind of designer wool or cashmere. She was flanked by two other women, all holding champagne flutes as they stood at the rail of the ship, the dark waters of a river behind them before blurred lights exploded in the background. "This page belongs to Trish Cushing."

"Wait, *the* Trish Cushing?" Ramos leaned in closer. "Damn, it is."

Chen squinted at the image. "Who's that?"

"One of the *Real Housewives* from way back." Ramos shrugged. "Guilty pleasure after a long day of dealing with sexual assault victims."

"You do what you need to do," Gemma said, reading over McFarland's shoulder. "From the photo description, it looks like she's on Horner's boat."

"Yeah. With those two gals." McFarland opened the next picture. "And that group."

The partygoers had moved indoors out of the frigid winter winds. Trish now stood in sky-high silver stilettos that matched her skintight minidress. Sewn with a sea of sequins and tiny seed pearls, it had a plunging V-neck that had Gemma hoping Trish had taped everything securely into place before leaving for the party. Her blond curls were down over her shoulder, and diamonds sparkled from long dangles at her ears, in a single drop between her breasts, and on her fingers. She was surrounded by five other people—men in formal suits with glossy ties, and women in multicolored party dresses of varying lengths and exposure.

It exhausted Gemma just thinking about how much time had to go into that kind of socialite getup. She'd rather spend the evening curled on the couch with Logan in her yoga pants and old NYPD sweatshirt. She suspected he'd prefer the same. It wasn't that she didn't like to go out, but this amounted to nothing short of a theatrical production in an effort to one-up every other woman at the party.

They always say women don't dress for men; they dress for other women.

McFarland moved on to the next photo, which was different people but more of the same—high heels, party wear, lots of jewelry, more alcohol. Most importantly, it showed Horner, who stood with his hands in the pockets of his charcoal suit pants, a magnanimous grin on his perfectly sculpted face below a swoosh of dark hair over his forehead.

Gemma knew well how good looks could curry favor. Being the second youngest of five, Gemma had watched her brothers grow up and take their places in the world. Joe, now a lieutenant in NYPD's gang squad, had been the serious older brother, the protector, the no-one-picks-on-my-younger-siblings-but-me type. Mark, now a patrol sergeant in NYPD's 5th Precinct, was the peacekeeper who would use words instead of fists. Alex, the youngest, her closest sibling, the one who'd weathered the worst of losing their mother at such a young age with her, had always focused on justice as a result, so much so his place in the NYPD was with Internal Affairs.

It was Teo, only a year older than Gemma, who'd been blessed with not only Sicilian good looks but charm as well. His face had always opened doors for him in a way that hadn't for Joe, Mark, or Alex. Girls and then women constantly vied for his attention, bringing first boys and later men to his side in hopes of sharing his limelight. However, he hadn't translated that into business as Horner had—for him, the lasting impact from 9/11 had carried him into the FDNY. Now that handsome face, and the body to match, helped sell firefighter calendars in support of the department.

But looking at Horner, Gemma had to think a less handsome man would have had to work a little harder to build his business. Horner appeared to have it all—looks, charm, business smarts, and a lucky flair for risk taking. It had made him rich, made him successful, and people flocked to him, as if they could absorb some of his good fortune.

Better than rubbing the brass balls of the Charging Bull on Wall Street.

But it was Horner's eyes that caught Gemma—icy blue, cold, and calculating, his magnanimous smile stopped just short of them. Even at his own party, she could see his intent to work the room. Always trying to win, always trying to climb higher.

Had that attitude landed him in this crisis? And everyone on the guest list with him? Finding out that answer was top of her list and could be key to solving this crisis.

"These photos are helpful because they're adding to the list of who's currently on the yacht," said McFarland, "but what this page gives me is other photos to dig through." He went back to the main page, scrolled down to a number of Christmas-themed parties. "Like this. Which led me to this."

He switched to another tab, which showed a group of people, once again dressed to the nines, holding drinks, and gathered around a Christmas tree. He clicked the photo, and a bunch of tagged names appeared. "These are people Trish knows personally—friends and family who aren't on the yacht tonight with her. Helpfully, Trish tagged everyone with an account. Now, not everyone has a public page and I don't have time to ask for access, but there are a few whose pages are open. I'm messaging them." He turned his laptop around to face him again, flipped back to the message tab, and sent another round of short messages.

Gemma imagined that somewhere in the city, in the middle of a ritzy party, someone's phone was exploding into repetitive alerts.

"You think someone is going to talk to a stranger like you?" Ramos asked.

"I told them I'm NYPD. I told them I needed to ask them about Trish, and I gave them the info as to where she is now so they know I'm not some internet weirdo. No details about the hostage situation, but hopefully, it will be enough to get their attention." He sent two more messages and then moved to another tab. This one showed a dark-haired man on a page with no socialite parties but many rounds of golf. "If not, I have a few others to do the same with." He'd just opened a new message pane when his computer alerted. "We may have just gotten lucky."

He flipped back to the message tab to find a short message and hunkered down, typing his reply. Several messages flew back and forth before McFarland glanced up to find everyone watching him. "Talk amongst yourselves?"

"As if." Gemma peered over his shoulder, reading the screen. "Nice job of convincing her you're who you say you are. You can't blame her for thinking you're phishing for personal info."

"Well, really, I am, just not her info and not for nefarious purposes." He stopped typing and stared at his static screen. "Come on, come on," he muttered. "Don't make me contact everyone in that damned image."

Three dots bounced at the bottom left of the screen, then they stopped briefly before jumping again.

Gemma leaned in.

A message appeared: **You better not make me regret doing this.** A phone number followed. Then: **If you're real, let me know Trish is okay. Whatever is happening.**

McFarland texted a reply: **I will. Thank you.** Then he sat back. "And we may have a better way to get through than the radio."

"Or we may have to use them together. One to tell them to pick up, one to actually have a conversation." Gemma pulled her pad and pen closer and jotted down the number. "Good work." She glanced at the time in his system tray. "Once we get the radio, we'll reach out. Then we'll finally be able to start the work of bringing them all home."

CHAPTER 5

AS HE REACHED FOR THE crash bar on the glass door leading out to the pier, Logan glanced to his right, toward the HNT table. He met Gemma's gaze for the briefest of moments—one last connection—then he slammed through the door, stepping from the warmth of the restaurant into the cold bite of winter's wind.

The bracing harbor wind slapped him into full awareness. He liked it. Time to get sharp, to get in the zone.

They had work to do.

"This way!" he called to the men and woman behind him as they followed him down the sloped ramp, framed on either side by metal fencing that enclosed the churning harbor waters and ringed the pier. They covered the distance down the pier quickly, passing picnic tables normally filled to overflowing during the balmy summer months but now deserted in the bitter temperatures.

Pier A was unlit except for the intermittent pairs of lanterns flanking each set of doors leading out to the pier down the length of the restaurant. Paired with the light of the moon rising overhead in a clear sky, it was enough to illuminate their way down the concrete path. As the pier angled to the right to join with the wide boardwalk that edged The Battery, an old breakwater jutted out into the harbor.

The rebuilt breakwater ended in an L-shaped outcrop upon which sat the American Merchant Mariners' Memorial—a bronze statue featuring the bow of a sinking ship and two mariners attempting to save the life of a drowning third in the water. For the A-Team, part of this rebuilt breakwater would function as their boat launch.

Three heavy metal cleats studded the length of the breakwater. Two men stood at the last cleat, tying off the bobbing RIB pulled between two pilings that rose four feet over the concrete span of the breakwater.

The waist-high metal fence that divided the pier from the harbor's winter water had a gate leading to the breakwater, with a thick, rusted chain looped multiple times through the metal bars of the fence and gate, secured by a heavy padlock. Logan held his carbine high against his chest with the safety engaged in his left hand, braced his right hand on the railing, and vaulted easily over the fence, landing lightly. As he strode to the end of the breakwater, he could hear his teammates, one by one, clearing the gate behind him.

The two men turned toward the approaching team. They were both dressed in NYPD navy-blue waterproof outerwear, overlaid with navy life jackets, their radios attached high on their left shoulders. Both wore knit caps with NYPD stitched onto the front to help manage the cold temps out on the water.

"Detective Logan, A-Team Unit 1," Logan said.

"Officers Clapton and Loakes." The taller cop indicated first himself, then his colleague. He extended a compact, handheld radio with a small screen, a keypad, and a thick antenna. "Your negotiation team needs a radio. Who can we give it to?"

"I'll take it to them." Johnson reached for the radio.

"Hang on." Logan glanced into the RIB. "I don't see body armor. We're heading into a potential live-fire situation. We can provide you with vests and helmets."

"Not our standard gear," said Clapton. "And this launch is too small for any kind of storage. Appreciate it."

Logan turned to Johnson. "Hit the truck on your way back. Grab two extra vests and helmets."

"Affirmative. Update me on what I need to know when I'm back." Johnson took off at a run down the breakwater, vaulted over the locked gate, and jogged toward the restaurant.

"We just got word from the Aviation Unit that they've identified the yacht. We have the GPS coordinates." Clapton pulled a handheld GPS unit out of his pocket in a gloved grip and woke it, angling it so Logan and his team could see. The unit displayed a color map of New York Harbor, showing the tip of The Battery, Governors Island, Ellis Island, and Liberty Island. A thin white line angled down the middle, splitting the harbor between Liberty and Ellis Islands and Governors Island—the division between the states of New York and New Jersey. To the right of the line, a bright-red isosceles triangle pointed its narrow tip at a spot just over halfway down toward the southern tip of Governors Island. "That red marker is the yacht. It's about four hundred yards off the coast of the island."

Four hundred yards. Logan made a rapid calculation. It was a shot he could make with his M10 sniper rifle and a good scope, but the blustery conditions immediately negated that idea. Even if a sharpshooter could take up a good position on the island, with a clear line of sight and nothing covering the yacht's windows, the choppy water and the gusty winds would make the shot nearly impossible. There were simply too many innocents on board to risk a wild shot. The direct approach was their only option.

"That location is well inside the state line," Sims said. "That makes things a lot less complicated. Otherwise, we'd be handing it over to the New Jersey boys, which would lose time we don't have."

"Which might have lost lives," Logan added. "At least this location looks like it's out of the main shipping lane."

"Just outside the Anchorage Channel," said Loakes. "We understand they dropped anchor, so they should be stable in that location. It's not a legal anchorage area, but they're in roughly twenty-five- or thirty-foot water only, so the Staten Island Ferry isn't going to route through them."

"The Harbor Unit knows to give them space?"

Clapton nodded. "As soon as Aviation gave us the location, word went out quietly to give them room. We don't want anyone listening in getting curious and deciding to get closer to rubberneck, because that could set the hostage taker off. All patrols were close enough that we could contact their cell phones and give them the exact coordinates."

"Good plan." Logan looked out over the busy harbor, thankful the northwest wind was mostly at his back and only wisps of it threaded between his collar and the bottom of his tactical helmet. "Did you spot it coming in from Brooklyn?"

Loakes shook his head. "No, but we followed the coastline from Sunset Park and stayed east of Governors Island going through Buttermilk Channel, so the island blocked our line of sight. Which is just as well." He glanced down at the RIB. "We're not marked and not overly obvious, but it's not a hospitable night to be out in an open boat for a pleasure cruise. Better not to be spotted."

Logan followed his gaze to the charcoal-gray inflatable they'd tied up. A sturdy rope was knotted through brass rings that studded the top lip of the inflated tubelike sponsons that formed the upper and outer edges of the boat. A pile of life jackets lay in the bow of the RIB, and a mesh bag about ten feet long lay along the center line. The RIB had no seats but had room enough to seat his team of six, plus the two Harbor officers either beside the tiller or kneeling on the rigid floor of the boat. But it was the engine that caught his eye, one with the smallest powerhead he'd ever seen. "We never heard you pull up."

"We swapped out the gas outboard motor for electric. Doesn't have quite as much power as a top-range gas outboard, but speed isn't our top priority. We're looking for stealth."

"That's the boarding ladder in the bag?"

"Yes. We can quickly put it together here and make adjustments on the fly if you need to adjust for size."

"We think we're going to need about thirteen to fifteen feet."

"We can work with that. We'll do twenty and drop the extra into the water. If plans change, we can snap-lock on another ten-foot section. Where are we boarding?"

"Starboard side, about a quarter of the way back from the bow. The only balcony on the yacht, leads to Horner's private bedroom."

"We'll then stand by in that position unless you deem it too dangerous and want us to pull back."

Logan glanced up at the sound of pounding boots as Johnson returned to the group, then handed off the vests and helmets to Clapton and Loakes.

Johnson's quick nod to Logan conveyed the HNT now had their radio and would try to make contact right away, so they needed to get moving. "There's a college kid we need to extract before we deal with the hostages. We believe the hostages are in the back half of the main deck. If so, we'll clear the front part of the boat on all levels before getting into position and waiting for instructions from the negotiators. The kid is below, on the hull deck. He's priority one—we'll find him and pass him down the ladder to you. I don't want him on the boat if this all goes to hell."

"Agreed, but we'll stay on-site. If the HNT can free hostages, we'll take them, too. If we're at capacity, the farthest I'd go is Governors Island to off-load. Could be there and back inside of eight to ten minutes tops, and that includes landing and debarking."

"Good info, thanks."

"Let's get the boarding ladder set up, then." Now wearing a helmet and with his PFD strapped on over a Kevlar vest, Clapton hopped into the boat and tossed up life jackets. "Put these on. They'll be a bit in your way, but at least while we're out on open water in a crowded area like this, you have to wear them. Take them off once you're on board the yacht."

Anyone who lived in and around New York City knew about the hazards of New York Harbor as well as the Hudson and East Rivers. These bodies of water could be a killer all year round, with strong tidal currents that could pull even the strongest swimmer under. Add in a winter water temperature that hovered around forty degrees Fahrenheit, and anyone who fell into the water could be in deep trouble. Additionally, tidal currents were always at their worst a few hours after low or high tide. They were about ninety minutes after a high tide that floated the top of the RIB close to the lip of the breakwater, which put the tidal pull near its maximum. The life jackets could truly be life savers.

"It's going to take about fifteen minutes out on the open water to get there. We're going to be running without nav lights once we get close," Clapton continued, "which increases the risk of collision but has the advantage of not announcing our arrival."

"Sounds good. We don't know if anyone will be on watch. We don't even know if it's a single hostage taker. If it is, chances of them being able to observe what's going on outside the confines of the boat are low." Ensuring again the safety on his rifle was engaged, Logan pulled the sling off over his head and handed the rifle to Perez, taking the life jacket he handed him in return. He shrugged into the life jacket, arranging it around his Kevlar vest, snapped the two buckles closed, and then took back his rifle, slipping the sling over his head and left arm to lie flat against his body.

Frowning, Logan shrugged his shoulders, settling his gear. Too many layers required for warmth and protection; he didn't like the way it felt and how it ever so slightly hampered his movements. In their line of work, milliseconds could be the difference between life and death, and freedom of movement could gain them those milliseconds. He understood the need for the life jacket, but the moment it was safe, he'd ditch it.

As the team finished preparing, Loakes extracted two ten-foot lengths of heavy titanium tubing with flat, triangular rungs welded into place in alternating one-foot lengths. Logan had used a boarding ladder a number of times before. The side rungs were just wide enough for both a boot or a handhold and were ingeniously anti-skid and perfectly spaced for a man of his height, allowing an easy upward climb. Turner, the shortest of the group, would have to work a little harder, but Logan had seen her run up a ladder quicker than some of the men, so he had no doubt of her ability to board the yacht.

Loakes attached a double structural hook with silicone wheels at the ends of both arms to allow the hook to be placed silently over a wall or railing. He snapped a second length of titanium on the end, then lowered the ladder, hook first, to the bottom of the boat to rest under the tiller of the motor, the other end propped on the bow, sticking over the end by roughly eighteen inches.

Loakes waved them in. "Ready for you. Get in and get down on the deck. Get a good hold of the lifeline because it's going to be a bumpy ride."

Logan climbed in first, moving to the front of the RIB, scanning the whitecaps raised by the strong gusts before lowering to his knees, his rifle across his thighs, the barrel pointing out toward the water, and grasped a section of the rope running along the top of the inflated sponson. Sims settled to his right, and he turned around to see Johnson and Perez behind him while Turner and Wilson were on their knees behind Sims.

At the stern, Clapton was seated on the sponson to the left of the outboard motor, his right hand on the tiller, while Loakes stood on the breakwater, untwining the nylon mooring line he'd looped in multiple figure eights around the metal dock cleat, coiling it as the line came free. When the boat was untied, he wound the end around the coil, tying it into a narrow skein, which he tossed into the stern of the boat. He climbed in and dropped onto the rear sponson opposite Clapton.

If Logan hadn't seen Clapton fire up the outboard motor, he wouldn't have had any idea it was running over the whistle of the wind. He'd been out with the Harbor Unit before, for both training and actual deployments, but this was his first time in a covert op requiring such a small boat and, especially, such a stealthy approach.

It gave him confidence they could pull this off.

As they pulled away from the breakwater, he tapped the button that activated his throat mic. "Unit 1 to Cartwright."

"Go ahead, Unit 1."

"The yacht has been identified by the Aviation Unit, and the Harbor Unit has the coordinates. Four hundred yards off the west side of Governors Island, just southwest of the halfway point. We are en route to board, ETA fifteen minutes. Will be going 10-7 on approach." Logan used the departmental code for radio silence.

"Understood, Unit 1. Good hunting."

"10-4." Logan turned off his mic and pushed up slightly higher on his knees.

Somewhere ahead, a group of innocent people could be only seconds away from a hostage taker losing it and ending lives in the blink of an eye.

They couldn't get there fast enough.

CHAPTER 6

THE A-TEAM HAD LEFT FIVE minutes earlier, exiting the restaurant in a long line through double doors that led out onto the south side of the pier. Gemma had caught a flash of Logan's cool blue gaze just before he went through the doorway; then he was gone. Bobbing lights to the side of the small breakwater that led to the American Merchant Mariners' Memorial told her they were headed out to the RIB, which had tied up close to Pier A for easy loading.

A minute later, Johnson had sprinted in with a handheld VHF radio, handed it off to Ramos, and run out just as quickly.

The A-Team was ready to move out.

McFarland held out a hand, his fingers curling in a *gimme* gesture. "Let me check the settings before we start."

Ramos handed over the radio.

McFarland powered it up and spent a minute zipping through menu options. "I want to make sure it's going to record all conversations in case we're forced to communicate more on this unit than we'd like." He made a few adjustments. "There we go. All set. It will capture both sides of the conversation." He fell silent for a moment as he set the channel and boosted the volume, then made a few more changes before handing it to Gemma. "It's on channel 16, and the volume should be high enough. I locked the controls with this button here"—he pointed at a button on the top right corner of the keypad—"so nothing gets accidentally bumped.

And I set the output power to the maximum of six watts. That's usually recommended only for emergency situations to ensure performance is sufficient to compensate for any issues with line of sight. For our purposes, it will assist with any issues due to the increase in harbor traffic tonight." When Ramos sent him a pointed look, he shrugged. "I did some research on the fly. We need to get that signal through."

"No argument here," Ramos replied.

"If you need to up the volume, hit the lock button, then arrow up. Then relock. The only button that's always unlocked is the push-to-talk button." He glanced at the throat mic Gemma wore around her neck, the earpiece dangling a few inches below her collarbone. "You know how that concept works."

"Definitely. Let's get started." Gemma glanced out the window to where the breakwater was now dark. "The A-Team is away."

McFarland tapped his earpiece. "Logan just radioed in to Cartwright. The *Salacia* is four hundred yards off the west side of Governors Island, a little over halfway down its length. They're going radio silent for the approach and boarding. I'll keep monitoring and will let you know if you need to listen in. Not sure when we'll hear from them via radio again. They'll stay silent until it's safe to talk or they're discovered and remaining invisible doesn't matter anymore."

"If they really need to get a message through when they can't talk, but it's safe enough to let go of the rifle temporarily, they'll send details via text." Gemma pulled her pad of paper closer. "I'll start with the radio, and we'll pass off to call Trish's phone next. Here we go. Let's try not to alarm the whole harbor." She raised the radio to her lips, depressed the push-to-talk button on the side of the unit, and gave it a full second to make sure the connection was established. "Hailing the *Salacia*. Hailing the *Salacia*. Come in, *Salacia*." She released the button and slowly counted to thirty in her head. Their table remained silent, while voices came from farther down the restaurant as other aspects of the response took shape.

"Either they don't have it on, or there's an argument about answering," McFarland said.

"My money's on the second." Gemma pressed the button again and repeated the message. "I'll give them three hails, and then I'll tell them we'll call one of the guests' phones and they should answer it. I won't identify myself yet; that could attract too much attention from anyone else listening in. If they're emergency personnel, then they've already been read in to the incident, but we don't want civilians getting involved. Using the name of the boat is bad enough, but we need them to know we're speaking directly to them."

The third hail garnered the same silence, but Gemma gave it a full thirty seconds more before she pushed a little harder. "*Salacia*, I need to make contact. I have the phone number of one of your guests. I'll call it now. Please answer." She set down the radio, and the whole team put on their headphones. McFarland tapped in Trish's number and placed the call.

It rang in their headsets. One…two…three…four…and then was picked up, flipping to voicemail. "Hello, lovelies." The voice was high, light, and a little tipsy to Gemma's ear. "Can't come to the phone right now, so leave a message. Kiss, kiss!"

Gemma declined to leave a message and ended the call. She didn't want to convey any information that might push them into not answering when she called back. If they wanted to call her, the return number would be registered in the call log. "Let's give them two minutes. We don't know where that phone is. They might literally be digging through purses to find it."

"There's no way they still have their personal phones on them," Ramos said. "Removing any form of communication had to be the first thing that happened after they were taken hostage."

"You would think," said McFarland. He met Gemma's gaze. "Kiss, kiss?" He rolled his eyes.

"You should put that on your voicemail," she replied. "You wouldn't get any messages because you'd shock anyone calling you into silence."

McFarland snorted under his breath.

She called again at the end of the two minutes, expecting it to go to voicemail again, and was unsurprised when it did. Often, first contacts with a hostage taker could be drawn out, as the suspect weighed whether to make contact or maintain their isolation. Gemma had never had someone not finally make that connection, but it could take an extended period, and sometimes she was met with rage because of her repeated attempts. She could deal with the rage; it was all about the connection, no matter the emotional level at the beginning. Her first job in any hostage situation was to lower the temperature, which was impossible to do without that initial discussion.

Another two minutes watching the clock, another phone call. One…two—

"Hello?"

Relief flooded through Gemma. *Contact.* The voice on the other end of the call sounded the same as the voicemail message, though overlaid with a layer of terror, giving it a shrill edge. "Is this Trish Cushing?"

"This is Trish." The voice trembled, and her words were followed by a squeaky gasp and raspy breathing.

Gemma could imagine the scene, right down to Trish's makeup and outfit. Imagined her standing in the luxurious lounge of the boat in her party dress and stilettos…with the black pit of the end of a gun barrel pointed at her forehead. Maybe with her arm in an ironfisted grasp, one that tightened to the point of pain, causing that gasp.

Time to cut to the chase. "Trish, this is Detective Gemma Capello of the NYPD. We know you're being held hostage. I need to speak to the person responsible."

"She wants to talk to you." Trish's voice was slightly distant, as if she'd dropped the phone away from her mouth.

Silence followed the request.

Then: "He says no."

He says no.

An abbreviated message, but one that still carried useful information past the meaning itself. *He*: likely a single man, less likely it was a team working in tandem, though not impossible. *Says no*: without speaking, because she'd heard no response. Whoever this sole gunman was, he didn't want to give away his identity in any way.

More than that, it told her something about the precarious nature of what was happening on the boat. Forty-one was a big group for a single man to manage. Based on the shots fired, he had at least one firearm, but one man could be overpowered by a group if the situation became desperate enough that the individuals within it were willing to risk injury for the greater good.

One firearm? He'd already spent three, maybe four bullets. Unless he had an illegal magazine, he was limited by state law to only ten rounds. Even with an illegal, higher-capacity magazine, it would be impossible to kill everyone with a single magazine, and then he'd either need a second weapon, time to reload a fresh magazine, or to load his existing magazine from a store of rounds. And that was when everything could go to hell. It could happen so fast that even if Logan and his team were right outside the door, they wouldn't be able to stop it.

Gemma couldn't stop it either if she was stuck speaking with a hostage and not the hostage taker. Using a hostage as a go-between was never a good idea, mostly for what could happen after a call as the hostage tried to spin what was said on the phone into what they thought the hostage taker wanted to hear, often misrepresenting the HNT. It could set an otherwise progressing negotiation back a long way.

More than that, she needed to build a rapport with the suspect. The whole point of negotiation was to connect with the person in crisis, to calm them and lower the emotional temperature in the room, and to work with them so they could exit the scenario with their head held high... even if it was in custody. Most importantly, it was to bring everyone—including the hostage taker—out alive.

It was time for a little parallel pressure. Negotiations were one thing, but she'd learned over her career that sometimes showing a little of the NYPD's potential force could keep a hostage taker on the straight and narrow. It could show the hostage taker the risk they took in resisting working with the negotiators.

Mute me, she mouthed to McFarland, then looked across the table at Ramos after McFarland hit the button. "Can you find out where the Aviation Unit chopper is at this point? I know they're lying low, but I think it might be time for a flyby with full lights. We need the hostage taker to know we know where he is and there's no easy escape. If they're close, keeping an eye on all harbor traffic, I need them to return to the *Salacia*."

Gemma paused, reconsidered. "Actually, what I'd like them to do is hang over them and focus the spotlight into that rear area of the main deck. If they've shaded the windows in any way, we won't see in, but the light will show through, and that will put a little more pressure on the hostage taker. It could give him a kick to actually pick up the phone and talk to us."

"Give me a second." Ramos pushed away from the table, rose, and headed straight for Cartwright.

"Put me back on." Gemma waited as McFarland unmuted her mic. "Trish, I'd like you to put the phone on speaker, please. Can you do that for me?"

A pause, then, "You're on speaker." Her voice now reflected a little distance.

"This is Detective Gemma Capello from the NYPD. I'd like to speak to the individual or individuals in charge. We're aware you're holding hostages. We know your location in the harbor by Governors Island. Now, I want to be extremely clear. I'm a negotiator. I just want to talk to you. More than that, I want to listen to you. There's a reason you took this action. I'd like you to share that with me. Maybe we can work something out."

Gemma paused, then closed her eyes, straining to hear any clue as to what was going on a little over a mile away in the harbor. But there was nothing—not a peep from Trish or the hostages, no sound of wind or water, no roar of helicopter rotors.

She let the silence hang heavy for a full twenty seconds, letting the hostage taker stew in the conflict he must be feeling, but wasn't surprised when there was no response. "How about I let you think about that for a bit? I'll call you again in five minutes." She ended the call, marked the time, slipped her headphones down to lie around her neck, and exchanged a glance with Chen. "No surprise there."

"No. To begin with, he may not believe you really know where they are. The helicopter is a good idea to reinforce that."

"I think you should let them stew under the spotlight, let them see the show of force," said McFarland. "You could tell them you have a team on board the chopper who could rappel down onto the swim platform at the rear of the boat. I know we don't like to lie to suspects, but this is one that will never impact him, as there isn't actually a team on the helicopter to board the *Salacia*."

There were a few golden rules when it came to hostage negotiation, and one of the most important was to never lie to a hostage taker. If they found out you'd lied to them, they'd never trust you again, and any progress you'd made would crumble. It would nullify the negotiator in the eyes of the suspect and could lead to one or more of the hostages being injured or killed.

Gemma's gaze fell to the blueprints in front of her. "That's a good idea. And while I agree on not lying, I think we can stretch the truth a little here for some crucial leverage to get his attention." She tapped a fingertip to the stern of the boat. "It would keep their focus down on this end. It could give the A-Team a little noise cover as well." She looked up as Ramos and Cartwright approached slowly until they realized Gemma wasn't wearing her headphones. "The Aviation Unit?"

"Will be in position in about sixty seconds," said Cartwright. "They're coming in from the north and just passed over Unit 1 on their approach."

"Can you let them know we want them to spotlight the stern windows on the main deck level? I'd like to apply a little pressure, and that might give Unit 1 a little boarding cover as well."

Cartwright changed the channel on his radio. "Affirmative. Unit 1 is boarding on the starboard side, so I'll specify the port side of the stern. We don't want the RIB lit in any way. The helicopter itself will already attract attention."

"Good call, thanks."

"I'll radio them now." Cartwright stepped away, already reaching out. "Cartwright to N482PD."

Gemma checked the time. "Two more minutes; then we'll call back. That will give them a minute to stew after they're lit up."

Ramos pulled out her chair and sat down. "Even if you can get the hostage taker, we still need to know who's out there with him."

"I've asked someone to reach out to Horner's personal secretary," McFarland said. "If anyone will know the guest list, it would be him. A..." He checked his notes on his laptop. "Darryl Foy."

"You're sure Foy won't be out on the ship managing the party from on board?" Gemma asked.

"Maybe. But that's what the kid's aunt, the chief steward, is for. It's doubtful, however, that she organized the guest list."

"Considering how rich that guy is, I'm sure he has an army of staff." The set of Ramos's mouth said she was unimpressed. "I'm sure he notices none of them. His kind rarely do."

"Or only notices the most important few." Gemma studied McFarland's monitor. "Speaking of 'his kind,' how goes the dive on Horner?"

"His AI is actually pretty good and has produced a lot of data," McFarland stated. "At this point, I've changed the prompt to highlight a different aspect and put it back to work. I'll update you when I have a little more. But the basic gist is he's pissed off a lot of people. This won't be a small pool of suspects, and we're in a time crunch. Anything you can get from the hostage taker will go a long way to narrowing that down."

"Understood." Gemma pulled on her headset. "Dial me through, please."

McFarland placed the call and ensured the recording was live, then sat back, his eyes fixed out the window toward where the helicopter had to already be in place.

The phone was picked up on the third ring.

"Hello?" Trish's voice again, but this time nearly a whisper.

If the helicopter was overhead, was it putting everyone on edge?

"Trish, it's Gemma." She'd made her introduction once, including her designation, and now it was time to drop it in order to make personal connections. "I'm going to make the same request—please put me on speaker."

"Okay."

Gemma waited for about ten seconds before continuing. "I'd like to speak to whoever is in charge." Again no one spoke, but Gemma thought she could hear the thrum of helicopter rotors in the background. "A helicopter is above you now, so you know I'm telling you the truth. We have the capability from that helicopter to rope a team down to board you. You have that convenient swim platform just outside your window as a perfect landing spot. Or the open deck directly overhead. But I don't want to do that. Please don't force my hand. Just talk to me."

An extended pause; then, from a distance, came a male voice. The words were only a murmur, too far away to be distinct. *Keeping his distance from the hostages, threatening them from afar.*

"Trish, please let him know I can't hear what he's saying. Either you need to get closer, or you need to pass him the phone." She was hoping for the latter. It was never optimum to negotiate in public, as she had done on occasion when the only way to negotiate was via a bullhorn back behind police lines. Or at South Greenfield High School, when the PA system had been her only option to reach a boy in crisis who threatened a class of students and their teacher.

"She can't hear you." Trish's raised voice carried clearly this time. "She says I need to get closer to you." Another murmur from the background, then Trish's voice up close. "Here he is."

"Why would I talk to you?" The voice was male, with a faint thread of fear edging the defiance. "You're not on my side. You're going to fuck me over."

The blatant distrust wasn't uncommon, but Gemma saw it as an opportunity to build from a place of division to one of cohesion.

It wouldn't be easy, but now they could begin the process of bringing the hostages home.

CHAPTER 7

FOR NOW, FAR FROM THE yacht and out of the line of sight of so many other boats, the Harbor Unit cruised with the RIB's navigation lights on for safety—at the bow, green on the starboard side and red on the port side, with an all-around white light shining from beside the outboard motor at the stern. They'd kill those lights when they got closer, but for now, the illumination provided safety. It was early enough that boats were still coming into the harbor and moving into position, so they needed to be visible.

The harbor was alive with activity. New Year's Eve in Manhattan wasn't all about Times Square—while a million people shoehorned their way into the iconic square to watch the ball drop, it wasn't the only fireworks show in town. Central Park's Bow Bridge and Brooklyn's Prospect Park also hosted fireworks shows. But the other notable display was the annual fireworks in New York Harbor, with the Statue of Liberty as the focal point of an amazing light show.

New York City had a robust commuter ferry industry going south to Staten Island, north to Ferry Point Park, all the way east to Rockaway, as well as the route from Lower Manhattan to South Brooklyn, with a stop on Governors Island.

But it was the sightseeing cruises that really cornered the marine market around Manhattan, covering the Hudson and East Rivers, Liberty Island, Ellis Island, and Weehawken, featuring brunch, lunch, happy hour, and dinner cruises. And on the big calendar days—July Fourth and New Year's Eve—the ferry operators pulled out all the stops.

Years ago, on a rare New Year's Eve off—a day most cops had to work because so much crowd control was required—he and his girlfriend at the time had booked one of the many—*many*—party cruises. Their trip began at 9:00 PM and had taken them down the Hudson, past Hudson Yards, then back up the river, flanked on either side by sparkling skylines, to pause near the Statue of Liberty for the amazing fireworks show. Following the display, they'd cruised down the East River, under the Brooklyn and Manhattan Bridges, before returning to Pier 40 at Hudson River Park. It was a great evening—the wrong girl, but a great evening.

He remembered how crowded the river had been that night, how many massive vessels had filled the space, as any company who owned a ferry was doing a similar party cruise, with a huge number of private boats on the water as well.

Why squeeze into a massive crowd in the cold at Times Square when you could be in the comfort of your own yacht, with all the food and drink you'd want, with your friends at your side, only to put on your coat and step out onto the deck for as long as the light show lasted, then retreat back into warmth? Or, depending on the vessel, watch from your comfortable, heated lounge through huge picture windows.

As they bounced over the whitecaps, Logan scanned the harbor. It was early still, but the crowds were already on their way. Right now, there were a lot of smaller boats on the water, trying to grab a good spot for a superior view. Though it looked like a few boats were moving from their initial spots when a giant ferry wound its way through the crowd. You didn't mess with a boat twenty or more times the size of yours. Just not worth it.

A cabin cruiser sped through the water on their starboard side, blasting out of the Hudson River even as they passed behind the Staten Island Ferry, the vessel having left the Whitehall Ferry Terminal a few minutes before they cast off themselves.

A glance back at Clapton showed the officer's eyes constantly on the move, judging the traffic around them. Even if it took them longer, avoiding any other boat was paramount. If they were rammed by a fast-moving power boat, their mission would end quickly and there might not be a chance to save their own lives, let alone those on the *Salacia*.

The moon provided just enough light to see they were about to intersect the frothing wake left by another boat. "Hang on!" Logan yelled as he dropped down onto the hull and gripped his rifle, pressing its bulk into his belly. The front half of the boat rose up in the air before splashing down with enough force to pitch everyone forward over their knees. Droplets of spray stung like a swarm of tiny bees against his exposed cheeks, catching his breath as he automatically ducked his head to protect his face.

The boat veered to the left, and when Logan looked up, they were clear of the wake and circling a small houseboat trolling its way toward Liberty Island.

He brushed ice-cold spray off his right cheek with his gloved hand and pulled the collar of his winter jacket up around his chin, trying to block streamers of cold air from slithering down between his layers of clothing. Between the salt spray and the wind, the cold was vicious, quickly dissipating Logan's annoyance at the many layers that had made him a little overwarm by the time he'd left the restaurant.

A look over the stern showed Lower Manhattan shrinking behind them, the trees of The Battery a dark smudge at the foot of the brightly lit skyscrapers of Manhattan's skyline, One World Trade rising like a torch above the city. The lights of Pier A shone against the darkness of the trees, leaving Logan wondering if Gemma had been able to make contact.

Facing forward again, he studied the lights before them. Far to the right, Ellis Island sprawled, hugging the harbor waters, the curved windows of the Ellis Island Immigration Station shining with warm radiance, its four domed towers barely visible against the New Jersey glow behind it. Just south of Ellis Island, the Statue of Liberty commanded the harbor, brilliantly lit, the pedestal shining from below and within, as Lady Liberty stood gloriously tall, a striking, vibrant green emblem of the city, of the country.

Somewhere at her feet, the fireworks barge was already anchored, calling boats of all shapes and sizes to gather near Lady Liberty to celebrate the New Year. Out of the main passage of New York Harbor, large anchorage areas lay around the smaller, westward islands, safely drawing in boats who wanted to see the show up close and personal. To start the New Year with a literal bang.

The goal for this deployment was to get the hostages through to the New Year and then beyond. The hostage taker? Logan couldn't say.

He'd killed before in the line of duty. It wasn't an act he took lightly, and he bore marks from the lives he'd taken, individual scars etched deep in his soul. Some had been in defense of an innocent victim, some had been to prevent a more heinous crime, and one had been to safeguard Gemma's brother, Alex. Would he be forced to kill again today? He fervently hoped not, but if that was what was required of him to save lives, he would do so without hesitation.

He would add yet another scar.

Rather than taking on another role in the NYPD, he'd followed his skills, followed his desire to use those skills to help those who needed it, straight into the ESU. And that meant often being thrown into situations requiring deadly force. But while he was prepared to make those hard choices, it was never his preference. Especially in a position where they might come into contact with those experiencing a mental health crisis, entering a situation with an aggression level dialed up to eleven wasn't necessarily the correct choice. For him, it wasn't just the life in play, but those around that individual who would be affected by his actions.

Sometimes there were no good options. And sometimes you made your own. He loved his team, and their ability to think on their feet and to work outside the box. They could handle this situation, no matter what got thrown at them.

The RIB cleared what had to be a 150-foot yacht, and a brutal crosswind slammed into them from the northwest. His body swaying, Logan gripped the rope more tightly, spreading his knees a bit on the deck to firm his foundation. He bumped knees with Sims, who looked up, the green of the starboard lamp painting his face with an emerald wash.

Ahead, boats filled the harbor around Liberty Island. It was breezy, but the skies were clear, a great night for fireworks, encouraging boat owners out onto the water. Had it been raining or snowing, the crowds would be thinned out, but even as early as 9:30 PM, private vessels were already getting into place. The larger party boats wouldn't be arriving until after 11:00 PM, and Logan missed the cover they'd have provided. Though there were a number of larger yachts already in position that could definitely help.

They'd been out on the water for almost ten minutes when the lights went out, pitching the RIB into darkness. Maintaining his death grip on the rope, Logan swiveled around to study his team. The moon cast enough light to highlight each face all the way back to Clapton, who stared out over the straight end of the boarding ladder, out into the harbor. Each team member was braced, though swaying with each contact with the choppy waves.

A faint light flashed, and the GPS unit Clapton must have held against his thigh glowed dimly. Clapton glanced down, then back up again, adjusting their direction slightly westerly.

No longer easily visible, Clapton gave each boat a much larger separation, slowing his speed a little more when they were passing a vessel blind, then picking up again once he could see their path was clear. He steered them downwind of a yacht, each of its three decks above the water glowing brilliantly. The wind instantly died, and Johnson's relieved mumble sounded behind him.

"The *Salacia* is about six hundred yards ahead. Can't see it yet, but when we get close, Aviation says it's the biggest vessel in the area by far." Clapton's voice was low but still managed to carry to the front of the boat. "Its bow faces toward Governors Island with the stern facing the Claremont Terminal Channel, which says to me they originally dropped anchor with the stern facing Liberty Island, but with no one at the controls, the vessel is beginning to yaw—meaning the stern is spinning with the wind while the bow is held in place by the anchors."

"No one at the controls of the yacht is a concern," said Sims. "This whole operation could go sideways if something goes wrong with the ship and there's no one there to compensate."

"Once you clear the ship, one of us could go on board," said Loakes. "We've both piloted the largest launch in the unit. It's not as big as that yacht, but we have the experience to compensate. And I guarantee she has significant power. Keep in mind, if we have to fire up the engines, there won't be any hiding the fact that someone else is on the boat. But if it's more important to move the boat than let them know they have company, we can cover you there." A quick silent conversation passed between Clapton and Loakes before Loakes nodded. "Clapton will stay close to ferry hostages if we get that opportunity. I'll go on board and can keep in touch with you via radio if there's an emergency. Otherwise, I'll hold tight."

"Affirmative." Logan stared ahead, but they were still too far away with too many obstructions to spot the yacht. However, Clapton's description revealed the captain's original intention—he'd angled the yacht to take in the fireworks most conveniently, for Horner and his guests to stay inside in the warmth and then step outside the party space just before midnight to take in the light show. They'd picked a location that gave them a little distance, to be able to see the panorama of color with Liberty Island as a backdrop. It was a spot with a spectacular view, while still providing a little more privacy and quiet, rather than the crowd of boats already clustering around Lady Liberty. Constant traffic through the Anchorage Channel required the middle of the harbor stay clear of anchored vessels, so it was either the party zone directly under the fireworks or the quiet and panorama of the other side of the channel. Horner wasn't the kind of man to jockey for space. He took what he wanted, and that included a little distance.

There would be no fireworks viewing tonight. If things went pear-shaped, some or all of them might not even make it to midnight.

Their location was a double-edged sword for the boarding party. Less surrounding traffic increased the safety zone around the ship in case of gunfire. But it meant their own cover would be minimal. They intended their arrival to be quiet and dark; they could only hope that on a night of increased activity on the water, they could remain hidden. One glance out a window, and they could be under fire. And while they may be wearing Kevlar and tactical helmets, the PVC of the RIB sponsons had no protection from the killing power of a bullet.

Then they'd all be in the water and even easier targets. Not to mention that Logan had questions about how well the life jackets would work to counteract seventy-five pounds of body armor and equipment. He wasn't sure they wouldn't each sink like a stone.

"I'm going to bring us in close to Governors Island." Clapton's words broke into Logan's thoughts. "I'll come at them from the bow, pulling up on their starboard side with our starboard side. I'll be throttling down so we stop precisely; still stay low and keep a tight grip. If we have to abort under gunfire, we'll be moving quickly. I don't want to lose anyone in the harbor."

"Copy that," Logan said. "Everyone down. Hang on."

His team dropped, and Logan gave Clapton a thumbs-up just before he pulled his carbine in closer, folding over it to crouch farther into the bow.

They started moving again. Logan tilted his chin up so his line of sight just topped the rise of the sponson.

The roiling dark water ahead was studded with boats as Clapton swung them eastward, straight for Governors Island. The massive bulk of Castle Williams—a circular red sandstone fortress, a remnant from the early nineteenth century—stood tall at the north end of the island, lit by encircling streetlights. The long run of the seawall lining the western side of the island was marked by the line of streetlights that stretched down its length. Flashes of light outside the line of the island showed a smattering of boats, significantly fewer than those grouped around Liberty and Ellis Islands.

In the dark night sky, a helicopter hovered, a single white spotlight focused down at a sharp angle. *There they are.*

They swung in closer to Governors Island, keeping it about one hundred feet to their port side, purposely staying out of any illumination thrown by the island's lights.

Just a ghost skimming the water.

The *Salacia* finally came into view.

Compared to the scatter of smaller boats on the east side of Anchorage Channel, the *Salacia* was a monster. But thanks to the blueprints the team had studied, a familiar one. Even from this distance and at an oblique angle, Logan could translate the two-dimensional drawings to a three-dimensional reality.

Clapton smoothly brought them around toward the yacht so they'd only be visible from the front of the vessel. A bright beam of light illuminated the rear port corner of the stern, focused squarely on the windows of the lounge area of the main deck. Beyond that, the yacht seemed to glow in the light of the moon. The body of the ship was a pure, clean white with long horizontal strips of windows, bright with internal illumination. The curved windows on the middle level, considerably darker and facing forward, had to be the bridge, now unoccupied. The top level was dimly lit and, on a night like tonight, would have only been meant as overflow for fireworks gazing, as its space was almost entirely exposed to the elements.

But it was the lower main deck level that had Logan's attention. The front-most windows, those enclosing Horner's stateroom, showed only minimal light. Possibly only a single lamp was on inside, but that would be enough illumination to move through the room easily without being highlighted for any external observation. Starting at the midpoint of the yacht, a metal railing edged the deck, running all the way to the stern. Brilliantly lit windows shone from behind the railing, stretching to about thirty feet short of the stern. The edge of the spotlight showcased steaming aqua waters of the small luminescent pool, stepping down to a swim platform splashed by icy harbor water.

Without a doubt, the best news for their deployment was the dullness of the light coming through the living and dining room windows—they were covered by blinds. Either they'd already been down for privacy while dining or the hostage taker or takers had insisted they be lowered so neither passing ships nor the helicopter could see inside. It didn't matter which, but it gave them a little more safety in gliding up beside the ship.

Logan glanced right to see Sims's calculating gaze fixed on the yacht. As if feeling Logan's eyes on him, Sims turned toward him and gave him a single nod. *We're a go.*

Five hundred feet away. Already in crouched position, the team members pulled in even more, and the boat slowed so any wake left in already choppy waters was only minimally visible.

As they came in line with the boat's position across from Governors Island, Clapton arced them in a curve to the right, so they were headed directly for the point of the *Salacia*'s bow. Their slower speed emphasized the choppiness of the water, and Logan kept his muscles loose, shifting easily as the boat heaved over the shallow waves, grateful he was fully healed from his injuries from weeks before or he'd have been in agony.

Two hundred feet away . . . One hundred.

As Logan tilted his head up enough to be able to see from under the rim of his tactical helmet, the boat's size struck home hard. The prow alone had to stand about forty feet above the water line, the clean, sleek lines of the bow meeting in what appeared to be a knife-sharp point.

Now fifty feet out, the RIB angled ever so slightly south, their speed easing down as they closed the distance. Then they were cruising by, passing the bow and the first thirty feet, slowing even more until Logan felt a slight push forward as Clapton briefly reversed the throttle to stop their motion entirely.

"Prepare the ladder." Loakes's words were barely audible.

Perez and Wilson freed the top section of the ladder from under the tiller and lifted it skyward, the remaining A-Team members shifting the bottom end to the stern of the boat until it stood vertical. With Loakes's assistance, the ladder's wheeled hooks slipped smoothly and silently over the top of the balcony railing. Johnson gave it a strong downward tug to test it, then gave the "okay" sign to Logan.

Staying low, Logan shifted into the middle of the RIB, then to the ladder. A quick look around the RIB showed him his team was ready to follow.

Logan's gaze followed the line of alternating rungs up to the lip of the balcony thirty feet overhead. Then he slung his carbine around so it dangled barrel-down at his back, braced his right boot on the bottom rung, and began to climb.

CHAPTER 8

"I'M NOT HERE TO FUCK you over." Gemma turned the hostage taker's own words around on him, F-bomb and all, as a subtle way of meeting him where he stood. If he wanted to set the tone with frank language, she could oblige; they wouldn't tiptoe through this conversation.

"What guarantees do I have if I talk to you?" the hostage taker continued.

A smile curved Gemma's lips at this first opportunity to draw him into the negotiation, one she hadn't even needed to fight for, as he'd opened the door all on his own. But she ensured none of her satisfaction was revealed in her tone. "I can guarantee that for as long as you talk to me, I can order that helicopter to move off. I can guarantee you some space. In return, all you have to do is continue to talk to me. Tell me what's going on. Give me an opportunity to help you."

"Why would you do that?"

"Because something is clearly wrong."

"Why would you think that?"

Gemma needed to be extremely careful to not let slip that Noah hadn't been rounded up with the rest of the hostages, or his aunt might come under fire. "Do you know how far sound carries over open water? And how many boats are on the harbor tonight for the fireworks?"

She was incredibly careful with her words, keeping in mind that implying facts wasn't actually lying, even if it stretched the truth, like she had with the imaginary helicopter team. It was true that gunshots were explosively loud even when suppressed, but Gemma didn't think he was using a suppressor, as Noah had heard the shots one level down at the front of the yacht. There was every possibility they might have been heard and reported by a nearby vessel. Better to let him think that rather than reason why Gemma was calling in the first place.

When the man didn't answer, Gemma continued, "Whatever it is, I'd like to talk it through with you. If you agree to talk to me, I'll ask the helicopter to pull back so it and anyone on it isn't an imminent threat. Let me do that for you. Then we can talk in peace without that kind of pressure on you."

In her mind's eye, she saw how even on a luxurious yacht, the generous space of the dining and lounge area would have shrunk dramatically under the enclosed pressure of law enforcement's spotlight. One man, with all those people in front of him and the NYPD at his back. It was the kind of pressure cooker where mistakes were made. Fatal mistakes.

Tension crawled up the back of Gemma's neck at the continued silence between them. "Do we have a deal?" she pushed gently.

"Fine." The single word was short, sharp, and filled with resignation.

Resigned or not, he still held all the cards.

"Thank you. Let me call you back once I have confirmation the Aviation Unit team has left the area. And when I call, please pick up. Let's not have this discussion via speaker phone for everyone to hear. Just you and me."

The phone went dead, the hum of the rotors cutting off abruptly.

"Let's hope that's a yes," Gemma muttered.

"It's progress," McFarland said.

"It'll be better progress if he answers and it's just him."

Ramos stood. "I'll have Cartwright order them to pull back."

"Thanks."

As Ramos strode away, Chen pulled the main deck plan toward him. "The pressure in there isn't going to play to our advantage. That space is maybe…twenty-five by fifty feet?"

"That's probably a fair estimate. But these plans aren't going to be accurate for this setup." Gemma scanned the blueprints that showed a table for twelve at the bow end of the room and then two separate seating areas with mixed arrangements of couches, chairs, and tables. "Even if the completed design was exactly like this—and who's to say it was, as this is just the designer's blueprints—they'd likely have moved things around to make room for that many people for a sit-down meal."

"Would they be able to do that?" Chen asked. "I'm not a boater, but wouldn't furniture be nailed down in case of rough seas?"

McFarland scratched his temple and frowned. "Fair question." He returned to his computer and started a search, then scanned the results. "According to a recent *Yacht World* article, apparently not. Modern yacht owners want flexibility and spend most of their time at anchor, so free-standing furniture is the norm now for the superyacht set." He looked up at Gemma. "Keeping that in mind, what are you thinking?"

"Got a pencil in your laptop bag?" Gemma took the pencil McFarland offered her, then spun the deck plans to face her. "Maybe something like this." She started to sketch. "It's going to still be at the bow end of the room because the service pantry leading from the galley is right there for serving. I'm thinking, unless you're going to do some sort of weird table shape, like a U, the best setup is still a single long table. One seat at each end, and then twelve seats on one side and eleven down the other, running straight down the middle."

She sketched a long rectangle down the length of the room, covering the dining table and one of the two seating areas in the original blueprint. She drew a half circle to represent a chair and then repeated them down one side and then one less, staggered against the far side, on the other. "Twenty-five in total." She considered the rectangles drawn against the outer walls. "These say floating buffets, but I'd be willing to bet some of them were either moved within the room or removed entirely. That would give the space for the seating from this middle area"—she tapped the end of the pencil on the couches and chairs now lying under the sketch of the long table—"against the walls under the windows. Not as cozy for after dinner, but if you were going to do a multicourse, extended dinner, this would be how I'd do it."

Ramos returned. "Cartwright's on it. He'll be over in a minute to confirm." She eyed the plans in front of Gemma. "What's that?"

"We're doing a best guess on hostage and hostage taker placement. From what I heard on the call, he's not standing close to the hostages."

"But he was close to the noise from the helicopter. We asked them to hit the spotlight on the port side of the stern." McFarland tapped the rear, port corner of the room. "Chances are good he's down at this end."

Still on her feet, Ramos braced both hands on the table and leaned in. "That sounds right to me." She indicated the area of the table and the adjacent seating. "He might keep everyone down here. After all, they fit in that space to eat dinner, so why not leave them there? Seated, too, as that gives a barrier to action. If anyone wants to make a run at him, they'd have to take the time to get out of a chair. Those extra seconds would give him an edge. He might also be using this outside seating area as a barricade between himself and the hostages—another way to give himself time to defend himself." She tapped a spot on the outer wall. "What's this under this window?"

"The couches and chairs from the middle area," Gemma said.

"What about the bar?"

"The bar?"

"In the original report, the kid said they'd hired on extra servers and a bartender because, unless they're teetotalers, they're going to be drinking."

"That's another issue," pointed out McFarland. "Who's going to be a loose cannon in there because they're drunk and overconfident?"

Chen nodded in agreement. "That's a bad combination. But a possibility."

"We're in agreement, then; there has to be a bar. And a bar means potential weapons. A whiskey bottle could be a club or—" Ramos mimed grabbing a bottle, striking it against the edge of the table, and raising the shattered remains. "Won't stop a bullet, but if enough people rush the hostage taker at the same time, it could be a fatal close-quarters weapon. So where's the bar?"

Gemma turned to McFarland. "You didn't see the bar in any of those social media photos?"

"Unfortunately for us, no. They were mostly just centered around the groups of people attending, so almost nothing of the yacht showed. Nothing useful, anyway."

"I would bet it's closer to the stern end," Gemma suggested. "They might keep some of the buffet space near the table for serving dinner, but move the rest. On top of that, they might not want a line for the drinks crowding the table. Down at the far end is my guess." She drew in a rectangle under the windows on the starboard side. "Could be on the other side, but this gives the idea. Assuming this is the setup, we likely have the hostages down here"—she drew a circle in the air over the dining table—"and he's isolated down here at the stern end." She set down the pencil. "That helps. I can see it now. There may only be about fifteen or twenty feet tops between him and the hostages."

"That's not much space if they decide to rush him. It depends on how threatened they feel. If they think he's not really going to hurt them, they'll give him space. If they think the end is near, they might take a page out of Flight 93's handbook and go for it."

United Airlines Flight 93. The flight on September 11, 2001, that went down over Pennsylvania when the passengers mounted a united resistance against the four hijackers. They'd all died in the attempt, but the hijackers' target—possibly the White House or the Capitol building—had been spared.

Might could overcome, though the price could be devastatingly high.

"Something we need to keep in mind." Gemma turned to McFarland. "That's enough time. Let's get him on the phone."

Chen extended a hand toward McFarland, stopping the call. "One more thing. Did you notice his accent?"

Gemma's head cocked as she looked at him. "Nothing significant. Why?"

"I caught something. I'm not sure if it's important or will be relevant, but listen for a vowel shift. I hear upper New York State, not the five boroughs. It's a classic northern cities vowel shift, but with that typical upstate increase and very little 'thought' vowel shift. He might or might not live in upstate New York, but if he doesn't, I think he learned to speak there."

When negotiators were starting at nothing and building a rapport with a hostage taker as well as an identity, every tiny scrap of information was important. When they were trying to determine who might hate someone enough to take hostages and threaten death, where that person came from could give them a valuable clue.

Getting into vowel shifts—where a vowel sat on the tongue during pronunciation—could be considered splitting hairs, but at the same time, it could tell a lot about a person's background. And because downstate New Yorkers had such a distinctive take on the "thought" vowel—where someone from Buffalo would say "*thahght*," while someone from the five boroughs would say "*thawght*" with the "*aw*" sound pushed forward on the tongue—it could be a true identifier.

Gemma closed her eyes for a moment, hearing his voice again in her head.

"What guarantees do I have if I talk to you?"

And there it was—the word *talk*, where she didn't hear the forward vowel shift to "*tawk*." Her eyes flashed open. "You're right. I didn't catch that."

"And that's why we have the team, because you're focusing on the message, so we can focus on the other stuff," said McFarland. "Call now?"

"Yes, please."

They settled in as McFarland put the call through.

It was answered before the second ring. Someone had apparently been waiting.

Good.

"Yeah." The voice was oddly flat—not excited, not terrified, not anticipating whatever prize for which he'd staged the standoff. Flat, like the life had been beaten out of him. As if their discovery of his actions had blown the wind from his sails. But the sound lacked the distance of a call put on speaker.

"Hello. Thank you for taking my call. The helicopter has moved on?"

"The lights are gone, but I'm not moving a blind to see. You could have me surrounded and you'd shoot."

"We don't have you surrounded."

"And why would I believe you?"

"Let me make something crystal clear as we're starting out—we're talking in good faith now, and whatever I say, I won't lie to you. I won't tell you what you want to hear to trick you. I'll only tell you the truth, even if it's not something you want to hear. It's important you know that. If I told you a lie and you figured it out, that would be more destructive than any bad news I might have for you, and our work here would be done. That would be bad for all of us, so nothing but the truth."

The silence from the other end of the line told her she hadn't sold him yet.

"Let's begin with something basic. I'm Gemma. What can I call you?"

"You don't need to call me anything."

"That seems rude. Disrespectful. Just your first name would do. I'm not asking you to identify yourself, just to let me know what to call you. Please."

The beginning salvo of a hostage negotiation was always one of the harder aspects. If a negotiator wanted to connect with a hostage taker, they had to start with conversation and the basics of polite respect, which included calling a person by the name they preferred.

The silence stretched long enough, Gemma thought she'd have to go for a different angle, but then he spoke.

"Kip."

The name was so short, Gemma wasn't sure she'd heard properly. She met McFarland's questioning eyes under bunched brows, then her gaze dropped to his pen as he wrote, **Kip?**

"Kip?"

"Yeah."

"Thank you, Kip. That's good. That makes me feel better, like we can really talk. Let's start with everyone in the room. Does anyone need medical attention?"

"No."

"Not of any kind? I know shots were fired."

"I said *no*." Stress edged Kip's tone.

"Glad to hear it." Gemma kept her voice low, the tone soothing, trying to settle him because he sounded like he was strung tight and ready to pop. "Keep this in mind, Kip, as you're in the middle of this. You haven't hurt anyone. You've scared them, but no one's been hurt. Serious charges come when someone is hurt." She decided to push a little harder, knowing from experience she wasn't planting an idea in his head. He'd come armed and taken hostages. Death was the ultimate threat he already offered with his choice of weapon. "Or worse, killed. Don't go down that road. That's a path you can't come back from." She paused for a moment, but he didn't speak, so she continued. "Let's talk about what you need. What are you looking for?"

"That's my business."

"That's your business." Gemma repeated his statement, reinforcing it, making it clear she heard him. "Normally, I'd agree with you that what you do is your business. But in taking hostages at gunpoint, in taking away the rights of others, it can't just be your business anymore. But maybe I can help, like I helped move that helicopter away. What is it you want?"

"To be left alone."

"I'm sorry, that's something I can't do for you. And it's clearly not your end goal, or you'd be somewhere alone and not in a crowd of people. Let me rephrase my question—why did you take hostages? You didn't do that just for kicks. What's the reason?"

There were typically limited motives behind a hostage taking—attention, revenge, money, political gain, or for a guarantee of safe passage for the hostage taker if they were in a tight corner, often after committing a different crime. The reason behind a hostage taking could be the key to ending the standoff.

It took Kip a long time to answer, and Gemma gave him that space. But the longer it took, the greater the chance he might not be telling her the truth if he was trying to come up with an alternate answer.

"Money."

"You want money from the hostages?" Gemma clarified.

"Yeah."

Possibly a correct answer, but too vague, too unfocused. If you needed money on New Year's Eve, you could hit any number of parties and steal jewelry from drunk revelers, rather than be trapped on a yacht in the middle of the harbor to become a sitting duck. "You're just looking for a payout?"

"Yeah."

"And if I could provide that to you? Meet you at a dock and exchange cash for the hostages?" Gemma met McFarland's eyes, saw the calculation there. He recognized she was pushing at Kip's story, knowing he wouldn't accept. Which was good because it wasn't in her power to show up with truckloads of cash to pass off to someone threatening the lives of others.

"I have it covered here."

"You sound like you know you're in charge. Tell me about that."

"I *am* in charge."

"Mm-hmm." Not satisfied with his answer, Gemma murmured encouragement and then got out of the way so Kip would feel free to talk. Seconds dragged by, and Gemma imagined Kip was feeling the weight of each one piling on.

"I'm in control," he finally said. "I have everything I need here. I don't need help."

Chen's head was tilted down, but his eyebrows arched at the half growl of frustration at the end of Kip's statement.

I have everything...Confirmation he's the only hostage taker. "I'm concerned you're not getting the help you need," Gemma stated. "You sound frustrated. Tell me about that."

"It's just—" Kip cut himself off, as if stopping himself just in time. "It's fine."

"It doesn't sound to me like it's fine. Kip, my job is to help you. But I can't unless you talk to me. I'm going to have a bunch of tactical guys breathing down my neck soon because they're going to want to get on board with you—"

"If that happens, I start shooting," Kip interrupted her, his words nearly tripping over each other with their speed.

"And no one wants that," Gemma finished calmly. "But remember what I said about working with me. You need to talk to me, but that means an actual conversation. This is a give-and-take between you and me. I give you something, you give me something, or vice versa. Right now, I'm giving you space from that helicopter. You're filling me in on what's happening on board, so I can find a way to help you." A negotiator's job was to listen more than he or she talked, but some hostage takers didn't want to pour out their souls, and you had to drag each detail out a bit at a time. "You said you have everything you need here. Does that mean someone on board has the money you need? Is it one specific person?"

With that particular crowd on board, collectively, there could be a lot of money in play. Not physically on them, though based on the few pictures she'd seen, there could be tens of thousands of dollars—if not more—of jewels in that room. People might be carrying a small amount of cash or a credit card or two, but even that was unlikely with phone and watch payments slowly taking over.

But when you considered what these people had in their bank accounts…it was enough to take your breath away.

"Why would I tell you? I don't need your help. Just back off and leave me alone." Stress edged Kip's tone, as if the pressure of her questioning was starting to unravel him.

Rising emotion could be deadly in a hostage negotiation, but at the same time, sometimes a little force was needed simply to get a hostage taker talking. Some people sang like canaries from the first moment; Kip clearly wasn't one of them.

Cartwright stood about thirty feet away, talking to another officer dressed in ESU black. Gemma snapped her fingers over her head twice, startling McFarland but creating enough noise for Cartwright to look over at her. Her arm still in the air, she pointed directly at Cartwright and then waved him toward her.

As he approached, she motioned for him to come and stand beside her and then pointed to her headphones and then her microphone. "Lieutenant, how fast can we get the Aviation Unit back to the yacht?" She held up two fingers and pointed again to her mic.

Cartwright followed along with no difficulty. "About two minutes. They're nearby." He spoke slightly louder than usual, making sure his words carried. "Would you like me to order them back?"

Gemma gave him a thumbs-up and mouthed *Thank you.* "What do you say, Kip? Are we going to have a conversation without you brushing me off, or am I turning the operation over to the Emergency Service Unit to deal with as they see fit?"

Silence stretched long. Five seconds, then ten, but Gemma wasn't about to break it. Dead air made most hostage takers uncomfortable, and they'd eventually feel the need to fill it.

A long sigh preceded his words. "We can talk."

Time to make it more personal. "I need everything, Kip. No holding back. I can't keep you safe unless you work with me." She stopped, took a breath, gentled her tone. "I'd like to keep you safe."

"Okay." The single word was heavy with defeat.

"That's good. Thank you." Gemma looked up at Cartwright, smiled her thanks, and nodded at him when he jerked a thumb back toward the A-Team staging area, then walked away.

She turned her attention back to Kip. "Let's pick up where we were, then. You said you have everything you need on board. With one specific person?"

"Yes."

"Who?" Gemma asked the question, even though she was sure she already knew the answer.

"Lucas Horner."

The flat stares around the table said she wasn't the only one who'd expected that answer. Which was unfortunate, because the list of people who held grudges against the venture capitalist was going to be *long*.

"What do you want from Mr. Horner?"

"He knows what I want—fifty million dollars in cryptocurrency."

Gemma was glad she was only a voice on the phone and not physically in front of Kip so he couldn't see her sagging jaw and shocked expression. She quickly schooled her features and made sure her tone was calm. "That's a lot of money."

"It is. But it's money he has. Money he can transfer."

"You've discussed it with Mr. Horner?"

"He's aware."

Gemma didn't like the sound of that. "Aware?"

"He's still thinking about it."

That was a surprise. Most people with a gun to their head and the ability to save their own lives would do so. But not Horner, apparently. "And if he doesn't agree to your transfer?"

"He's taking that into consideration, too. He has until midnight when the fireworks go off."

Gemma's gaze shot to the clock at the head of the table, its large red numbers shining bright—*9:48. Not much time to sort this out.* "And if he doesn't do the transfer?"

Kip hesitated briefly, then answered, "Then they're all going to die, one at a time. Horner will be last, but if he doesn't do it, there's a bullet with his name on it."

CHAPTER 9

THE LADDER WAS ROCK SOLID under Logan's boots as he climbed, his team steadying the apparatus from below. He'd climbed about six feet when the ladder shuddered under his hands as Wilson mounted the first step, following him. The ladder could safely carry four officers at a time, but with a climb this short, it would only fit three of them.

Overhead, helicopter rotors beat the air, a roaring *whop-whop-whop* entirely drowning out any small sounds that might have come from the ladder as they climbed.

Within seconds, Logan reached the top. Grasping the white metal railing that shot icy cold through his tactical gloves, he stepped up one final rung, then swung his right leg over the railing, landing silently on the rubber sole of his boot. He swung his left leg over, then looked down. Wilson was nearly on him, followed by Turner and Perez. Sims hung back behind Johnson, ready to bring up the rear.

Logan stepped back, giving Wilson space to climb over the balcony as he pulled his clear safety glasses out of a pocket of his cargo pants and slipped them on now that there was no risk of splashing or smearing. Eye protection was important, but if an officer's vision wasn't crystal clear through it, it was a liability.

Wilson climbed over, and Turner's head popped up just behind him as the team continued their ascent.

They'd stay in place until they could move as a unified group, so Logan took a moment to scan the area. He stood about fifteen feet above the water on the hardwood planking of a balcony that widened as it flowed from bow to stern. The tall railing—its outer side flat while the inner side was angled for comfortable leaning—broke into an open space below, contained by three lines of metal cord between slender silver support poles.

Opposite the water, two glossy floor-to-ceiling windows were contained by reflective silver frames while the middle section was a wide sliding glass door. Semi-sheer pleated shades had been lowered on the far side of the glass. Through them, Logan pinpointed the light source glowing at about waist height across the room and to the left. As expected, there was no sign of any activity behind the shades; everyone was forty feet away toward the stern and behind several likely closed doors, though that remained to be confirmed.

He ensured the safety on his rifle was still engaged, then slipped off his sling before handing his M4A1 to Wilson. He quickly released the buckles on his life jacket, shucked it off, and then dropped it over the side into the unoccupied bow of the RIB. Taking his rifle, he slipped the sling on, settled his rifle, and then held Wilson's rifle as he did the same.

Sims came over the railing, his extended thumbs-up to Clapton and Loakes below visible in the moonlight. As the rest of the detectives removed their life jackets, resettled their rifles for the op, and donned safety glasses, Logan moved to the sliding door and gave the inset handle a tug—locked. Pretty much what he had expected, especially during the winter when the door likely wouldn't be opened for months at a time.

He tapped Wilson's arm and pointed at the door. Wilson turned his back to Logan, presenting him with the three-pocket equipment pack attached to his Kevlar vest. Logan opened the long pocket and removed the glass-cutting device, which he passed to Wilson.

Using hand signals, he told his officers to give Wilson a little space, and they stepped back, forming a full arc. Each detective stood ready to fire, the buttstocks of their carbines braced against a shoulder so their red laser sight was at eye level, each with a finger lying along the trigger guard, ready for things to go to hell.

Hoping they wouldn't.

Wilson set up the glass cutter, sliding the cutting blade along the ruler arm to about a four-inch span, then tightening it in place. He did a quick adjustment of the depth of the cutting blade, then held the suction cup to the glass of the patio door, ten inches away and at the same level as the inset handle. He flipped down a small lever, sticking the suction cup to the glass, then applied the blade to the surface and smoothly rotated it in a full circle. He unscrewed the ruler arm, then used the end to tap just inside the score mark while applying a gentle pull on the suction cup. The glass snapped free, the sound lost in the rotor wash from above, pulling away with the suction cup still attached.

Reaching in with a gloved hand, Wilson unlocked the patio door. As he stepped back, he nodded at Logan, mouthed *Good to go*, and then handed the glass cutter to Johnson, waiting as Johnson freed it from the glass and stowed the cutter in his pack, then pulled his rifle into place.

Ready to roll.

Logan stepped into place beside the door and motioned to Perez to open it and stand back. Perez slid the door open on smooth runners with almost no sound as Logan stepped to the open doorway, pushed aside the shade, and swept the room with the barrel of his rifle.

Empty. As expected.

A quick scan showed him a room with spare modern furnishings done in quiet tones of beige, brown, and navy—hallmarks of a man's room. A king-size bed under a narrow modern oil painting in tones of blue commanded what would be a large bedroom on a yacht, though likely only a fraction of the size of Horner's bedroom in the city. Bedside tables flanked the bed under dark hanging lanterns. Wall-to-wall carpeting covered the floor, and a narrow desk with a closed laptop sat under the glow of a single angular desk lamp on the far side of the room. Beside it stood a padded reading chair and a small table with the curves of an hourglass. The shades in the windows were down, and the two doors leading toward the bow on either side of the bed—to his-and-hers bathrooms and a walk-in closet, as per the blueprints—were closed.

Logan stepped into the room and motioned to the two doors. Johnson and Turner broke off and went through them simultaneously, disappearing briefly into dim spaces lit only by the light of the bedroom. They both returned quickly, giving the "okay" signal for all clear.

Time to clear as much of the yacht as they could and find the terrified young man who'd alerted them to the crisis in the first place. There was no need to issue orders, as everyone knew their role, and each had a map of the vessel in their head.

They'd split into teams of two to clear the bow section of the boat before returning to the main deck foyer by the elevator to hold for a possible incursion into the dining and lounge area.

Sims and Johnson would finish clearing the main deck, including the guest stateroom, closet, and en suite bathroom before moving on to the galley, the adjacent service pantry, and all related storage areas. Their task was the most dangerous of the teams', as they'd be actively searching the area on the other side of a single door from the hostage taker and the hostages. One wrong move, one slight noise, and their silent arrival would be blown. After that, they'd use the main staircase that accessed all three decks to clear the four guest staterooms and their associated bathrooms on the hull deck.

Wilson and Turner would take the bridge deck, clearing the bridge itself, the navigation room, then the captain's stateroom and adjoining bathroom. After that, they'd move into the living spaces—the smaller lounge area with a gaming table as well as a larger TV-oriented seating area, and behind that, a small prep kitchen. Much of the bridge deck was outside, but they'd be able to check those well-lit areas—both the integrated seating in the bow and the dining, lounging, and bar area in the stern—from inside, negating the need to walk directly over the main deck lounge and risk giving themselves away.

Logan and Perez would take the stairs down to the hull deck to search the crew quarters, which were mostly isolated from the guest areas on the same level. That space was a warren of smaller rooms, cramming the crew in with none of the comfort of the guest spaces or the luxury of Horner's suite—the crew mess with additional freezer, cooler, and storage space; a large laundry room to manage crew, guests, and owner laundry; and six double bunk crew cabins, each tiny space holding two lockers, a folding desk, and a small bathroom with a toilet, sink, and shower. Noah Swift had called in from the laundry room—hopefully, he was still there. Either way, they'd find him as they cleared the ship one room at a time.

The only area of the ship no one would be able to access was the engine room, as the sole entrance to that space was camouflaged near the swimming pool and would be visible if the hostage taker looked out a window. It was doubtful anyone was there if the entire crew had been called up, but Logan would make sure it was searched once they had the freedom to do so. It was simply too risky while they didn't know what they were dealing with or the exact location of the hostages.

All eyes drifted toward the ceiling when the whir of helicopter blades faded as the chopper moved off. Their cover was gone; time to ensure no one else on the boat was aware of their arrival.

Logan snapped his left arm straight up with his hand flat—the hand signal for the unit to form into a single-column formation—then eased the door open from the stateroom to the study beyond. One glance showed the room to be empty, with a long desk stretched under the darkened window, a leather desk chair, and opposite, a narrow, closed cabinet only deep enough to hold books. The team moved forward to the next closed door, did a quick check, and then stepped out into the deserted foyer.

Luxury was all Logan could think. The floors were a soft white-and-honey marble against pale walls studded with modern art only interrupted by doors leading to a small powder room and a well-hidden utility room on their left, as well as a sliding door that led to the galley on the right.

They moved forward silently, Johnson and Wilson breaking off to check the powder and utility rooms before they continued past a plush settee to the main area of the foyer. To their left, a glass door to the deck was flanked by two floor-to-ceiling picture windows, the dark waters of the Anchorage Channel beyond broken by the southern tip of Governors Island and backlit by the suburban bulk of South Brooklyn. To their right lay both an elevator and a staircase of curving pale wood edged with an elegant silver banister, rising to disappear into the floor above.

After a short scan of the area, all eyes locked on the sliding door in front of them that separated them from the hostage crisis only twenty feet away. Everyone held their breath, straining to hear any sound.

Logan picked up the low murmur of a man's voice, then a pause, then a response. The words were indistinct, but the cadence carried the lilt and spacing of conversation.

Well done, Gem.

She'd gotten through, made contact, and now the negotiations were on. Which had the added benefit of keeping the hostage taker distracted by dealing with her. He was likely off-balance because his secret operation had somehow attracted the attention of the cops, which would make any idea of escape infinitely more difficult.

With hand signals pointing to his officers and their search locations, Logan ordered the team to split up. They moved, rubber-soled boots silent on marble. Wilson and Turner headed up the curving staircase for the bridge deck, Johnson took the door opposite the powder room into the guest stateroom, and Sims slid open the door into the kitchen with Logan and Perez following.

Luxury evaporated as they stepped into utilitarian efficiency. A row of tall, stainless steel fridges and freezers lined the passageway to their left, while a huge double-doored wooden pantry lay to their right. Sims checked the stairs leading down just off to the right, then opened the sliding door ahead of them, cleared the space with a sweep of his rifle, and stepped through. Logan took the stairs down, Perez close behind, their boots making almost no noise on the bare stair treads. A tall man, Logan had to duck to avoid the bulkhead as they stepped down to the hull deck, and then they were through the door at the bottom of the flight of steps to stand in a short hallway.

The images of the blueprints Logan held in his head told him the laundry room was immediately to his left, and the crew mess was ten feet ahead to his right, opposite the walk-in cooler and freezer. The crew cabins were straight ahead, behind first a sliding privacy door and then a watertight door. The hull deck was divided into watertight sections in case of a hull breach to avoid the entire level being flooded. For Logan, the layout provided an extra level of security and soundproofing so he'd be able to check in via his UHF radio, which would be able to penetrate the structure of the vessel.

Silently, Logan moved to the sliding door on his left as Perez peeled off to the right. Logan waited until Perez checked and then disappeared into the mess before sliding the door open and swinging in to clear the laundry room.

Three stacked washer-dryer units lined the right-hand wall opposite a counter for folding clothes beside a deep sink for handwashing more delicate fabrics. Otherwise, the room was empty.

Where's the college kid?

The only space under the counter was stacked with laundry baskets and rolling racks, and other than a shelf at the far end filled with laundry products, there was no enclosed storage space. Had he moved to another area of the ship with more places to hide?

Logan's gaze fell on the watertight door just to his left. Made of solid steel with a round glass window near the top and a single handle, it was inset into the wall, hanging on three heavy hinges. From the plans, it was the only access at this level from the crew section of the hull deck into the guest section, leading into one of the guest staterooms through a second door.

But there was about two feet of space between the two doors. Barely enough room to hide a scared college kid, but it could be done if he was small enough. Logan moved to the window and peered through the thick glass, going up on his toes to see as far down into the gap as he could. He could just see the top of a dark head.

Found you.

Not wanting to scare the life out of the terrified young man by jerking open the door so he came face-to-face with the barrel of Logan's rifle, he instead opted to tap two gloved knuckles against the glass.

The young man inside jerked in surprise—if he made a noise, it was muffled by the watertight door—raising wide, dark eyes to Logan. Not having a badge to show him—ESU officers' name and badge numbers were stitched onto their uniforms and hidden under his winter gear and

Kevlar vest—Logan gave him an "okay" hand signal and then stepped back to slowly open the door.

Keeping his voice low, he spoke as soon as there was a gap. "Noah, I'm NYPD. I'm here to get you off the boat." He opened the door fully to find a young man with a pale complexion and tousled dark hair, folded into a seated position on the floor with his knees at his chest. Gripping his carbine by the pistol grip with the barrel pointed at the floor, Logan extended his left hand. "Let's get you out of here."

"Thank God." Noah kept his voice equally low, but it carried an audible quaver as Logan hauled him to his feet. "I wasn't sure you guys could find us out here."

"Hard to miss a boat of this size, even when the harbor is busy. There's a whole team of us here clearing the front half of the boat. Once that's done, we're going to transfer you to the boat we used to get out here." He took in Noah's standard catering outfit of black pants and white shirt. "You're going to be out there for a bit. Do you have a coat? A hat and gloves."

"Yes. In the mess."

"Good. Give me a second. I'm going to radio in that we have you. The negotiation team needs to know you've been taken out of play." He activated his throat mic, thankful for it instead of the boom mic in the helmet they sometimes used. With the two small contact transducers pressed on either side of his larynx, it allowed him to keep his voice way down and still communicate clearly in an environment where camouflage was paramount. "Logan to Cartwright."

The reply was almost instantaneous. "Cartwright here."

"Unit 1 has successfully boarded the *Salacia*. Currently clearing the bow portion of the lower three decks. Noah Swift is with me now; no injuries to report. As soon as the decks are cleared and there are no other confirmed crew or guests outside of the hostages, we'll move Noah to the RIB. Officer Loakes will then board the boat and move to the bridge to be ready to take the helm if the boat runs into trouble. Lounge location for the hostages is likely, as I could hear a single male talking through the connecting door to the foyer."

"HNT has made contact. Location confirmed. Capello is in contact with the suspect and is starting to make headway."

"Good to hear. I won't be able to talk when we're staged but will contact you via double mic click. You can confirm our position at that time. If I need to convey any information after that, we'll have to rely on text communications."

"10-4."

"Logan out." Logan disengaged his mic. "Follow me. Only crucial communications down here—none above on the main deck. Whoever is responsible doesn't know we're on board, and people could die if they find out. Let's get your outerwear. *Quietly*."

They made their way into the main hallway and across to the now deserted mess. The room was approximately eight by sixteen feet and had an L-shaped bench with seating for two tables opposite a large-screen TV, a fridge, microwave, sink, and counter. Not a space to cook large meals—that was clearly done in the main galley upstairs—but a place for the crew to congregate to eat and relax when off duty. Noah grabbed a winter jacket off the end of the bench, pulled a hat and gloves out of one arm, and tugged them on.

Logan turned at the *shush* of a sliding door to find Perez returning to the kitchen. "All clear?"

"Affirmative." Perez's gaze landed on Noah, whose hands were shaking hard enough that he struggled to get the jacket's end tab into the zipper head, finally succeeding on the third attempt. "We ready to move?"

"Affirmative." Logan turned to Noah. "We're going to take you up the crew stairs and then through to Horner's stateroom. Absolute silence all the way."

The speed of Noah's repetitive nod carried the edge of panic, and he remained wordless, as if reinforcing the instructions.

"I'll go first. You follow me, and Perez will bring up the rear. Let's move."

They moved in single file into the corridor, through the door to the staircase, and up to the galley corridor above. Back in the foyer, they found Sims and Johnson waiting out of sight of the door to the lounge in the lee formed by the bulk of the elevator. Sims gave Logan an "okay" signal to report their search was negative.

Logan signaled to Perez to take Noah to the RIB, and then indicated for Johnson to assist. He joined Sims as the three men disappeared into Horner's study. Only the tiniest sound had him looking to the top of the stairs as Wilson and Turner appeared. An "okay" from Turner told him the rest of the boat was clear.

Within three minutes, Perez and Johnson returned with Loakes, who then followed Wilson upstairs to the bridge. Minutes later, Wilson rejoined the group.

Logan signaled Cartwright with a double mic click.

"Confirmation you're in position outside the lounge door." Cartwright's voice sounded in his earpiece. "One click for negative, two for affirmative."

Logan replied with a double mic click.

"Confirmation the boat is clear, Noah has been removed to the RIB, and Loakes is in control of the bridge."

Double mic click.

"10-4. Will convey to HNT. Cartwright out."

They were ready for whatever happened next.

The ball was now firmly in Gemma's court.

CHAPTER 10

"AND IF HE DOESN'T DO the transfer?"

"Then they're all going to die, one at a time. Horner will be last, but if he doesn't do it, there's a bullet with his name on it."

A little over two hours to save all those lives.

"That's an extreme threat," Gemma said, careful to keep condemnation out of her voice. Just stating facts.

"I need his attention."

That stopped Gemma for a moment. I need *his attention. Not I* want *his attention.* That spoke deeply to motive and the lengths to which Kip would go to get this payout.

"It's hardly going to make a dent in his fortune." Kip was talking again, filling the silence as Gemma was thinking through his messaging. "He's a billionaire. He won't even notice it's gone. Anyway, if he was really in trouble, he could collect from this crowd. They're all rich. I'm sure they could help make it up."

"Maybe he can't give you the fifty million because he doesn't have that much. What about if it was a lower figure? Would Horner be amenable to twenty-five million?"

"I don't know. I haven't asked. And I'm not going to. It's fifty, and nothing less. I need that money. And I'm going to get it."

Need again. "Talk to me about that. Why do you need it?"

"Because I do. Why does that matter?" His tone was rising, taking on a shrill edge with a defined waver.

Losing control? "You sound scared, Kip. I don't want you to feel that way. Perhaps if you tell me why, I could help."

"Because I'm here, on this boat, with one simple request, and he won't do as I say." Kip's voice continued to rise, nearly a shout by the end.

Beside her, McFarland wrote on his pad of paper and slid it toward her. **Losing it. Needs separation.**

Gemma nodded in agreement. "Kip, do me a favor. I want you to move to the rear of the room, toward the stern. Give yourself some space from the hostages; give yourself some breathing room while we talk this out. They're not a part of this conversation, so let's keep it private. You'll still be able to watch them from there, but they won't be able to hear you so well. Can you do that for me?"

"Yes." The single word was nearly a growl. A long pause followed, then a heavy exhalation, as if he'd fallen back against a wall, expelling air from his lungs. "I'm here."

"Thank you." She picked up her pen and quickly wrote: **Position confirmed – Kip at stern, hostages at bow end of lounge. Have Cartwright update Unit 1.** She pushed the pad at Ramos, who read it and quietly slipped from her chair. "Let's back up a bit, Kip. I'd like you to tell me about yourself."

The sigh that came down the line was heavy with frustration. "How does that help anything? It's just wasting time."

"It's not wasting time. It helps me get to know you. It's hard for me to help you when I don't know you. Are you married? Do you have kids?"

"Yes."

"Married?"

"Yes, with a daughter and a son."

"Is that why you need the money? For them?"

"I'd do anything for them." His tone overflowed with emotion, his voice cracking on the final word.

For the first time, Gemma heard genuine pain, and she latched on to it as a possible connection point. "It sounds like you love them very much."

"Yes." His whisper was barely audible.

"You want the money for them?"

There was a pause—much too long to suit Gemma—before he answered. "I could give my kids anything with that kind of money."

"Tell me about them."

Kip started to speak, then cut himself off. When he spoke again, his tone was pure suspicion. "Why do you want to know?"

"To learn about them and, through them, you," she said honestly. "You can learn a lot about a person by how they talk about their children."

"Do you have kids?"

It wasn't the turn she expected, but she followed it. "No. But I'm a proud aunt. Three nephews, two nieces." She let pride flow through her tone. "I'm very lucky. They're amazing kids. The youngest is ten months old and has just started to take his first steps. He's a firecracker and is going to give his parents a run for their money. I love him to bits."

"Olivia was like that, though she walked late. She was so good at crawling; she mastered that early and then could go everywhere. Probably delayed her walking for a good month or more. She'd crawl to where she wanted to be and pull herself up. After that, she was into everything. Her brother, Riley, is the less active sort. The artist, the dreamer, the reader. Incredible skills even now, though I may be a little biased."

Ramos returned, slipping silently into her chair and putting her headset on again.

"How old are they?" Gemma asked.

"Olivia just turned nine. Riley's five."

A sound came down the line, and Gemma's head snapped up to stare directly into Chen's eyes across the table. She tilted her head in question—*Was that a sob?*—and he nodded in response.

"You want to get back to them. Your kids and your wife." It wasn't a question, but a statement, a sign that she could see his pain.

"Yes." The word was a barely intelligible mumble.

At risk of him sinking too low, sinking into despair. Time to pull him into the present. "What was your plan for getting back to them? You're out on a yacht in the middle of the harbor. Were you planning on having the captain sail to the marina and you'd hop off there?"

"I don't want to hurt anyone. Once the money is transferred, I'm going to take one of the jet skis from the boat and get to shore."

A jet ski? In this weather?

She'd seen the watercraft in the blueprints earlier. Where were they? Gemma pulled the plans closer and found the outline of two jet skis situated on the main deck level just forward of the owner's stateroom and connected baths. They'd have to be lifted out of the bow section from the bridge deck above to be launched. "You brought a wet suit for that?"

"It's not that far to shore. I'd manage."

"You'd manage." This time Gemma's repetition wasn't to reinforce Kip's words, but as a disbelieving statement. "It's the end of December—a jet ski will need to be launched. Can you do that on your own?"

"No, but the whole crew is here. Someone must know how."

Beside her, McFarland jotted a note and pushed his paper toward her.

This feels like a strange lack of planning.

Gemma was in complete agreement. So much of this negotiation felt off to her—from his vague motivation to his rigidity about his needs to his lack of a realistic escape route. What was going on?

"Let's try to make sure you don't have to make that attempt," she said. "What if we sent a boat out to get you?"

"To take me into custody?" Kip's tone was laced with resignation.

"Kip, I think you and I know that since we're talking, and now that we know where you are, there's no escape through the harbor."

"You're not boarding this boat." The resignation and exhaustion fell away, replaced by steel. "I have a job to do. Nothing gets in the way of that. *Nothing.*"

Gemma could hear she needed to back off, give him some time to come to grips with the end of whatever plans he'd made, plans that might have worked had his attack been kept secret. But now the NYPD had been brought in, that dream was dead, and he needed time to come to that conclusion on his own, without her constant pushing. "Why don't we take a break? I appreciate that you've been so open with me, but you might like a few minutes to take a breath." Gemma glanced at the clock, seeing the minutes crawl by. They couldn't pause for long, but it could be time well spent. "Let's take five. Then I'll call you back, and we can figure out together what we can do to settle this peacefully."

"You're not going to get what you want." Steel backed Kip's tone.

"Let's see what we can do. I'll call you in five. But remember, the helicopter stays away only if you continue to talk to me and no one is hurt. If we hear more reports of gunfire, or if you don't pick up the phone when I call again, it's out of my hands. I'm asking you to continue to work with me on resolving this situation, Kip."

A noncommittal grunt came from the other end of the call, and Gemma disconnected. She pulled off her headphones, then clasped her hands, tipping them against her mouth as she gazed out the window into the darkness, in the direction of the *Salacia*.

"Before we discuss, I have a radio update from Unit 1."

Gemma turned back toward McFarland. "Are they on board?"

"Yes. Logan did a quick check-in once they'd cleared the lower decks and found Noah. He was far enough away from the incident he could radio in. They were about to transfer Noah to the RIB, and one of the Harbor boys was coming on board to monitor and take the controls only if needed. Then when they were in position, Logan confirmed their location. They're here."

McFarland half rose out of his chair and picked up the pencil. On the main deck plan, in the alcove between the sliding door into the lounge area and the bulk of the elevator, he wrote *U1* and circled it. "They're ready to move whenever you need them." He fell back into his seat. "What are you thinking when it comes to Kip?"

"That it's not adding up." When McFarland simply arched an eyebrow at her, Gemma met his stare. "It's adding up for you?"

"Not entirely. But I'm interested to hear your thoughts on it to see if we picked up the same things."

"It's just not ringing true for me. He's gone to this length at considerable personal risk to isolate himself on a boat in the harbor with a crowd of hostages who could easily overpower him if they all put their minds to it, even if there would be some casualties. He's doing it for an ungodly sum of money but can't identify why he needs it. And he needs it. It's not that he wants it; he *needs* it. But can't say why."

"That's my read on it, as well." Chen looked down at his page of notes. "He's hiding his motivation. Related to something criminal?"

"That's what I'm thinking," Ramos said. "Considering where he is now, essentially surrounded for all he knows by NYPD boats and helicopters, at risk of being detained at any minute, he's trying to protect himself, possibly from the ramifications of a worse crime?"

"Like if he killed someone to get on the boat?" McFarland suggested. "Because he's on board and was flying under the radar until he made his move. And everything was rolling along fine until it wasn't." McFarland sat back in his chair and interlaced his hands over his belly. "I agree with everything you've said, but there's one other aspect that's bugging me. His escape plan."

"It's weak," Gemma said.

"I'll say. Does he really think he's going to grab a jet ski out of the hold, jump on it, and zip off to shore in winter waters with no wet suit? A, he's going to freeze to death, especially if he falls off or is hit navigating the harbor on a high-traffic night like this. Or he'll straight up drown." McFarland ticked items off on his fingers. "B, he'll get caught by one of the Harbor Unit boats. C, even if he made it to shore, he's going to be greeted by the NYPD upon docking. There's no way out for him. So why set up this scenario? Why didn't he do it last night when Horner was alone at home or working late in his office? Or why not tomorrow, or the next day? Why pick a high-profile night in an isolated spot without any easy means of escape? It makes zero sense."

"And why did he involve all these people?" Gemma asked. "From what I understand about Horner, threatening his guests with death might not be the deterrent Kip thinks it is."

"Horner has a reputation for being unforgiving and selfish. Cutthroat. It's how he got to where he is, by having no mercy."

"No mercy…" Gemma murmured. "If so, he's going to watch everyone in there die if we can't stop this. What do you know about cryptocurrency?"

"A fair bit. It's replacing cash as the currency of crime because it can be untraceable."

"We have a ticking clock if he wants the transfer done by midnight. How fast can it happen? Does midnight actually mean the transfer has to be initiated at eleven o'clock? Eleven thirty? Eleven fifty-nine?"

"That's going to depend on a few things. Which cryptocurrency, where it's held, if he's considered a VIP at that exchange, if he's willing to pay higher transaction fees to get it moving faster, as well as network speeds and congestion. It can also depend on the regulations of the country you're banking with. Granted, I think a lot of that won't apply to Horner."

"Why?" Ramos asked.

"One of the things you need to do if you're doing a large crypto withdrawal is justify the providence and legitimacy of those funds. Because crypto is becoming the currency of criminal activities, reputable exchanges want to know where those funds came from. The one exception to that is early adopters. If you went all in on crypto early and had a small amount initially that's now immensely overvalued, then those funds won't be questioned and will be released immediately. Horner is well-known as one of those early adopters, and he has a fortune in Bitcoin at his fingertips. The negative with Bitcoin is it tends to be a little slower than other currencies, like Solana, which is essentially instantaneous. Bitcoin can take ten to sixty minutes. But as long as Kip can see the transaction has gone through, he might be fine with waiting for notification of the transfer, then trying to get off the yacht."

"Would a transfer go through at midnight?" asked Chen. "No bank would be open at that hour."

"It's not a bank; it's a decentralized exchange. On top of that, the global crypto market never sleeps. You want to move fifty million dollars at midnight? No problem. So we'll deal with that when we get to it." His gaze focused on Chen, who was staring at his notes again while tapping the end of his pen on the edge of the paper. "Something bothering you, Chen?"

"Yes. It's just..." Chen's tone was indistinct, as if he was trying to put his finger on something that continued to elude him. Everyone stayed silent for a moment, letting him work it out. "Did you notice when he said he had a job to do? That struck me at the time as being odd wording. Not a mission to finish. Not a goal to achieve. A *job*."

"A job," Ramos echoed. "Like work for hire? You think he's being paid to do this? That makes zero sense to me. The payout would have to be massive."

"Even a fraction of fifty million would be massive to us regular folks," McFarland said. "Money can be a great motivator. It doesn't do anything for you if you're behind bars, but maybe he thought he could pull this off with law enforcement entirely out of the picture. It's why everyone was supposed to be in that room. That way no one could reach out for help."

"Which went sideways as soon as Noah was left behind," Gemma said.

"That may be true, but it still doesn't fit for me," Chen said. "I agree with Gemma—the pieces aren't adding up. There's a level of…" He petered out again with a shrug, struggling with the effort to express the nuance he sensed. "I'm not sure what I'm picking up."

"If you ask me," Ramos interjected, "I'd say there's a level of grief backing a lot of what he says. That's driving him. I've seen it before in my days with Special Victims. For some, there's rage at what's been done to them driving the need for revenge or retribution. But it's what's under the rage that's the real bedrock emotion, and often that's grief. Grief at what they've lost, at what they'll never get back. He's determined to do what needs to be done, at least as far as he's concerned, but under it all, I think I hear a deep grief. Just for an instant, but it was there. Possibly from loss? Or what he's going to lose? If you can get to that grief, as long as you can keep him from falling into fatalism, I think you'll have him. But if he has walls up, it might not be possible in the time we have."

Getting to the most personal, the most private. That was always a challenge. Another glance at the clock—9:57.

Two hours before the first victim slaying. Could she pull off a save in that scant amount of time?

CHAPTER 11

"HI, KIP. THANKS FOR TAKING my call."

"Uh-huh."

Apparently, the short break hadn't done anything to change his attitude. Sometimes that happened. Sometimes giving the hostage taker time to think made them realize their best exit strategy lay with the negotiator. But sometimes it gave them time to dig in their heels. There was no way to tell ahead of time how it would go.

Gemma wanted to know so much more—how he'd come on board, as a guest or staff; what weapon he carried and its firepower; what his actual motives were—but there was simply no time. She needed to concentrate on finding a way for him to end this standoff with his head held high but no hostages injured or killed. Now was the real high-wire act. "I'm watching the clock, and I know your deadline. What does Horner say?"

Ransoms could be a tricky issue. When the Grand Central Terminal standoff had happened weeks before with members of Sinister 13 demanding the release of their compatriots responsible for a bombing that had killed 129 victims, the fact that the government didn't negotiate with terrorists had been rammed home forcefully. Companies didn't want to negotiate ransoms with foreign countries who kidnapped their employees because it simply emboldened those bad actors to take similar actions again and again. But when it came to personal ransom requests, negotiators were more likely to leave that decision in the hands of the families involved.

No one wanted to see suspects rewarded for their crimes, but when it came down to money for a loved one's life, Gemma could never fault anyone who decided to pay. Her job was to bring everyone out alive. If a monetary payment could facilitate that, she considered it another tool in her toolbox.

But did Horner think fifty million dollars was worth the risk of his life? Or the risk to the lives of his guests? Did he take Kip's threat seriously?

"Horner's not willing to do the transfer." Kip's tone was heavy with resignation.

Normally, in a situation like this, Gemma would be able to discuss ransom options with the family involved as they'd be outside the hostage situation. But this time, Horner was both hostage and payment target, so there was no way to easily discuss their options.

But that didn't mean she couldn't try. "How would you feel about me talking to Horner?"

"Why would you do that?"

"So far he's only heard from you. You're the one applying pressure. I could be a voice of reason."

"You're crazy if you think I'd hand the phone to him so you two could conspire against me."

That would have been nice, but Gemma knew Kip would have to be a complete fool to allow that to happen. "I'm not asking for that. Put the phone on speaker so you can hear every word." Her gaze dropped to the blueprints in front of her. "You're still down at the stern end of the boat?"

"Yes."

"Is there a seating area between you and the hostages? Something with a table and chairs?"

"Yes."

"Then call him over and put the phone down between you. I understand you don't want him close, but you could put the phone in between you on a table so I can still talk to him, but he can't touch you or the phone. Would that work?"

Kip didn't answer Gemma, but instead barked, "Horner! The cop wants to talk to you!"

The cop. Not exactly the image Gemma wanted front and center during a negotiation. It was always better if she could make a connection with the hostage taker that made her official role a little less in-their-face.

"If you want to talk to her, come stand on the other side of this couch. You come near me, I'll blow your head off." Kip's voice was distant, like he'd put the phone down and was walking away from it.

This conversation was going to be done entirely at a near shout. "Mr. Horner, can you hear me?" Gemma mouthed *sorry* to the group when Chen winced ever so slightly, even as he kept transcribing the conversation. "My name is Detective Gemma Capello of the NYPD Hostage Negotiation Team."

"Hostage negotiation, huh?" The man's voice was deep and carried a harsh edge. "You're not doing a great job."

Gemma jerked in surprise. This wasn't the response she expected. Most hostages displayed fear, or at the very least, caution. Not belligerence.

Beside her, McFarland hissed and rolled his eyes.

"Mr. Horner, we're doing our best to settle this incident."

"You obviously know where we are. Taking care of situations like this is what we pay you for. Do your job."

Ah, one of those people. The "I pay taxes, so I pay your salary, so you work for me" type. This man was turning out to be exactly as big a jerk as McFarland had implied.

"Mr. Horner, the safety of everyone on board is our first priority. The goal is to end this standoff with no one injured, no one killed."

"He caused it. Ever heard of natural consequences?"

Gesù Cristo. This man was going to get himself killed with his arrogance. Or one or more of his guests, though that didn't sound like a priority for him. One more question, and then she was getting off the phone before bullets started to fly and didn't stop until Kip's magazine was empty.

"Mr. Horner, I understand a request was made of you for a ransom in cryptocurrency, and everyone will be released once it's paid. I'll help guarantee that if you're willing to pay the ransom."

"What happened to not negotiating with terrorists? Am I the only one with the balls to tell him to fuck off?"

Across the table, Ramos looked dumbstruck, a feeling Gemma mirrored. Two years as a negotiator, she'd never dealt with a hostage with this amount of agency digging in so deep. At Grand Central Terminal, Elliott Redmond had been outraged at his treatment and had paid the ultimate price for it in his single, brief attempt at freedom. But Horner wasn't trying to win his own freedom—he was demanding it from those around him who he essentially considered his employees.

Not the way it works, buddy.

Normally, a negotiator had to work hard to keep any dislike she felt for the hostage taker out of their tone or they risked tanking the entire negotiation. She'd never had to use that same strategy on one of the hostages.

"When we're negotiating a situation, all options have to be considered." Gemma was careful to keep her tone moderate and measured. "I asked for a chance to talk to you so we could discuss those options. From what I understand, from a technical standpoint, such a transfer could be done in fairly short order. Somewhere between ten to sixty minutes." She glanced at the clock. "We have just under two hours at this point, so there's still time to make a decision."

Gemma was so focused on the silence coming from Horner that she jumped when McFarland elbowed her. She turned to find him writing on his pad again, grateful for the many incidents they'd negotiated together, or there wouldn't have been a chance in hell she'd be able to read his hurried scrawl.

Pending deposit notifications to stall for time

Email about pending deposit, then another after block confirmation

Last when deposit is processed

She had no idea what a block confirmation was, but she didn't need to as long as McFarland did. And she had every confidence he knew his geek-related stuff. She mouthed *Thank you* before turning her attention to the call. "As I'm sure you know, it's not all about the actual deposit, which could buy us some time." Her attention was briefly distracted by Ramos, who leaned forward as the phone she left faceup on the table woke, a message notification glowing on-screen. She scooped up her phone, read the notification, and then silently pushed away from the table and hurried down the restaurant.

Whatever that was would have to wait.

"If you decide to pay the ransom, you have a midnight deadline to beat anyone's life being in jeopardy. But as long as Kip can see the pending deposit notification after block confirmation, he might be satisfied to wait. The final notification will come a little later, but he'll know it's in progress. You have time, so think about it."

"*You* have time. I shouldn't be the one saving the day. Do your job. Get this clown the fuck off my yacht."

Temper shot to the surface. "*Sei proprio uno stronzo,*" Gemma muttered under her breath, knowing no one on the other end of the line would hear her. "Kip?" she said loudly.

"Hang on." Kip's voice sounded from a distance. "Go back to your chair. Fifty million. That's chump change for you. You could end this all right now with one transaction."

"No." Horner's voice, barely perceptible now.

Gemma tipped her forehead into her palm, her elbow braced on the table. If no one was willing to compromise, her hands were going to be tied and it was going to be Logan's show after all.

Would it be better or worse for the situation to reveal her hand there? Would Kip stand down in the face of all that firepower? Or would he go down taking as many hostages—and possibly officers—as possible during an incursion? The thought made her mouth go dry, as did her insecurity that she couldn't read him well enough yet to guess at what he'd do.

"I'm here." Kip's voice was strong again, off speaker and close.

"I've tried to give him something to think about," Gemma said. "Let's give him a little time. Can you do that for me? Let's say…fifteen minutes?"

"He's cutting into his time."

"I know. His time. Your time. I want you both to take that time to think about what you really want out of this situation. I want to help you find a way out for yourself and for everyone in that room. Separate yourself from them again and take the time to think this through. Think about how I can help you."

"There's no help." Again with that flat tone.

"Think about it for me anyway. There have to be options. I'll call you in fifteen. We still have time to work this out, but I need you to help me find a path for you. Talk soon."

Gemma motioned to McFarland to end the call as she noted the time. She pulled off her headphones and sagged against the spindles of her chair, rubbing both hands over her face. "We're getting nowhere." She dropped her hands. "Am I the only one who thinks we're getting nowhere?"

"Definitely not," said Chen.

"He keeps saying there's no help for the situation. He's in charge. He can make that call. But he won't."

"It doesn't help that Horner is an absolute SOB." McFarland's tone carried an edge of disgust. "Is that what you called him in Italian?"

"Close enough."

"Someday I'm going to take Italian for fun. Not the whole language, just the curse words and phrases, so when you lay it on someone, I'll be in on the joke."

"You do that." Movement drew her gaze up as Ramos came in at a jog. "What's going on?"

"We just got a real break. Well, for us, not for the family of Jerome Vann."

"Who's Jerome Vann?"

"Vann was supposed to be the bartender on the *Salacia* tonight. Let me back up." Ramos pulled out her chair and sat. "While we're running this case and while McFarland is doing his own research, the NYPD has assigned detectives to do the legwork on tracking down Horner's personal assistant. Which they did."

"The PA could hold many of the answers we need," McFarland said.

"He's certainly opened some doors. For starters, he provided the guest list for all those who RSVP'd they'd attend, which was pretty much everyone, because who wants to miss a Lucas Horner event?" She scrolled through her phone, opened her email, scanned the contents, and selected one. "Here's the list. I'll send it to you." She quickly forwarded it to the team and then returned to her inbox. "And this one, too. This is the catering help hired for the party with all their associated roles. He had the names of everyone who was coming on board, because Horner likes to run backgrounds on temp staff to make sure they're not some kind of investigative journalist looking for a scoop to make him look bad. Apparently, he's a control freak."

"That's no surprise."

"Definitely not. The detectives ran all the names, only to find out a body later identified as Jerome Vann was pulled out of the East River early this morning."

"How did they identify the body so quickly? Wallet in the pocket?"

"No, the body had been stripped of all identification. But his fingerprints were in the system. He'd been arrested for petit larceny in his early twenties and then released due to lack of evidence. No conviction, but his fingerprints remained in the system, leading to the identification of his body."

"That can't be a coincidence," said Gemma. "So the assumption is that Kip killed Vann and then took his place on the yacht?"

"That would explain how he got there. Now, whether he's pretending to be Vann or came on board saying Vann was sick and he pulled in a favor so Kip was working his shift, we don't know yet, but somehow, Kip got on board. Presumably as the bartender."

McFarland thoughtfully drummed his fingers on the palm rest of his laptop. "Dumb question, because I've never done either role, but wouldn't we think being a bartender requires some skill? Or at least a more specialized skill than just being a server?"

"I worked as a server when I was in college," Ramos said. "There's more to it than you think, but I get your basic question. Unless they wanted someone to just pour beer and wine, knowing how to make cocktails requires some knowledge, especially if you're working off the top of your head. Though, to work in New York State, you don't need a license or certification to bartend. Real-life bartending is as much about crowd control, cutting off those who've had too much, and restocking on the fly as it is about making a dozen drinks in five minutes. That's the kind of experience you learn on the job."

"With a party like this, they'd likely have had a cocktail hour before dinner," said Chen. "Adult beverages, hors d'oeuvres, et cetera. You're right, if he didn't know how to serve a negroni, a whiskey sour, or an espresso martini, he would have been forced to make his move likely more than an hour earlier because his lack of knowledge would have been suspicious. Horner can pay for the best of the best. He's not going to have a bartender who needed to refer to a cocktail book."

McFarland glanced at the clock. "We have ten minutes, so let's test the theory that Kip is a real bartender with the experience to serve and he knew all the drink recipes when one was requested to avoid raising red flags." He opened a new browser tab on his laptop. "It's a long shot, but let's look for a bartender in New York City named Kip."

Gemma watched over his shoulder as he typed in "bartender kip new york city" and started the search. Then blinked at the first page of results. "No way. Only three?"

McFarland scanned the results. "Only one. The top one, Kip Slater, is the head bartender at The Wandering Flask."

"I know that place," said Chen. "It's a hot spot in the East Village. One of those places built around the skills of a particular bartender." When McFarland pinned him with a pointed stare, Chen shrugged. "I went there for drinks once on a date. It was fun."

"It's always the quiet ones who surprise you with their exciting social lives." McFarland rolled his eyes, then turned back to his laptop. "So we have Kip Slater. The next two listed aren't in the city—one's in Syracuse, next is in West Virginia. We have a few entries for Kip's Bay locations, but we're looking for a person, not a place." He moved to the next page of results, then the next. "That's it. Let's try one more angle." He opened a new tab and repeated the search but used the name Christopher instead.

"Christopher instead of Kip?" Gemma asked. "Because Kip is a short form for Christopher?"

"Yeah." Contradicting his words, McFarland shook his head. "This isn't going to work. At least not without significant time or a team of people searching. *Way* too many entries." He flipped to his original search tab. "Let's look closer at Kip Slater. This link leads to his Instagram page."

The page he opened led to blocks of colorful photos of the dark wood of a restaurant bar backed by shelves of multicolored bottles. "He describes himself as a 'mixologist' on his profile page." He opened a few photos of drinks and then one of a man in his late thirties or early forties with a slender build and spiky dirty-blond hair sporting a huge, teasing smile. "It looks like custom drinks is this guy's specialty."

He scrolled a bit farther and then whistled. "Look at this." He turned his laptop around so everyone could see. In the image, Kip Slater stood in a kitchen with bright white cabinets and marble-look countertops. He was flanked by two children as they stood at a chopping block, cutting strawberries, which went into an adjacent blender. "'Teaching the kids the fine art of the virgin daiquiri.'" McFarland leaned in closer. "This is from September. How old you think those kids are?"

"If you said the girl was nine and the boy was five, I don't think you'd be far off," said Ramos. "Exactly the ages Kip told us. No names?"

"Not in this one." McFarland spun the laptop toward him and scrolled down the panel of images to find only a few more family pictures. He opened a few more photos, the kids getting progressively younger in each one. "Mostly his Instagram page highlights his professional career, but his wife is featured—her name is Katie—and the kids get a few mentions. Never named though. Likely for privacy."

"His kids' faces are on the internet, and he's a local public figure," said Gemma. "He can kiss privacy goodbye." She glanced at the clock. "Five more minutes. We need to confirm his identity."

"It's New Year's Eve and he's the head bartender at a local hot spot," said Chen. "He should be there. Go old-school and call them."

"They may be too busy to answer, but it's worth a shot. McFarland?"

"Hang on. Searching." A few clicks and he had it. "Calling now."

The team put their headphones on.

The phone rang four times, and Gemma was sure it was going to go unanswered when it was finally picked up.

"The Wandering Flask. Lia speaking." The voice was young, female, harried, and nearly drowned out by the background cacophony of voices.

"This is Detective Gemma Capello of the NYPD. I need to speak with Kip Slater."

"You and me both, Detective." Lia's words carried an undertone of anger.

"Mr. Slater isn't there?"

"No."

"If I can't speak with Mr. Slater, I'd like to speak with your manager."

"You already are."

"Good. I need to ask about Kip. You expected him tonight?"

"It's New Year's Eve, for God's sake. We've been planning tonight for weeks, planning it around *him*. But he didn't show. We're swamped, and he didn't show."

"Does this happen often?"

"Every now and then. Kip likes his marijuana a little too much sometimes. If he gets tense, he likes to take the edge off. Sometimes he takes it off too much and he greens out."

Not a user herself, Gemma was familiar from her work on the force with "greening out"—essentially overdosing on cannabis, which could lead to dizziness, nausea, vomiting, headaches, hallucinations, and in extreme cases, blackouts. "You think that's what happened?"

"There's a lot riding on tonight. We'd be managing a lot better if he was here." Her voice rose with frustration on her final sentence. "We built this place around his skills. Tonight of all nights, he needs to be here. I thought he'd be here."

"He was excited for tonight?"

"Sure seemed to be."

"Do you think there's any chance something could have gone wrong?"

The pause on the other end of the line went on so long, Gemma wasn't sure the call hadn't been dropped. Then: "You think he's in trouble?" All anger was gone, leaving only stark fear. "That's why you called? Kip's in trouble?"

"We don't know, but we want to reach out to him."

"I've been calling him all evening. He's not picking up."

"Can you give us his number and home address? I'd like the NYPD to do a wellness check."

"Hang on. I need to move into the office. I don't leave that kind of personal information out for patrons to see." Another long pause before the noise level dropped significantly, then the sound of a door closing. "Here's his phone number and address." She read out both, the address being in East Elmhurst, Queens. "You'll let us know if something's happened?"

"We will. Can I get your full name?"

"Lia Thomas." She spelled out both names. "I have to go. It's crazy in here. If Kip's in trouble, you'll help?"

"We'll do everything we can." Gemma was about to hang up when Kip's words echoed in her head. "One more thing. Does Kip have kids?"

"Two. Olivia and Riley."

Bingo. "That's helpful. Thank you. We'll be in touch if we have any more questions." Gemma signaled to McFarland to end the call, then looked up at Ramos. "Kip Slater's our guy. You got that address?"

"I did. Start your next call without me. I'm dispatching officers there now. Let's find out if Kip is passed out on his couch or AWOL." Ramos grabbed her notepad and her phone and left the table, already placing her call.

Gemma swiveled in her chair to face McFarland, whose eyes were fixed on a document on-screen. "You've been doing that dive into Horner. How does Kip connect there? What axe does he have to grind with Horner that he'd go to this extent?"

"That's the question, isn't it?" He met her gaze. "Kip Slater is nowhere in this document. I already knew 'Kip' wasn't, but this is that extra bit of detail."

"Christopher Slater? Anything Slater?"

"No Slater to speak of."

"*Dannazione.* I was hoping there'd be a straightforward connection to save us time."

"We're never that lucky. Anyway, I've been using Horner's generative AI search, but to cover my bases while we're on the next call, I'm going to set up ChatGPT and Claude to do their own searches, looking specifically for Kip in any of his potential names or someone who is related to or associated with him. See if Horner's AI missed something. They can be working in the background, and hopefully, by the time we're off again, we'll have a lead to jump on."

"Are you going to find some kind of data that's not available anywhere else?"

"Most of what we're looking for isn't secret. It's just finding the needle in the haystack. Do you know how many people are affected by Horner and his scads of businesses?"

"I'd have to guess a lot."

"*A lot* a lot. Thousands. *Tens* of thousands. Our window of time won't allow us to search by hand. But a handful of AIs can do it." When she gave him a look, he continued, "TARU would do the same thing for the same reason. They all have different aspects of search as strengths. Do a few on the same question, get a rounded answer."

"I have no idea why you didn't apply to TARU," Gemma said, referring to the department's Technical Assistance Response Unit.

"It's been suggested more than a few times, but I like to be in the action, not constantly adjacent to it. So I find a way to work my tech skills in here. They actually appreciate when I'm in an incident. Unless we need additional equipment support at that moment, forensic support later, or have some extraordinary ask, I can usually cover for them and they can focus their attention elsewhere. Oh, one other thing. As soon as his name and address were confirmed, I did a quick check of NYPD gun licenses."

"Any luck?"

"Yes. I have a Christopher Slater at that address who applied for, and was granted, a premises license for a handgun. A Beretta 92FS, specifically. Kip had a break-in while the family wasn't home a few years ago and applied for a license shortly thereafter."

"Likely in case of another home invasion," Chen reasoned. "He'd want to protect his kids."

"And while a premises license is supposed to be restricted to uses at a residence or business only," Gemma said, "that puts a weapon into his hands."

"We won't know for sure until we get him, but it appears so, yes. So that's another charge to be added to the rest." McFarland jabbed an index finger at the clock. "One minute to call-in time."

"I'm ready. Set up your AI searches fast, then let's put that call through." She straightened her boom mic in preparation. "We now have a good idea who we're dealing with. If we can find out why he's done this, we have a chance of talking him down. Without that, he has all the leverage and the lives of the hostages in his hands."

CHAPTER 12

"HI, KIP. HOW ARE THINGS going?"

"The same."

"Still no injuries and no one in need of medical attention?"

"No."

"Good. Then let's work on getting you home to Olivia and Riley. Has Mr. Horner changed his mind at all?"

"He hasn't said anything. He knows the time is ticking down."

Again, that same flat affect, but this time Gemma was listening for the grief Chen and Ramos said they'd been able to hear.

"Then you and I need to discuss your options. There have to be options."

"No. I need that money."

"You have to consider that he might not give it to you."

"Why would he rather die than part with a fraction of his wealth?" The words were a low, sharp statement, but this time the grief flooded his words.

Gemma met Chen's eyes, and he nodded. *He heard it, too. What are we missing?* "Some people never get over growing up without money. Always scraping by, never sure of their next meal or how to keep a roof over their head. For some of those people, even when they have money later in life, it's not a mindset they can break. They were born into it, raised into it, and can't lose the feeling there will never be enough. Maybe that's how

Horner feels, as incredible as it seems to us, who live normal lives, part of the ninety-nine percent." She let silence beat for a few seconds. "So that's why we need a plan B for you. What happens if he doesn't pay?"

"He has to." A whisper now.

"Let's think this through. I want to help you, Kip. I want to help Olivia and Riley. What do we need to do to get you back to them?"

"There isn't anything. It's all..." His voice drifted away, followed by several beats of silence.

"Kip?"

"*What are you doing?*"

Kip's bellow was so loud, Gemma's headphones buzzed, and she reflexively slapped her hands over them. Across the table, Chen visibly jumped, his pen skittering across his paper.

Gemma shot upright at the force of the words that had screamed through her headphones. "Kip? *Kip!* What's going on? Talk to me!"

A bang sounded, then: "Who are you talking to?" Kip's voice was distant now; he must have thrown the phone down and walked away from it.

A woman's shriek sounded in the background.

Gemma pushed her left earphone behind her ear, grabbed the earpiece dangling over her collarbone, and jammed it into her left ear. She wrapped her fingers around her boom mic. "Mute me."

McFarland jabbed at a button. "Muted."

Gemma hit the button on her throat mic. "Capello to Logan. Double click to acknowledge."

Two clicks sounded in her earpiece.

"I need you and the team to stand by for incursion. He's put down the phone, so I'm not sure what's going on in there. Depending on where they are in the room, you may be able to hear better than me. Acknowledge."

Two clicks.

An upward glance showed Cartwright bearing down on them.

"I'm leaving my radio on so you and the team can follow along. Adjust your volume; it's about to get loud. McFarland, unmute me."

McFarland hit the button and leveled an index finger at her. *Unmuted.*

"Kip? Kip, pick up the phone and talk to me. *Kip!*" She pushed her volume harder, not knowing how far the phone was from him. She pulled the blueprints closer and stared down at her altered version of the lounge.

Her attention was attracted when her departmental cell phone lit up where it sat faceup and silenced near the window. In the notifications bar on the lock screen was a tiny circle with the initials *SL*.

Sean. She lunged for her phone, opening Logan's text message.

Only way to talk. Suspect is yelling inside. Female in distress. He thinks she's talking to someone but it's not clear who. Orders?

McFarland intuited what she'd need and muted her call.

She read out his message to Cartwright, then, "I want him to hold. We don't know enough yet, and we may be able to get control. If we can't, we have no choice but to send them in."

Cartwright's expression was grim. "Agreed."

Back to the radio, as it was the fastest way to convey a message while she was muted. "Logan, Cartwright is with me. You're to hold pending more information. Be ready to move if needed. Let me know if you hear specific language coming from inside the room."

Double mic click.

In the background of the phone call came the sound of indistinct female pleading.

Then Kip's voice. "Who is Noah? Where is he?"

Merda. "Logan, the hostage taker knows about Noah."

Double mic click.

She pointed at the audio equipment, and McFarland unmuted her.

"Kip!" Footfalls sounded, coming closer, as was the sound of ragged breathing—he must have brought the woman with him. "Kip, I need you to tell me what's going on."

The sound of fumbling, then, "I'm here." Fury kept his words tight.

"All I could hear was yelling. What happened?"

"I noticed one of the hostages still had her phone *even though I'd told them to hand them all over*." The emphasis in the final part of his statement was pure outrage at her rebellion against his commands. And likely some fury he hadn't been able to pat everyone down as a double check, but that would have been impossible to manage without being jumped while he was searching one of the other hostages.

If Gemma didn't talk fast, that woman would be their first casualty. Every hostage negotiator knew once a hostage was hurt—or, worse, killed—and the hostage taker had catapulted over the line of serious charges, additional casualties were sure to follow, as the hostage taker would consider at that point they had very little left to lose and violence could be a direct way to get what they wanted. One small act of brutality could open the door to ever-widening circles of breathtaking violence.

It was up to Gemma to stop it. "What was she doing with her phone?"

"Texting someone named Noah. Who she told to *stay hidden*."

This was what Gemma had feared when she heard someone was hidden on board. That the hostage taker might find out and threaten the hostages until the missing man appeared.

Gemma stifled a sigh of frustration. It was evident the woman in question had to be Noah's aunt, Rae Swift. When Kip had stripped the hostages of their communication devices, he might not have paid as much attention to the staff, assuming they'd either use radios or intercoms to connect with each other. She might have been carrying a phone for this one shift just to be able to communicate with her under-the-table nephew if she felt she couldn't do it within Horner's hearing.

Rae had likely been trying to take advantage of Kip's distraction as his emotions had welled—maybe telling Noah to lay low and to alert law enforcement. Little did she know he'd already done those things and she'd endangered her own life for nothing.

"Where is he?" Kip yelled. A shriek carried down the line, then a moan, now much closer to the phone handset. "Tell me, or I'll put a bullet through your skull."

"Kip, stop, this isn't the way." Gemma attempted to pull Kip's attention back to her, back to her pragmatism as the situation continued to spin out of control. But she was afraid the emotion that had welled high in him only moments before was now playing against her. "Remember how I said you haven't done anything to deserve serious charges? Don't go down this road now. It's not too late. Let her go."

"I will, once she tells me where he is!"

"Belowdecks." Rae's voice shook.

"Then text him." Kip's voice took on a condescending tone. "Tell him to join us."

"And if he won't?" A tremor ran through the woman's voice.

"Tell him you'll be the first to die."

More weeping.

They were in trouble. Noah was currently off the yacht. Gemma assumed the RIB was nearby, possibly still at the bottom of the ladder, but Noah would be cold and wet, definitely not someone who was hiding belowdecks. And if he wasn't belowdecks, Kip would surely wonder where he'd gone and how he'd been helped to get there.

Rae Swift was about to blow the A-Team boarding party out of the water, and the body count could skyrocket.

Gemma's phone lit up again. **Ask if there's an intercom system on the yacht.**

She didn't question Logan's instruction. She just went with it. "Kip? Is there an intercom on the boat?"

"How the hell would I know? Is there?" Nothing in the background but sniffling for a few seconds, then Kip was back. "She says yes."

If there is, have them call Noah over the intercom.

"Did Noah answer that text?" Gemma asked.

"No."

"Maybe he doesn't have his phone with him. Maybe he's been separated from it. Why don't you use the intercom? Does that go all over the ship?"

"She says yes."

Sean, you better know what you're doing. "Then get in touch with him."

"You call him." Kip's voice was slightly muffled, as if he'd lowered the phone. "Tell him to come up here. Don't tell him why."

"What if he won't come?" The woman's voice.

"Then the first bullet is yours. Maybe a knee at a time. When he hears you screaming, maybe he'll move his ass."

If he was actually on board, maybe it would scare the life out of him and he'd never set foot in there.

"I'm watching you," Kip said. "Don't do anything funny. And tell me what you're doing."

Gemma had to strain to hear the distant voice. "I'm going to set it to call all the crew areas on the hull deck." A pause followed, then, "Noah, you're needed in the dining room. *I* need you in the dining room. Come up immediately."

Dead air dragged on for a long stretch of seconds, and Gemma's heart started to pound. *You asked for this. Make something happen.*

Then there was a crackle of static followed by a male voice. "I'm here. I'm coming."

Perez?

She suddenly understood Logan's plan. They were leaving Noah out of the loop, but he was going to send in his youngest officer as "Noah." Only the aunt would recognize the switch. Hopefully, she would be smart enough to keep her mouth shut, or Perez was a dead man.

She looked at McFarland and pointed at her mic.

He hit the button. "You're muted. What just happened?"

Gemma looked up to meet Cartwright's gaze, saw the same knowledge there. "That was Perez. Logan, can you talk?"

"Affirmative." Logan's voice was clear but muted, as if ensuring his voice didn't carry. "Yes, that was Perez. We're belowdecks finding him a crew uniform to wear."

"You're sending him in as the college student?" Cartwright clarified.

"Yes, sir. We can't pull that kid out of the RIB without looking like a cold, drowned rat and giving us away. Perez can carry off the role, with command approval."

"Approval granted. Are you sending him in unarmed?"

"I think we have to. At the very least, after what just happened, we have to assume Kip is going to search the kid for his phone, even if he didn't answer her text, because he won't want the risk of any more external communication. But I'm sending him in with my knife."

Logan never went anywhere without his folded tactical blade. The habit had saved his life, which then allowed him to save hers during the

Grand Central Terminal incident. Early in the incident, they'd hidden his weapon and both of their badges by shoving them deep into their boots, an area missed during the hands-on searches.

"They're going to miss his boot in the search," Gemma stated.

"You know it. We found him a crew shirt that should fit him. It won't be exactly like the catering staff, but it will do."

"Tell Perez the aunt's name is Rae Swift."

"Will do." Logan paused briefly. "He's almost ready. We'll be heading up shortly. Watch for him to be coming out in under two minutes."

Cartwright bent over the blueprints on the table. "Send him in through the service pantry. That way there's no risk the team will be seen when the foyer door opens."

"Yes, sir. We'll be going silent now. Capello, keep your radio on so I can monitor once we're upstairs, but I'll be back to clicks at that point for radio communication. One more thing, if we can swing it, Perez won't be wearing his earpiece, but he's going to keep the throat mic on as long as we can hide it under his collar. That way you'll be able to hear what he says a bit better."

"Good idea. Wish Perez good luck and tell him to be careful. I have to get back to Kip." She turned to McFarland. "Unmute me."

She settled her right earphone more securely, leaving the radio earpiece in place in her left ear, though the radio chatter was now silent. "Kip? Kip, are you there?" Ten seconds went by, then twenty. "He must have put the phone down. Let's end the call and place it again. The ringing phone will attract his attention."

Kip answered on the third ring. "Yeah?"

"Hi, Kip. Has Noah arrived?"

"Not yet."

"Give him another minute or two. Who knows where he was down there."

They stared at the clock at the head of the table. 10:28:24…10:28:25… 10:28:26…

Gemma made herself look away, staring out the window at the boats on the harbor. Every minute brought them closer to Kip's midnight deadline, and she didn't feel she was making enough progress. No need to literally watch the seconds tick by.

A full two minutes later, she heard Kip mutter, "Finally."

Then, clear as day through her tactical earpiece, she heard Perez say, "I'm here, Aunt Rae. What do you..." and then trail off, as if he was shocked at what he was seeing.

Silence. Most importantly, no exclamation through the phone from Rae that this wasn't her nephew.

Perez had done well. He'd not only passed on the message to Rae to play along, he'd also faked not knowing about the previous gunfire—and therefore couldn't have been the one to bring the NYPD into the situation—and had communicated shock at the hostages. All things that could help save his life as he walked into the incident with a giant bullseye on his chest.

It was good work. But would it be enough?

CHAPTER 13

LOGAN OPENED THE DOOR FROM the service pantry to the staircase climbing to the small kitchen on the bridge deck. Bracing the door open with his boot, he shouldered his rifle, ready to swing out to protect his officer, if needed.

Perez stood in the service pantry.

Logan would have preferred to take on the role himself, using his experience and skills to see the job through. But there was simply no way a man of thirty-five could convincingly pass as a college student. Perez, already pushing it at twenty-seven, was his unit's youngest member and their best chance to convince Kip this was the kid. Lucky for them, he had a boyish face to hide his considerable tactical skills.

If they were lucky, Kip would focus on Perez's face and not look at the whole of him too closely. They hadn't had much time to get him ready without the delay being overly suspicious. Perez still wore his heavy boots and his black tactical pants—the pockets now empty, as the bulky tactical accoutrements would have been a dead giveaway. His helmet, Kevlar vest, duty belt, uniform shirt, winter jacket, and tactical gloves had been left downstairs, as well as his safetied rifle, spare magazines, and his holstered Glock. Logan had stuffed everything into an empty crew locker, its key still in place in the cylinder, which he pocketed after locking it. It was doubtful anyone from the crew would be belowdecks until this incident was over, but he wasn't about to take any chances leaving a deadly weapon out in plain sight for someone to pick up and use to possibly harm themselves or others.

A few of the occupied crew lockers were unlocked, revealing extra crew uniform pieces of white pants and a white shirt, and they'd been fortunate to find a shirt big enough to fit Perez. It was well made, of good quality material, collared, and buttoned up the front, with left and right breast flap pockets, each secured with a button. Above the left breast pocket, *Salacia* was stitched in a flowing script over the outline of a trio of waves.

There'd been a brief discussion about whether Perez could get away with wearing his tactical vest under the shirt, but in the end, they'd both agreed it was likely Kip would pat him down, looking for both a weapon and a phone. The vest would simply be too obvious, and it could cost Perez his life if he was identified as law enforcement. That would leave Logan with a dead officer and an exposed tactical unit.

No vest it was.

Perez wore the shirt buttoned to the top, the high collar hiding his throat mic. Throat mics had positive and negative aspects. Positive—unlike a boom mic, it could be hidden under a collar, pick up speech in a noisy environment, and also allow mumbled speech to be heard clearly if clandestine communication was required. The overwhelming negative with throat mics was that it didn't pick up any of the local environment, just the vibrations coming from the larynx. Once Perez was inside, they'd only be able to hear his voice through his throat mic; they'd once more be dependent on Gemma's calls to hear what was going on in the greater room.

Some hostage negotiations were conducive to visuals—either from a clandestine camera or a convenient window. But in this case, the dining and lounge area of the yacht was a black box with its remote location and drawn blinds. If they were on land, they'd have called in equipment to run a tiny camera into the room, like they had at South Greenfield. However, they'd needed to board quickly and only carried the essentials, not knowing what extras might have been useful. Still, it was advantageous to have a man inside, a man who could cut to the chase and give directions they wouldn't question. Everyone knew if things blew up, there'd be no time for questions anyway.

Perez was unarmed except for Logan's tactical blade, safely hidden inside his left boot, the boot laced loosely enough he'd be able to extract the knife in under two seconds. It would have to do. Anything more could blow his cover and earn him a bullet.

Logan gave Perez a nod and then held still, waiting for the need to act. He heard the sliding door open, then start to close just as Perez said, "I'm here, Aunt Rae. What do you…" His voice trailed off as he pulled the door closed, except for the final four inches on the side of the room opposite from where Logan stood.

Now for the moment they hadn't been able to plan for. Was the door weighted to close naturally, or would it stay open? Inching around the corner, Logan studied the edge of the door and what lay beyond.

A trio of floor-to-ceiling windows were shielded by opaque white pleated blinds, dark against the night sky beyond. Centered in front of the windows was a sleekly modern, dark-wood buffet with a marble top and shiny chrome accents, bearing several wine bottles and a number of platters.

Seconds passed and the door didn't move. Excellent news. As long as the ship didn't suddenly pitch, rolling the door, this was enough space for Logan to hear what was happening inside.

Logan stepped into the service pantry unseen. He moved to hold position immediately behind the door, waiting. Ready for whatever came next.

"Aunt Rae?" Perez's voice paused in Logan's ear. "Who are you? What are you doing to her?" Perez's tone was rife with confused outrage.

"Kip, what's going on?" Gemma's voice now.

"The stowaway is here." Kip's voice was low, but the lounge and pantry were so quiet, every word was clear. "Come here."

"Why?" Perez's tone held caution.

"I don't have to explain myself to you," Kip snapped. "Come here, or your aunt takes the first bullet."

These were the first few seconds where it could all go to hell. Where the aunt could give them away and bullets could fly. Logan was both fast and accurate, but he'd lose precious seconds getting the door open, taking in the room setup, finding Kip, and making the shot. He held his breath, his rifle in position, balancing on the balls of his feet as he prepared to go through the door to protect his officer, knowing Sims and the rest of the team were about twenty-five feet away through the wall at his back and past the elevator, ready to join the fray if needed.

"Noah, please. Just do as he says." A woman's voice, likely the aunt, buying into their pretense. Saving both her life and Perez's. At least for now.

"Don't hurt her." Perez's voice duplicated between earpiece and filtering through the door on a fraction-of-a-second delay, the voice from inside seeming a little more distant as Perez moved into the room full of hostages.

The second test was about to begin, because there was no reason to get Perez to come closer unless he wanted to check him for a phone or a weapon.

"Turn around. And don't try anything funny. The gun is still pointed at her."

"I'm not going to do anything funny. And you won't find anything on me."

Fifteen seconds passed as Logan leaned closer to the gap in the door, listening intently, but from this distance, he couldn't hear anything.

"You're fine. You both go stand over there," Kip ordered.

You both go stand over there. This was good. It meant Perez would be on his feet and ready to react to whatever came next. While he couldn't see into the next room, he imagined Perez guiding the yacht's chief steward away, making sure she had some distance and he was in a position from which he could act, if needed.

"Kip, can we talk now?" Gemma asked.

Logan silently crept closer to the gap so he could hear Kip's response more clearly.

"About what?"

"About what I can offer you or what you'll do if Horner refuses to transfer the money."

"I've already told you how it will go down. He pays, or people start to die."

"There has to be another way."

"There isn't. And don't threaten the helicopter again. By the time you get officers on this ship, people will be dead."

That's what you think.

"Let's look at this from another angle." Gemma again tried to find a middle ground with a man who was so rigid as to doom everyone in that room. "A show of good faith while we're working things out."

"There's nothing to work out. And I only need one thing."

"No one only needs one thing."

"I do. I need Horner. That's all."

"Then you don't need the hostages."

Logan couldn't help the smile that curved his lips. Leave it to Gemma to latch on to such a salient fact to spin the situation into her favor.

"You just said it—all you need is Horner," Gemma repeated to drive the point home. "What do you know about him?"

"Everyone knows about Horner. He's a gold-plated son of a bitch."

"But what do you know about him personally? Do you think it will matter to him if people around him die?"

"Wouldn't it matter to most people?"

"It would, but does it matter to him?"

In the silence that followed, a new realization struck Logan—Kip didn't know. He'd based this entire hostage situation and the leverage of the deaths of Horner's guests on the fact that normal people would act altruistically to save the life of someone they knew. Would pay a fraction of their immeasurable wealth to save lives.

Maybe Horner wasn't one of those people. Perhaps he'd change his tune when it was his own life on the line, but at that moment, it appeared Horner could live with the deaths of the forty people standing in line before him.

Logan couldn't wrap his head around that kind of thinking. As an officer who risked himself to save the lives of others on a regular basis, this kind of selfishness, egotism, or, hell, evil, was something he could accept as a failing in others but would never understand. It didn't matter your skill set—when someone needed help, you stepped up, stepped in. It didn't take someone with defined skills to save a drowning child, volunteer at a soup kitchen, or donate money to someone who needed it for staggering medical bills or simply to feed their family. It didn't have to be a grand gesture like dragging people to safety under a hail of bullets; small moments counted, too.

Horner clearly wouldn't know a small moment if it strolled up and bit him in the ass.

"Kip?" Gemma broached the silence of Kip's lack of response. "You don't think it will matter to him that people will die for him, do you?"

More silence.

This time, Gemma didn't let him stew, cutting right to the chase. "If it doesn't matter to him, then are you prepared to kill everyone in the room, and then Horner, only to never get what you want? Kip?"

A sharp *crack* came from behind the door. Logan braced for entry but then eased back as silence followed it.

"He ended the call," Gemma said through the radio. "He knows he's in a truly impossible situation now. Let's give him some time before we call again. Logan, can you hold position?"

Logan keyed his radio twice.

"Good."

"Stand by, Unit 1." Cartwright's voice this time over the radio. "Acknowledge."

A double click came through the earpiece, likely from Sims, before Logan followed it with his own.

He stood for a moment, listening to the silence in the room, wishing he could see inside. Then the sound at the end of the call echoed in his head. Carefully lowering his rifle and pulling out his cell phone, he sent a quick text to Gemma: **You may not be able to call him. I think he threw the phone across the room. From the sound, it may have been enough to break it. He may have cut off communications.**

Her response came quickly: **10-4**

If Kip had truly ended communications, then Logan and his men needed to be ready. If there was no talking to him, they'd have no choice but to storm the room before midnight to save lives.

But how many lives would be lost in the process? And would Perez be one of them?

CHAPTER 14

GEMMA KNEW THE TEAM REALIZED something had gone wrong, simply from the grim set of her mouth. "Logan thinks Kip threw the phone, possibly hard enough to break it. We may have lost communications."

"Shit," McFarland muttered.

"My sentiments exactly. And I'm sure Trish also shares them. Hang on a second." She activated her throat mic. "Capello to Unit 1. We're still here, but we're working on how to give Kip an exit strategy that doesn't involve the hostages. We'll be silent so you can concentrate on what's going on in the lounge, but reach out if you need us. Acknowledge."

One set of double clicks, then a second.

"10-4. Capello out." Gemma deactivated her mic. "So we do have one other option if Kip won't answer Trish's phone."

"The aunt," Chen said.

"The aunt. We know she had her phone on her because she got caught trying to contact Noah. I'm not sure if that was a blessing or not. Kip found out about Noah's presence, forcing Unit 1 to improvise."

"You know the A-Team," said McFarland. "They're good at thinking on their feet. And now Perez is in the room with them, which could be good or bad. He has no body armor and only a close-range weapon. But now we have a direct line of information out of that room."

"Perez can't hear us," Gemma said, "but you can rest assured everything he says will be angled to feed us information. We have Noah's cell number, so we can reach out to him for the aunt's. Actually, let's do that now so we have it. Then let's look at why we keep banging our heads, time and again, against the same wall. We need to figure out why Kip is so focused on Horner to the exclusion of all other options, and potentially at the loss of his own life. I've never had a hostage taker shut negotiations down to this extent. Normally we can find some kind of side offer they'll consider. Nothing like that for Kip. We need to know exactly what it is Horner did that pushed Kip to this extreme." Her gaze slid down the restaurant. "I wish Ramos was back for this."

"If she's not, it's because she's on the trail of something," Chen said. "She'll be back as soon as she can."

"Hopefully on the trail of something that moves the needle." McFarland's fingers hovered over the keypad. "Call now?"

"Yes, please."

Minutes later, after a short call with an extremely cold college student, communicating through chattering teeth from the RIB, they had Rae Swift's cell phone number. But before Gemma could do anything with it, her attention was attracted by activity down the restaurant. Ramos had reappeared and stood with Cartwright with their backs to the HNT table, with several other officers gathered around. "What's going on down there?"

"Not sure." McFarland's eyes were narrowed on the group. "Want to check it out?"

"If it's important, they'll let us know. In the meantime, anything new from your research into Lucas Horner?"

"Horner has enough fingers in various pies that Kip could have been affected by Horner's business dealings without it making headlines. Or it could be his new venture, which is too new and isn't sexy enough to hit the headlines yet. And it's local."

"How local?"

"Extremely. Which is likely why Horner is here."

"Here in the harbor or in Manhattan?"

"The five boroughs, to be exact. He and SagAIcity are trying to sell New York City on a smart infrastructure system based on AI. Everything from traffic optimization to public transit scheduling to water maintenance to urban planning to law enforcement. AI can have a part in it."

"Law enforcement." Disapproval was etched into the lines around Chen's eyes and mouth. "I don't like the sound of that. Why do they have to integrate stuff like that into how we work?"

"Many people think AI is the wave of the future and can assist in pretty much every aspect of our lives," stated McFarland. "Try to buy something as simple as a toothbrush lately? AI."

Gemma rolled her eyes. "Why would I need AI to tell me how to brush my teeth? But I'll bet there are some on city council who like the idea of automating part of city management. The budget is a constant battle, and they'll do anything to cut it back. AI means more computers, which costs money, but those computers don't pull down an annual salary plus benefits. *Voilà*, savings in the long run."

"Got it in one. Horner is pushing a frugal city run by AI, one with efficient planning, smoothly flowing traffic, 24/7 chatbot citizen assistance, clean air and water, and an optimized, coordinated emergency response."

"All for a mere king's ransom, I'd assume."

"Possibly two kings' ransoms."

"Am I the only one seeing this could be a complete disaster?" Gemma asked. "Maybe someday, but we're not there now. This could cripple New York City."

"It could, but Horner can be very persuasive. It is, however, creating some deep waves in council."

"Not just council, I'd bet," Chen suggested. "Labor unions around the city, current procurement groups, upper management—who would feel their control of their departments slipping through their fingers—and even the citizens of the five boroughs. There could be a lot of resistance to the city moving in this direction once word gets out."

"But this can't be the only reason you could see for someone objecting to Horner and his AI advances," Chen reasoned.

"It's definitely not. Over the years, Horner has invested in a number of companies, mostly involved in finance or some kind of technology. A thing to note is he has never actually started a company from scratch. He simply researches and then invests in that company."

"So he chooses well and invests wisely but doesn't have any ideas himself," Chen said. "Doesn't do the hard work of building a company from the ground up."

"He doesn't even have a related degree. He has a BA in Philosophy."

"Actually, that probably helped him," Gemma interjected. "I took a few philosophy courses as electives at NYU during my psych degree. Those courses were great for teaching big-picture ideals, as well as communication and problem-solving. That could play into his business acumen and subsequent successes. What did he do before SagAIcity?"

"He got in early on a food delivery service. A small local group, but one so successful it was then bought out by Uber Eats, raking in a huge profit for him. He's angel invested in search companies, Web advertising companies, and a company that makes software to turn your car into a self-driving vehicle, among others."

Gemma sat back in her seat, her gaze trailing to the harbor again. "But would this particular act make sense through that lens? Fifty million is an obscene amount of money to most people, but Horner could lose it and not notice with his wealth." She swung back to face the table. "And how would this stop him? It won't slow him down personally or professionally. More than that, this feels too personal. David versus Goliath. Not David versus Metropolis, which is what his proposal to New York City would be. And even if Kip killed Horner tonight, his company still exists. Whatever deal is in the works could still continue."

"The personal is where I keep tripping up, too," McFarland agreed. "I ran a search on Kip Slater again, looking for any points of intersection. There simply aren't any. Horner's done business all over the world, big business, wrecking lives more than a few times as employees were downsized or companies failed after Horner took a big risk. Kip's world is very small, all centered in Manhattan. I even expanded the search to related names—mother's maiden name, et cetera—and found nothing. Though Chen called it on the upper New York State accent—Kip was born and raised in Rochester."

"We have a major disconnect between Kip and Horner," Chen said.

"Which I've been saying from the beginning," Gemma said. "This is simply not adding up. Unless they find a manifesto at his residence, I'm not sure we're going to figure this out in time. And with Kip not willing to bend in any way, I'm not going to have a choice but to send Unit 1 in before he starts firing. He doesn't know we have a team on the boat with him. Surprise may be our only option."

"There's one angle on this that might make sense, but I haven't been able to find any way to connect Kip. Horner has a habit of getting in with a company and then using his investment for leverage to streamline processes that he sees as wasteful."

"Eliminating waste in that kind of company usually means cutting staff," Chen pointed out.

"Correct. And that's exactly what's happened again and again. We can't track the connection to Kip, which leaves us with the question of whether some kind of financial hardship has come to someone close to Kip to justify this."

Gemma kept working it through in her head, but every time, the pieces didn't fit together properly. "It would have to be a pretty damned close relationship for him to go to this extent. Or something catastrophic happened, like a bankruptcy causing someone to take their own life. Any deaths in his family that you can see?"

"Nothing obvious from Kip's socials. We could get information from government records, but we'd have to go through the usual legal channels, so it's not something we're going to get tonight. If we could reach Kip's family, which could help move that angle along." McFarland's gaze slid sideways, froze. "Incoming."

Gemma followed McFarland's gaze down the restaurant. Two men were striding down the main corridor. From a distance, they could have been brothers—both with shorter, stockier builds and graying hair despite the twelve years between them. But only one had the olive Sicilian skin tone of each of her blood.

Chen twisted around in his chair to see the HNT's supervising officer, Lieutenant Tomás Garcia, and Chief of Special Operations Tony Capello, approaching. "There goes everyone's New Year's Eve."

Instead of continuing down the restaurant, the two men stopped at the A-Team table, leaning in to look at something on the tabletop. Cartwright picked something up, and Gemma had a flash of a video screen between bodies before it was set back down again.

"They're watching something down there."

McFarland stood, craning his neck for a better view. "I'd bet they have a tablet to stream the search of Kip's place via helmet cams."

As if aware the HNT was watching him, Cartwright turned around as he tapped his microphone button.

Gemma studied him as he spoke to someone over the radio, but not Unit 1, as her earpiece stayed silent. "I don't like his expression. Something's gone sideways."

McFarland lowered into his chair. "They're coming over, so we're about to find out." He waited as Tony Capello, Garcia, and Cartwright approached to stand at the table while Ramos pulled out her chair and sat down. "Chief, Lieutenant. Sorry this has interrupted your evening."

"Rowland interrupted my evening." Garcia's cocked eyebrow expressed his irritation in a way his tone of voice didn't. "As the NYPD has been building a list of who's on that yacht with the help of Horner's personal assistant, word has started to spread. One of those people is Rowland's chief of staff."

McFarland groaned. "Great. We all know what that means."

Gemma certainly did. Kevin Rowland, mayor of the City of New York. The man who had interfered in the hostage standoff in City Hall last August in his rush for a quick resolution and whose actions had likely contributed to the death of his longtime friend, First Deputy Mayor Charles Willan. Rowland had also reached out during the Rikers Island hostage taking in one of the Enhanced Supervision Housing units, pressuring them to quickly wrap up the crisis because it made the city look bad. That emergency had taken days to resolve, finally requiring an armed incursion by Logan and two teams of ESU officers when prisoners had killed Correction Officer Garvey on the fifth day of the incident.

Now he had a reason to be involved again.

"You told the mayor we had the situation in hand and that our goal was to get everyone out alive?" she asked.

"Of course." Garcia looked like he was putting a lot of effort into not letting his opinion of the mayor show in his expression in front of his superior officer. "It had its usual effect of bouncing off him without actually getting through to him. He wants to be kept in the loop. We'll do that, hopefully once this is all resolved. But things just took a turn."

Gemma met her father's eyes, the unease in their depths giving her a jolt. *Something is very wrong.*

"Which we'll get into in a second," Tony said, his eyes still locked on his daughter's. "First, what link do you have to tie your hostage taker to Lucas Horner?"

"That's our big issue—we don't have one. We have two people who seem to live in entirely different worlds. Worlds that have never collided, at least with the information we have now. It's caused problems. I've tried to get concessions from Kip, tried to get him to consider other options besides opening fire on everyone at midnight if Horner doesn't come through with the fifty million he's asked for, but he won't consider a single option. It's the money or the hostages' lives, including Horner's. That's his only endgame."

Tony nodded thoughtfully. "That actually makes sense in light of what we've learned."

Gemma's gaze flicked to Cartwright. "Which is?"

"Sergeant Nilsson took a team over to Slater's house in East Elmhurst. He lives in one of those townhouse rows, the ones right on the street but with a laneway in back with a place to park behind the house. Slater's place is an end unit. It was locked, so Cummings and his team breached the front door. Cummings streamed his helmet cam to us so we could follow along because we're squeezed for time. Straightforward single-floor, two-bed, one-bath layout. It was empty."

As McFarland opened his mouth to speak, Cartwright jerked up an index finger, telling him to wait. "But that doesn't mean we didn't learn anything. There were signs of an abrupt exit—the TV was still on, snacks were sitting in the middle of the table, a novel was dropped onto the living room floor. The sliding back door had been left ajar. Most importantly, there was a note left on the kitchen counter. Written to Slater specifically."

The pieces began to fit together in Gemma's head. Even before Cartwright finished his explanation, she understood why they couldn't find a connection between Kip and Horner.

There was never one to begin with.

"The note was a typical eight-and-a-half-by-eleven sheet of paper, printed off a home printer," Cartwright continued. "It instructed Slater that if he wanted to see his wife and children again, he was to join the catering staff for the *Salacia* as the bartender at five thirty that afternoon at Chelsea Piers Marina. He was to bring his own gun and any extra ammunition he had on hand. After dinner, he was to use whatever means necessary to take everyone on board hostage and then force Horner to transfer fifty million dollars in cryptocurrency to a specific wallet address. The instructions were to give Horner until midnight, and then to start shooting hostages, one per minute, until Horner gave up. If he didn't, Horner was to be the last to die."

McFarland whistled. "Suddenly his inflexibility makes total sense. He was blackmailed into this job. He's doing what needs doing to save his family, even at risk to himself and his own freedom. Though you have to wonder why he didn't let us know about it once we contacted him."

"That's because Slater was informed in the letter that one of the guests was wired and would be watching him. If he didn't follow the instructions, the spy would give the command to kill Slater's family."

"Wired? From that distance?" McFarland's expression reflected his disbelief. "No way. I mean, they're good for hundreds of feet. You're running an op with a wired subject, you can pick up their signal from the van outside the building. But out there? In the middle of the harbor? Unless the person responsible for this is sitting with a receiver at the edge of Governors Island—which he's not, because how would he also hold Kip's family hostage in such an open area—there's no wire in play here."

"You know that, but you're the tech guy," Ramos pointed out. "If Kip doesn't know anything about tech, he likely bought it hook, line, and sinker."

"He's also not thinking clearly," said Chen. "He's not analyzing what's in the letter, just reacting to it. Given time, he might have thought it through or done some research, but he didn't have that luxury. It's enough to keep him on the straight and narrow. He thinks he's being watched and will act accordingly."

Gemma tipped her head into her fingertips, massaging her forehead at her hairline, her eyes closed as she gear shifted into a new reality for this case.

"What are you thinking?"

It was her father's voice, directing the question at her. She opened her eyes and raised her head. "We've known there was a disconnect for an hour. I couldn't reach him no matter how we tried to find accommodation for him—he won't release any hostages, won't accept transportation off the yacht, won't accept a smaller amount of money from Horner. This is why. He hasn't been in control from the start. He's been following a script." She met Garcia's eyes. "He's as much a victim as every hostage on that boat."

"Agreed." Garcia's expression reflected her own belief this information didn't give them any kind of advantage; more than anything else, it simply highlighted why they were at a dead end. "And that will be taken into account as long as no one is hurt. The moment he hurts—or worse, kills—someone, things get a lot more complicated."

"Do we think he left the note behind as evidence?" Ramos asked.

"He might have left it behind so there was no chance it could be found on him, possibly blowing the incident before it even started," Chen suggested.

"He likely took a picture of it with his phone," said McFarland. "Nothing to find on him and more subtle than unfolding a note if he needed to check details like the crypto wallet address. Everyone is always on their phone, so him looking at his wouldn't be suspicious in any way."

"What are the instructions for after everyone is dead or the money is transferred?" Gemma asked.

"That his family will be released, unharmed."

McFarland's laugh held no humor. "That's not going to happen. Because of their age, the kids might not be considered credible witnesses, but the wife would be. Whoever's done this will likely hold on to them in case proof of life is needed before the end of the crisis, but then they're entirely disposable."

"I think this just became both simpler and considerably more challenging all at once." Gemma looked from Garcia to her father and back. "We need to send in Unit 1, not to apprehend Kip, but to rescue him." She looked at the clock. "We have just over an hour until midnight. What was the exact wording in the letter about the transfer? It has to be complete by midnight or initiated?"

"That's a good point." McFarland turned to the three men standing at the head of the table. "It can take up to an hour for a Bitcoin transfer, so if it's only initializing it, that gains us some badly needed time."

"Hang on." Cartwright pulled his NYPD phone from his pocket. "I asked Cummings to snap a picture of the letter so I could pass it on to you." He scrolled for a moment. "Here it is. I'll send it to you, but for now, take a look." He passed the phone to McFarland, and Gemma leaned in to read it.

The bare-bones message was exactly as Cartwright had described it, and Gemma felt a burst of sympathy for Kip. The terror he must have felt while reading it must have been suffocating.

"The transfer has to be initiated by midnight," McFarland clarified, jumping to the salient information while Gemma was still reading through to get a feel for what Kip had internalized. He paused for a full twenty seconds, realizing she was reading from the beginning. "Done?"

"Yes." She sat back as McFarland passed the phone across to Ramos so she and Chen could read the full letter. "I wanted the full impact so I knew exactly what Kip was dealing with. He must be hanging on by his fingernails in there."

"What do you mean?" Garcia asked.

"He's a bartender. A family man. And he's been catapulted into this role of aggressor. He was so angry when we first got him on the line. Was that playing a part or lashing out at the situation?"

"Could have been both."

"If he doesn't follow the exact instructions, his family dies. If he does, he's told they'll live, but he's going down a road he may never be able to come back from himself. It's likely he would either be killed or captured; either way, the life he knew as a family man would be over."

"That's if he believes they'll survive tonight," Ramos pointed out. "He may have already come to the conclusion himself there's no way they'd be allowed to live to identify the suspect afterward. His life being over might pale in comparison to their deaths."

"He has to be lost as hell out there." McFarland stared out the window to where the harbor was noticeably more crowded than it had been when they first sat down.

"We need to help him." Gemma looked up at Cartwright. "We need Logan to get to where he can talk to us. I don't want to just issue orders; we need to explain what we've discovered and get his take on the situation. Better still, we need both Logan and Sims, as they're in different locations, and I suspect this needs to be a two-pronged attack. They're on board and can advise if anything isn't arranged as indicated by the blueprints."

"Logan radioed in from the hull deck. I'll tell them to go there." Cartwright activated his mic. "Cartwright to Logan and Sims. We need to discuss strategy. Move to the hull deck where your communications won't be heard on the main deck. Radio in when ready. Acknowledge."

Two sets of double clicks sounded.

Gemma pulled the main deck plans toward her again. They needed to come up with a plan, to think this through.

How could they possibly pull this off to ensure everyone survived? Worse, assuming the spy was actually real, how would they identify him or her in time to neutralize the threat?

CHAPTER 15

"LOGAN TO CARTWRIGHT. WE'RE CLEAR to talk."

Sitting on the lower bunk, Logan took in the tiny crew sleeping cabin they'd selected for this conversation. Almost all the way to the bow of the ship, it had twin bunks, a desk that folded up flat against the wall with a chair beneath it—now occupied by Sims—two lockers, and a connected bathroom. Not only was the area lacking in the luxury evident one floor above, but space was at a premium. Every aspect of the room was compact and squeezed together as tightly as the designer had been able to manage. Clearly, the crew was only expected to spend a minimum of time inside.

Logan was willing to bet that included a minimum of sleep. Horner would expect his staff to be at his beck and call any hour of any day. The rich so often did.

"Cartwright to Logan. You're far enough away?"

"Affirmative. Hull deck, and we took the extra precaution of ensuring one watertight door is between us and the staircase. We'll keep our voices down, but they won't hear us. At the same time, we're now cut off from the standoff but left the team split between the two entrances. Wilson is in the service pantry. Johnson and Turner are in the foyer. They'll let us know if something happens that requires our attention while they're on the radio with us."

"Good. Capello, you're up."

"Thanks," Gemma said. "We need to loop the A-Team into a situation we've just discovered. We were able to determine that Kip is Kip Slater, a bartender at The Wandering Flask in the East Village. The man who was supposed to be the *Salacia*'s bartender for the party was found floating in the East River this morning. Kip took his place in order to take hostages and give Horner the ransom demand. But here's the kicker—he's a hostage in his own right. When Nilsson took a team over to Kip's townhouse in East Elmhurst, they found a ransom note left for Kip. Someone has his wife, Katie, and his young kids, Olivia and Riley. They'll die if Kip doesn't do exactly as he's doing now. The fifty million also isn't going to Kip. The letter outlines the exact account info for deposit."

"I'll be damned," Sims murmured.

Logan remained silent, but his mind was racing. No hostages had been killed; none had even been injured. Logan had thought the hostage taker didn't have the stomach for it or hadn't been pushed far enough, but maybe that wasn't it at all. Kip was only following orders, Logan suspected, to the letter.

"What were the instructions?" he asked.

Gemma quickly read out the entire letter.

"He's following the instructions," Logan said. "This could be why he hasn't hurt anyone up to now. He's going through the motions, but it's not his motivation driving him. Still, a man desperate to get his family back will do what needs doing."

He knew he would in those circumstances. And damn the consequences.

"The instructions were to take his handgun and extra ammunition," Logan said, "but didn't say how much. Whoever wrote that note knew about the party but possibly didn't know the number of attendees, so couldn't be specific."

"Also didn't know the number of crew or catering staff," McFarland said.

"The person behind the letter also may not care," Gemma pointed out. "Horner is the bottom line. Either Horner pays, or Horner dies. The rest is just window dressing."

"What are the chances Kip would have enough ammunition to work his way through the guests and staff so he'd still have a bullet left for Horner?"

"He was told to bring his own gun," said Sims. "What does he own?"

There was a pause, then McFarland said, "A Beretta 92FS."

"Unless he's obtained an illegal magazine, he's going to be limited to the standard ten-round magazine," said Cartwright. "If he wanted more rounds in New York State, he'd have to buy a second magazine."

"Unless he just brought a box of ammunition. This isn't a gun expert with a concealed-carry license," Logan said. "This is a guy with a premises license who just wants to protect his home. Someone who buys a gun for premises protection might only buy a box of ammo to go with his gun because in his wildest dreams, he'd never assume he'd fire more than ten shots at anyone. The kid reported three or four shots already fired, so he might be down to as little as six or seven rounds in that magazine. Which could be his only magazine."

"No matter what he's carrying, he needs to be neutralized by midnight." Cartwright, his words clipped and precise.

"He needs to be taken into custody before midnight." Gemma's voice, coming hard on the heels of Cartwright.

The term *neutralize* didn't sit well with Gemma. This was the crux of the disconnect between the A-Team and the HNT, one that could sometimes create real difficulties between the two groups. When push came to shove, Cartwright and the ESU had the final decision, so it was always a fight for the HNT. The HNT considered it their job to get everyone out alive, including the hostage taker. Let the justice system deal with him, rather than the morgue. The A-Team's entire purpose was the protection of the citizens of New York City. Right now, there were citizens under threat one deck above, and Logan and his men were trained to do what must be done. Sometimes that meant the death of the hostage taker. Logan would take the shot if he had to but would be happy to find other ways if they presented themselves. Gemma would do everything in her power to provide those other paths.

Logan had known Gemma for fifteen years in some capacity—starting when they attended the academy together, where they'd spent six months trying to competitively best each other for top spot. But it was only during the last weeks that he'd truly come to know her intimately, giving him deeper insight into how she viewed her role as primary negotiator.

Bottom line—she would fight like hell to safeguard everyone in that room, from hostage to spy to hostage taker. He would do everything in his power to back her up as long as the hostages stayed safe. If they didn't, then he and Gemma might have a difference of opinion, depending on the circumstances. They'd cross that bridge if they came to it.

"The instructions are to give Horner until midnight to do the transfer," said McFarland. "If he hasn't by then, pressure is to be applied to get Horner to get the job done. One death per minute."

Logan could see where McFarland was going. "That means, assuming he has the ammunition, it could be forty minutes before he gets to a kill shot for Horner. From what I understand about Horner, if he's really that self-centered, forty deaths to save his own skin might not make much of an impact."

"And if whoever this suspect has on board as his spy was still able to communicate before phones were taken away—and he or she should have had more than enough time—the real suspect should have a good idea of how many were on board. How many guests and how many crew members and caterers they'd seen, knowing that a few more, like the chef and sous-chef, et cetera, would be downstairs."

"There's possibly a bigger window to save Kip's family," said Logan, "but it would come at too high a cost. We need to preempt that midnight cutoff."

"Agreed," said Sims. "What's the plan?"

"Is there anything on board that differs from the blueprints?" McFarland asked. "All entryways are as originally planned?"

"Affirmative."

"Can you confirm the hostages are at the forward end of the lounge?" Gemma asked. "We think the table is at that end and the diners are being kept in their chairs. The crew and catering staff are likely standing around them."

"Affirmative," Logan replied. "When Perez went through the door from the pantry, he purposely left the sliding door open about four inches. It gave me a narrow view into the room, including a buffet loaded with food and the lowered blinds. And while I couldn't see the hostages, I could hear movement near the door, material shifting or the odd cough. When Perez went in, I could hear him through the radio and through the door. What came through the door moved away as he went farther in to where Kip is on the far side."

"Then he went to stand with the hostages."

"He's on the port side," Logan confirmed. "Kip told him to stand with the hostages. A few minutes later, after Kip had thrown away his phone and while you two weren't talking, I heard Perez clear his throat. He was letting me know he was near the open doorway. He may actually be purposely standing to block the gap in the door. It could give us cover. Wilson, you'll have to be silent, but can you confirm?"

Two clicks.

"Check. One click for you can't see him, two if you can."

Silence stretched for a full twenty seconds. Then two clicks.

"Excellent," said Cartwright. "Is he standing to block the doorway from someone at the far end?"

Two clicks.

"How close is he?" Logan asked. "Ten feet?"

Two clicks.

"Five?"

One click.

"10-4. So between five and ten feet away." Logan met Sims's eyes. "We go through that door, one of us should be able to arm him with a Glock."

Sims nodded in agreement.

"With this change in motivation, is an incursion now on the table?" Logan asked.

There were a few beats of silence, long enough for Logan to throw a raised-eyebrow look at Sims. He could imagine the silent discussion going on in the restaurant—Cartwright and Gemma staring each other down.

"Possibly," Gemma said. "What are our options for entry?"

"The obvious option is going through the two doors simultaneously," Sims said. "There are only five of us now, so three through the double-width foyer door and two through the pantry door?"

Logan closed his eyes, seeing the blueprints in his mind, seeing the lounge area. Focusing in on the stern end. "I'll take the outside entrance."

"The sliding doors by the pool?" Cartwright clarified.

"Yes. That's going to be the better way to go."

"Chances they'll be locked?"

"I'd say close to zero. It's a fireworks cruise. They're expecting people to wander outside to watch. They could go upstairs where there's more room, but some would just step out right there to watch where it's more convenient. It'll be open. We'll time the entry so Kip is distracted by what's happening behind him, so he doesn't simply open fire on officers coming through the doors, because the hostages lie between those two points. If he fires, someone will likely die. He'll have his back to those doors, considering himself safe from that angle of attack because he's not aware of the team on board, and if the helicopter returned, he'd be able to hear it. Just a few seconds will be all I'd need to catch his attention, then everyone else comes in. Whoever goes through the pantry arms Perez, and then we're at full strength."

"That puts you in the line of fire." Gemma's statement was flat, emotionless.

Here it was, the first real test of their being able to work together. She needed to trust him to do the job, to not get himself killed. And if he couldn't, she needed to accept that she held no responsibility for his death. This was what they did. If they couldn't pull off this first incident as a couple, they'd never work together again. In his opinion, that would be a loss for both of their units.

"Yes, it does. Bottom line, do you think he'd fire on me? You've talked to him. What's your gut impression? I trust your take on him."

She was silent for a moment as she considered. "I don't think so, no. I think shock will stay his hand, at least initially. But you'll have to work fast. This isn't naturally his fight and he's not a natural aggressor, but if you give him enough time for his brain to kick in, for him to remember his family's survival lies in the balance, even though it's not in his detailed directions, he may act against you."

"I'll have him disarmed before that happens. You're correct that speed will be crucial here. I think we can do it."

"What about the wild card of the spy?" Cartwright asked. "Is the whole thing made up, or is there actually someone there? Someone to literally hold a gun to Kip's head as backup. Or to simply take over if Kip folds?"

"We can't discount it," Logan said. "We go in prepped for one of the hostages to be a threat. Do we have command approval on an incursion?"

"You have command approval."

That wasn't Cartwright. That was Gemma's father, Chief Capello. There were more people in this briefing than he or Sims knew. He'd been sitting back, listening, letting his teams do what they did best.

Definitely extra pressure on Gemma to perform like this was just a typical op.

"I want you to put this into motion immediately," Tony continued. "Time is ticking. And we need every moment to track down where Slater's family is once this situation is contained. We'll follow your camera feeds from here."

"Yes, sir." Logan stood from where he sat on the bunk, Sims following suit. "We're heading up now. I'll need a few minutes to get into position outside, but then we'll go in."

"Good hunting," said Cartwright.

"Logan and Sims going 10-7." Logan keyed off his mic. He cut off any thoughts of how Gemma was feeling right now. She'd done her job. Now it was time for him to do his.

He turned to Sims. "Time to move."

CHAPTER 16

LOGAN STEPPED ONTO THE OUTER deck, easing the door shut behind him. Through the glass, Sims and Turner flanked the double-wide pocket doors leading into the lounge. Both stood braced, their rifle butts pressed against their shoulders, ready to go through the door on the anticipated signal.

Sims's gaze darted to Logan, visible through the door by the light thrown from the foyer, and he gave him a nod. Logan returned the nod, then started down the deck that hugged the outside of the ship, flanked on his left by a waist-high white wall topped by a metal railing.

Almost immediately to his right, floor-to-ceiling windows ran in a long line, broken only by a four-foot stretch Logan knew from the plans camouflaged ventilation ductwork. Each window was covered by semiopaque blinds, and Logan paused before the first one, trying to discern any kind of movement inside. But the blinds went past the edge of the window, so there was no view from his angle; otherwise, only indistinct shapes of bodies standing near the windows were evident. Anyone seated at the tables was too far inside to be visualized.

He moved on, keeping his body hunched low, being a smaller visual target in case anyone looked out the window.

After so much time inside in his winter gear, the cool rush of winter wind was refreshing. He knew that wouldn't last if he ended up positioned outside for long enough, but for now it was decreasing his overheated core temperature. He pulled his collar away from his damp neck, letting the wind that blew from the northwest directly into his face slip inside.

One boot in front of the other, moving soundlessly behind the rhythmic slap of the choppy harbor water against the starboard side of the boat, he quickly covered the more than fifty feet of the dining and lounge areas, then slipped around a pillar. And froze.

The stern wall of the lounge was a series of six glass doors on runners Logan imagined would slide into a stacked row on each side, opening the rear of the lounge area to summer's temperate marine breezes. But because this was a dual wall and entrance, it wasn't covered by opaque blinds but by semitransparent curtains, giving him a view of the internal space.

But also giving anyone inside a view of him on the lighted deck.

A quick scan showed the pool area to be only slightly darker. Out from under the bridge deck, it was lit by the radiant aqua lights thrown by the shimmering waters of the pool, its stern edge a glass wall to give that popular infinity appearance. But lights under every step and under the mirrored L-shaped couches hugging the pool would still illuminate him, even as the pool backlit him as a shadow, which would be worse.

He was going to have to hang back until he was ready to move. Then he'd have to move fast.

Keeping his rifle braced in place, he took a small sidestep, enough so he could better see through the diaphanous curtains and yet keep himself at an oblique angle so the only person who might see him was Kip, and only if he turned around and took his eyes entirely off the hostages. It was doubtful that would happen, but Logan wasn't taking any chances.

A single man stood with his back to the curtains, feet shoulder-width apart, shifting restlessly. Both hands hung at his sides, but Logan was sure the dark mass in his right hand was a firearm. It was impossible to tell if he had pockets or if those potential pockets held extra magazines. Logan had to assume they did.

Beyond that single silhouette was a large amount of empty space, then a mass of dark blurs filled the background.

They'd been correct in their assumption of the setup, which was good. It meant that even if Logan had to struggle with Kip, there was at least twenty-five feet between him and the nearest person. There was some safety in that distance—not a lot, but some.

Logan's hope was the sight of a rifle pointed at his chest would make Kip second-guess making any kind of stand.

A quick glance at the sliding door showed a simple nickel-brushed D-shaped handle with a keyhole that likely had a matching handle with a thumb latch inside for an easy exit.

There would be a gap in the curtain at that spot where the two sides came together. He'd have to cross the ten to twelve feet in a rush, unlatch the door, slide it open, and go through the curtain in only seconds. By that time, Kip would be bringing his gun around. At such a short distance, if he pulled the trigger, there was no chance he'd miss.

The only saving grace was it would likely be a center mass shot, and the 9mm rounds used in Kip's handgun would be stopped dead by Logan's Kevlar vest.

Logan could only hope to not take another round—or four—in the chest again. He was essentially healed, but every once in a while, he'd do an exercise in the gym and there'd be a twinge. Deep healing wasn't totally complete yet. Hopefully, he wouldn't be taking a giant step backward tonight.

Or worse.

"Cartwright to Logan. Are you in position?"

Logan sent back the affirmative via a double mic click. Then readjusted his hold on his rifle, moving his finger from lying along the trigger guard to threading through it. He adjusted his left hand slightly on the fore-end. Ready.

"Sims?"

Affirmative clicks.

"Wilson?"

Affirmative clicks.

"All Unit 1 teams, you are a go. Logan, on my mark. Three…two… one…*mark!*"

Trying to keep his footfalls as light as possible while moving fast, he covered the distance to the door in seconds, dropped his left hand while still supporting his carbine with his right hand wrapped around the pistol grip, grasped the handle, and slammed the door to the left. It moved smoothly, gliding on the track as Logan grabbed a handful of curtain and jerked it clear of the gap, even as he stepped through.

"Other teams, *go!*" Cartwright barked in his ear.

"NYPD! Hands in the air!" Logan was conscious of the sounds of pounding feet coming from the other end of the room, but his attention was locked on Kip as he whirled around, the Beretta gripped in his hand rising into the air.

But Kip couldn't turn fast enough, and Logan had him pinned under the barrel of his rifle in a fraction of a second. "Freeze!" He decided it was time to take a page out of Gemma's book. "Do it for Olivia and Riley. For Katie. Don't force my hand."

Kip froze at the names of his family, only three-quarters turned toward Logan, the gun frozen at a forty-five-degree angle from the floor.

"We know about the note. We know about your family." Logan kept his voice low as a furious shriek sounded from across the room. "Let us help you. Let us help them. End this. Come in and help us save them."

An anguished moan bubbled up from Kip's throat, and he dropped down to his knees, both hands in the air. Keeping his finger on the trigger of his rifle in case Kip lost his mind and tried something stupid, Logan reached over with his left hand and pulled the pistol from the other man's grip. With his left thumb, he engaged the safety. "Hands on your head."

Kip put his hands on his head, interlacing his fingers across the back of his skull, then bowed his head, his breaths coming hard.

Only then did Logan look up to take in the rest of the room. The setup was exactly as Gemma had described—a long table, flanked by chairs at both ends and along both sides, filled the forward end of the room, while a couch-and-chair seating area stood between Logan and Kip and everyone else. The partygoers who had been seated around the table were all on their feet, as were the crew and catering staff.

But it was Perez who had his attention where he stood behind a blond woman with his hand clamped onto her shoulder and Logan's tactical blade opened and pressed against her throat. Apparently, the team hadn't had time to arm him, because he'd leaped into action as soon as the op started.

The woman wore a silvery one-shoulder floor-length gown with some sort of floral appliqué on the top and down a long side slit that rose nearly to the top of her thigh. A cutout at her waist began near her left hip, angling high above the top of the skirt to the bottom of her right breast. The woman's hand was frozen, tucked into the lower section of her bodice, reaching in from below. With a shit-eating grin, Perez murmured something in her ear. Her eyes narrowed in fury but she dropped her hand, even as she bared her teeth in a snarl.

Sims moved to stand with his rifle trained on the woman, allowing Perez to drop the knife. But he kept his hold on the woman.

Wilson approached Logan, pulling cuffs from a pouch on his duty belt. "I got him." He secured Kip's hands behind his back.

"Read him his rights, then watch him for a minute." Logan's eyes were locked on the woman and Perez as a tall, handsome man stalked toward the group, his expression a mixture of confusion and outrage. Logan knew from news reports he was looking at Lucas Horner. "I need to check that out."

Wilson's gaze cut to Horner. "Yeah. Horner looks like he's aiming for Perez." He took the Beretta from Logan. "Johnson, come bag this handgun."

Logan approached the group standing around the woman, just as Horner lit into Perez.

"What the fuck are you doing? Get your hands off her. Sylvia, are you okay?"

Logan raised an index finger, telling Perez to let him handle it. "Mr. Horner, Detective Logan, NYPD Emergency Service Unit. Please step away from my detective."

"I will not. This server is threatening one of my guests with a switchblade."

"It's a tactical knife, and that server is one of my men. Perez, nicely done."

"Are you out of your goddammed mind?" Color suffused Horner's complexion as he turned on Logan, stepping in close.

"Not at all. And I'd advise you to step back, sir. I understand emotions are high, but we have this under control."

"Hardly. And this is my yacht. I make the calls here." Horner took another step closer, bumping against Logan's Kevlar vest.

Temper rose, but Logan brutally tamped it down. "Not during a police operation. Sir, step back or you risk charges. I won't ask again."

Something in Logan's tone must have registered with Horner because he took a single step away.

"Turner! Need a hand here," called Perez.

"What do you need?" Turner jogged around the table.

"She's carrying. Check for a flashbang holster," Perez said, referring to the small custom holster meant for women that snapped onto the middle section of their bra at the front for concealed carry.

Turner stepped in beside the woman and slid her gloved hand into the woman's bodice through the side cutout. Turner's smile went sly, then she jerked free a compact black pistol.

"Thanks." Perez pulled Sylvia's hands behind her back. "Sims, my duty belt is downstairs. Can you do the honors?"

"Happy to." Sims pulled out his cuffs and secured Sylvia's hands behind her back.

Horner started to protest, and Logan cut him off with a single look as he turned back to Perez. "How did you know she was armed?"

Perez returned Logan's knife. "When Ms. Swift and I went to stand with the hostages, I purposely picked a spot that blocked the door to the pantry I'd left open. That left me at an angle to where that woman was sitting. Unlike most of the other guests, she'd turned her chair sideways so she was facing Kip. She also had a different attitude from the others."

His gaze shot to Horner. "Well, most of them. Most of them were clearly terrified. But she…wasn't. She seemed weirdly invested, weirdly calm. Almost like she was enjoying it. And then she shifted sideways in her seat, and I caught a glimpse of the outline of the pistol grip before the material relaxed. Someone else seeing it might not have realized what it was, but I knew. From that point on, I kept my eye on her. When Kip was occupied, I'd managed to palm your knife under the guise of adjusting my boot, so when the incursion started and she went for her gun, I had her cold." He turned to Turner. "What's she carrying?"

"A SIG Sauer P238," said Turner. "The cutout in the dress allowed her access when we came through the doors. We wouldn't have been in time to stop her. You, however, were right there and knew what she was doing."

"I knew what but didn't know why. When she stood, I suspected she was aiming for line of sight on Kip, so I moved in."

"Why did you stop her?" Horner snarled. "She could have rid us of that one." He turned his furious gaze on Kip.

"Because he's actually an innocent party." At Perez's and Turner's surprised expressions, Logan said, "I'll explain later. But you." He turned to Sylvia. "You're another matter. What's your full name?"

Sylvia said nothing, her green eyes snapping with anger.

Logan looked at Horner, his flat gaze asking the question for him.

"Sylvia Lansing," Horner said. "But there's been a mistake."

"Wrong. Turner, do a full pat down. I don't believe the wire story, but let's cross that *t*." As Turner started the pat down, Logan read out her Miranda rights.

In short order, they had their answer—the wire story was simply extra pressure for Kip. As McFarland had suspected, it wasn't possible from this distance to get a signal to shore.

"I don't understand." Horner looked uneasy, shifting his weight from foot to foot, his eyes darting between Logan and Sylvia. "Why would she be wired?"

"Because she's been in on the hostage taking from the beginning. She's in cahoots with the real perpetrator." Logan stepped in front of the woman. Wearing sky-high stilettos, she was nearly eye to eye with him. "Who's responsible for this?"

Sylvia turned slitted eyes toward Horner. "He is."

"Pardon me?" Both Horner's expression and tone telegraphed his offense at her accusation. "I'm not responsible for anything more than throwing a party."

"You're responsible for much more than that. He should have had it all. *We* should have had it all. But you ruined it. You stole from us. We're just taking our own back."

Logan stepped between Sylvia and Horner, blocking Horner from view. "Who are you working with?"

Sylvia simply smirked.

"He's taken children hostage. They could die. Who is he and where did he take them?"

The smirk slid into a smile. "I want a lawyer."

Legally, Logan had no choice now other than to step back, but the frustration of having someone right in front of him who could identify both the suspect and potentially his location, and not being able to question her, ripped at him.

He knew very well that by the time they could question her with a lawyer present, it would be too late for the Slater family.

"You'll get one." The knowledge there would be additional charges for her, potentially full charges in connection with Kip's crimes under New York's accessorial liability laws, didn't make him feel better. Even knowing Kip might get off with fewer or no charges when the full scope of his situation was taken into account.

He left Lansing with Sims and Turner and walked away, activating his radio mic. "Logan to Cartwright. Kip Slater and Sylvia Lansing are in custody. Lansing knows who the suspect is but has invoked her right to an attorney. Request additional Harbor support to assist in bringing the boat in."

"Affirmative. We need you to bring Slater to Pier A in the RIB. Bring Perez with you, since he was in the room and may be able to fill in some details for us. We've received additional information from units on-site about the kidnapping of Slater's family, and we're working on determining where the real hostage taker is holed up. I'll have the Harbor Unit send in extra officers and a boat to bring Unit 1 back here ASAP. Otherwise, the Harbor Unit can be met by additional officers at the Chelsea Piers Marina."

"10-4. Logan out." He turned toward the dining area, pulled a key from his pocket and tossed it to Perez. "Get your equipment out of the locker, get back into uniform, and meet me on the balcony ASAP."

"Yes, sir." Perez disappeared into the pantry.

Logan returned to Kip, knowing Wilson and Johnson had already heard their orders to stay on the ship. Kip was now on his feet, though Wilson still had a hold of one arm. At a nod from Logan, Wilson released him. "Slater, you're coming with me. The Harbor Unit is going to take us to Battery Park."

Kip's face was an undulating mix of hope and fear. "What about my family?"

"That's why we need you back on land. We're going after them."

CHAPTER 17

"YOU DID WELL."

Gemma spun around at the sound of her father's voice. She was standing near the main entrance to the restaurant, alone, looking out through a large picture window along the waterfront that stretched east along the south end of The Battery. She met his smile with her own. "Thanks. I wasn't so sure for a while there. Things weren't making any sense."

"Now we see why they didn't."

"Finally, yes. At least when I felt lost in there for a little while, the whole team was with me."

Tony came to stand beside her. "You're handling things okay?"

Gemma knew this wasn't a question from her chief, but from her father. Her chief knew she'd done the job; her father wanted to know how much she'd had to cover. If she was hurting. "I'm handling things. I admit when he was putting up that brick wall and nothing would shift him, I was concerned I might not be able to pull everyone out alive. Now that we have a brief break in the action, I wanted a minute of peace."

Normally, the Capellos worked hard to keep their family relationships out of their work life, but Gemma allowed herself a moment of comfort for both of them while she took three minutes away from the HNT table. She wove her arm through her father's, tipped her head against his shoulder, and exhaled.

They stood in silence for a full thirty seconds, watching the crowds gather on the waterfront as the minutes ticked toward the midnight fireworks show.

The crawl of time pulled at her. She'd needed a few moments, but her time wasn't her own right now. She blew out a long breath, releasing some of the stress with it. "Thanks for sharing my peace. It's been a while since we spent New Year's Eve together."

"Not the way I'd prefer to spend it, but yes, at least we're together."

"Are you heading out, or are you going to stay?"

"I think I'll stay. I don't have anywhere to be, and I'd like to see this through. The teams have the situation in hand—you don't need your chief issuing additional orders—but there's a family involved, and I'd like to see them safely home."

Gemma understood what her father didn't say. Tony Capello wasn't just the head of a large Sicilian family—he was a man who'd once had to stand outside the hostage situation involving his wife and his daughter. Who'd followed the leading wave of officers into the bank to rescue the hostages. Who'd knelt over his wife's dead body to say a final goodbye. Who'd pried his daughter's grip from his wife's cold hand to carry her away from her mother, away from the life she'd known, forever. Her father would have a personal interest in a case that involved a father fighting to get his wife and children back.

He'd done the same but hadn't been successful. That's why he'd stay.

"I get that." She gave his arm a squeeze and released it. "Break time's over."

When the Capellos walked back down the corridor, the father and daughter pair was gone, the chief and detective firmly in their places.

Time to get back to work.

Tony split off to get an update from Cartwright while Gemma continued on. Back at the table, she pulled out her chair and sat down. "Logan and Perez are on their way here with Kip now?"

"Yes," Ramos said.

Gemma rubbed the heel of one hand over her forehead, trying to ease the tension headache currently holding at a low throb. "We have to figure this out ourselves. Sylvia Lansing knows who's responsible, but she's lawyered up." She remembered the frustration she heard behind Logan's words when he talked to Lansing. He'd kept his emotions battened down, but she'd heard his fury that they'd come so close, only to be blocked from a quick resolution to Kip's family's disappearance. Sylvia Lansing was useless to them now because by the time she had her lawyer in place, it would be far too late to help the Slaters. It was all up to them.

"Nothing we can do about it unless this situation stretches on for hours. Which is doubtful," Ramos said, her eyes fixed on McFarland.

Gemma realized then that McFarland was wearing the mic'd headset, and she leaned in to look at what he was working at on-screen. He'd tiled together six different windows, each a different camera view of a street or thoroughfare.

"Yeah, I got it," McFarland said. "On the Brooklyn Queens Expressway, just past Queens Boulevard. Moving southwest."

Gemma looked back across the table. "What's this?"

"Neighbor across the back lane and down one has a security system, and one of his cameras covers his driveway behind his house," said Ramos. "An eagle-eyed A-Team officer spotted it and approached the neighbor for the footage. Neighbor was extremely helpful and provided said footage. A navy panel van pulled in behind the Slater house at 3:08 PM. A single individual got out and walked to the rear sliding door. Tried the door, found it locked. From the size and stature, it appears to be a man, but we can't confirm because whoever it was had a hood up, so we never see a face."

Gemma's stomach sank. "Unless they have a security bar, those doors are a snap to force open. One hand on the handle, one hand braced on the glass, lift up and to the side. Disengages the latch and the door slides open. Takes about three seconds. Unless someone was watching, no one in the neighborhood would realize it was a brazen middle-of-the-day break-in."

"That's exactly what happened," said Chen. "The suspect opened the door just enough to slip through, then slid it shut behind him. Nothing after that for seven minutes."

"Do we know if the suspect was armed?"

Ramos shook her head. "Nothing was evident on the footage, but they walked in wearing a winter jacket over the hoodie. There could have been a knife or firearm in a coat pocket, which was pulled as soon as they were out of any neighbor's eyesight. My money's on a handgun."

"After the seven minutes?" Gemma asked.

"The sliding door opened and they came out. Check your email for some screenshots forwarded from Cummings."

Gemma picked up her phone, opened her NYPD email, and found the emails from Cummings forwarded to the HNT team by Cartwright. The first of the attached color images showed the rear of a redbrick townhouse with a concrete driveway behind it as well as a thin line of a winter-empty flower garden lining one side of the driveway. The next showed an unmarked navy-blue panel van pulled into the driveway, and the next, the dark shape of an individual disappearing into the house. Gemma agreed with Ramos's estimation of a male suspect from the figure's height and bulk. "Detail's not great. Pretty pixelated."

"The camera wasn't focused on that driveway," McFarland said, splitting his attention between his team and whoever he had on the phone. "We're lucky we got it at all."

Gemma pointed at the headset and mouthed *TARU?* McFarland nodded. She turned back to Ramos and Chen. "So, not enough detail for something like the license plate, but you got the color and possibly the make of the van."

She flipped to the next image, showing a woman and two children exiting, followed by the kidnapper. The next showed the woman and kids climbing into the back of the van. The last photo in the sequence showed the van backing out of the driveway, angling for a southern exit. "And an indication of direction."

"As soon as he saw the pictures, McFarland logged onto DAS and started tracking. The first camera picked up the van at 24th and Astoria."

DAS—Domain Awareness System, the NYPD's network of over 18,000 closed-circuit cameras spread across the city to track traffic and do visual surveillance, including facial recognition. If they could use DAS to track the vehicle…

"They're trying to figure out where they went. Find where Kip's wife and kids are being held."

"Yes." Ramos looked pointedly at McFarland's laptop. "McFarland started the search and pulled in a team from TARU to speed things along. While he's working off a hot-spotted laptop, they have the department's systems with a direct connection to the network."

McFarland's gaze flicked up. "I'm holding my own." His gaze dropped again.

Ramos rolled her eyes. "Apparently, it turned into a competition when I wasn't looking. Is there a trophy for the winning geek?"

"I'd love a new 8K monitor for my system at home," McFarland quipped. "Still on I-278 at 49th." A pause. "Yes, continuing south through the interchange."

"So he forced Kip's family into the van, locked them in, and drove them somewhere," stated Gemma. "They drove past the house with the camera. Any chance it got the front plate?"

Ramos shook her head. "Not at the right angle. But we got lucky. There's a DAS camera at the corner of 83rd and Astoria. McFarland grabbed an image and was able to enlarge and clarify with what he had on his laptop."

"So we know the registration?"

"Sort of. It's registered to GEA Electrical."

"What's the connection to Horner?"

"We don't have one yet. But it's there somewhere. Someone didn't go to this amount of trouble for kicks."

"Agreed. And while we haven't seen the abductor's face, we have to assume this is someone who isn't worrying about showing their face to Kip's family."

"It's possible the abductor is masked under that hoodie," Chen pointed out. "We couldn't see a face when the suspect left the house with Kip's family. If they've seen their abductor's face, chances of them surviving this are astronomically small. Even if the kidnapper thought the courts wouldn't trust the word of a five- and nine-year-old, Kip's wife is a problem."

"Assuming he pulled off this nested, convoluted scheme, law enforcement will already be after him for the theft of fifty million dollars, as well as being responsible for the hostage situation and any injuries or deaths that might have occurred there, so what's a few more murder charges added on at that point?"

"Not to mention, he's likely responsible for Jerome Vann's death, so, yeah, that could be how he's looking at it. If so, then likely no mask. So it's even more important to find where they are before the time frame is up."

"I don't have that," McFarland said. "There's not enough cameras on the expressway. Hang on. I'm switching to the DOT feed."

The Department of Transportation was the other agency that could help the teams at this point. And whereas any citizen could use the 511NY traffic and transit map to determine current conditions, the DOT made recordings of all cameras available to law enforcement for up to three months. McFarland obviously knew how to access that information.

It was always good to work with McFarland, but sometimes it was the little things that could kick an investigation to the next level.

"Got him." McFarland's mumble wasn't actually meant for anyone to hear, but the voice on the other end of the call must have caught some of it. "Yeah, sorry. I have him. Still on I-278 traveling west, between the Manhattan and Brooklyn Bridges at Adams Street."

Chen turned to look out the window. "Boat coming directly for us. Looks like the RIB."

"Good." Gemma checked the clock. "We're running out of time." A sideways glance at McFarland told her she didn't need to impress upon him they needed a location pronto, or there'd be nothing left for them to do. From the speed with which he flicked through windows and the occasional low curse, he knew it.

Minutes were going to make the difference tonight. And minutes might be all they had.

CHAPTER 18

MOTION AT THE SIDE DOOR of the restaurant attracted Gemma's attention as Logan led in a tall, lean man wearing a short winter jacket with his hands secured behind his back, Perez bringing up the rear. Even though his spiky hair was now windblown and disordered, Gemma recognized Kip Slater from both his Instagram account and from Unit 1's incursion feed.

Somehow, McFarland had managed to cobble together a number of tablets from somewhere, and by the time Unit 1 was ready to go in, he had them connected to the helmet cams from the five team members in split screen, and they were able to watch the operation in real time. As expected, everything had gone smoothly, as Logan easily contained Kip, and Perez had gotten the upper hand by surprising Sylvia Lansing before she could pull her SIG and attempt to fight her way free.

Things might have been a little more touch and go if Lansing hadn't inadvertently telegraphed her intentions, allowing Perez to take control of the situation, as Logan's attention had been rightly fixed on Kip and his firepower. But with a team this experienced and well prepared, it had all gone off like clockwork. Gemma was especially proud of how Logan had minimized the usual force of the A-Team officers and had instead used HNT techniques and tried to connect with Kip on a personal level as a way of deescalating the situation rapidly.

The A-Team regularly tangled with the hardest and most out-of-control factions of the city's criminals. Kip, however, seemed to be cut from an entirely different cloth. Forced into this situation, he wasn't a natural killer, as evidenced by how easily Logan had been able to subdue him—it wasn't in his nature to fight back. Gemma no longer wore her throat mic and earpiece but had been in hearing distance of Cartwright when he approved Logan's request to remove Kip's handcuffs to transfer him to the RIB for the trip in. God forbid the boat was hit or capsized; they didn't want Kip to drown because his hands were cuffed behind him. More than that, it was clear neither of them considered him a real threat.

As per protocol, Kip was now cuffed again, but Gemma knew Garcia had already been in touch with the New York County District Attorney's Office. The prosecutor he'd been able to rip away from their evening of frivolity had been open to the consideration of reducing or entirely dropping Kip's charges because of the kidnapping of his family forcing his hand. For now, they'd take him into custody, but everyone was prepared for an ongoing discussion of mitigating circumstances.

Tony had decided to stay, and so had Garcia. Gemma knew Garcia's wife was likely unhappy her husband had felt obligated to answer the mayor's call, but Gemma understood his desire to see the case through now he was here.

Garcia had kept his team intact, with Gemma taking lead questioning Kip but with Ramos there as the more experienced interviewer to ask questions if anything was missed. They had a little extra space at the table now after McFarland piled as much of the equipment at one end as he could. He and TARU were still tracking the navy van, but they were narrowing in.

They now knew the driver had exited I-278 to drive south through the Columbia Street Waterfront District, heading for Brooklyn's Red Hook neighborhood. The guys at TARU knew McFarland needed to be present for the interview and would continue on, tapping into CCTV cameras and tracking the vehicle. They'd reach out as soon as they had something concrete.

It better be soon, or they were in trouble. And so were Katie, Olivia, and Riley Slater. Gemma could see McFarland knew it, too, because he continued to work from his corner of the table while Kip was still incoming. Gemma had initially tried to follow what he was doing—flipping between camera views on his laptop—but gave up when he stayed focused, occasionally mumbling to himself and scratching notes on his notepad.

Seeing Logan arrive, Cartwright strode up the aisle. "Bring him to the HNT table. We need to do this fast and get teams in motion."

Logan guided Kip to the left and down to the table, directing him to the chair across from Gemma that Chen had cleared, standing instead behind Gemma. The interview would be recorded, so Chen didn't need to note every word, but he held his notes from the negotiation in his hands in case Gemma needed to refer to previous conversations.

Logan indicated the chair. "Sit down."

Kip lowered himself into the chair, his whole body collapsing in as far as his bound hands would allow.

Garcia and Tony moved to stand at the head of the table, with Ramos and Chen standing behind Gemma's chair, and Cartwright, Logan, and Perez forming a solid wall behind Kip. Logan and Perez had both removed their safety glasses and unsnapped their chin straps. Otherwise, they stayed dressed in their winter gear, ready to move out as soon as they were needed.

Gemma met Logan's eyes, held there for a fraction of a second, and then flashed over to Cartwright. "Any reason we can't take the cuffs off for now? Every officer in this room is armed, and the three of you are ready for an assault. I'd prefer it if Kip is comfortable."

Kip's head raised at the sound of Gemma's voice. His face was deathly pale, his blue eyes hollow with dark circles of exhaustion. "You're the voice on the phone." His voice was husky.

"I am. Lieutenant?"

Cartwright nodded at Logan, who asked Kip to stand, produced a key, and unlocked the cuffs.

As he did that, Gemma left the table to walk to the bar, where someone had dumped a twelve-pack of water bottles. She grabbed one and returned, setting it in front of Kip as he sat down again. "You sound dry. Have some water."

His hands free, Kip briefly rubbed each wrist, then chafed warmth into his cold, pale hands. "Thank you." He clumsily unscrewed the cap and downed half of the water in a continual series of swallows. He wiped his mouth with the back of his hand and then screwed the cap on. "Have you found my family?"

"We're working on it." McFarland didn't raise his eyes from his laptop screen. "Give us a few more minutes. TARU and I are onto something. It will save us time in the long run to get this nailed down. And yes, I know the clock is ticking."

Progress was progress, so Gemma was happy to leave him to it. He was correct—they'd have one chance to get this right, and even though TARU was happy to take over, McFarland's skills might be more useful working with them than with Gemma, who was already surrounded by cops more experienced than her.

"Kip, we know you came home to an empty house, a missing family, and a letter left in their place." She woke her phone, brought up the image of the note, and set it down in front of Kip. "This is the letter you followed?"

Kip's lips twisted for a moment, then he smoothed his expression. "Yes."

"Tell us what happened."

"I'd gone to the Flask for a last-minute check of everything for tonight, then I came home to take a nap for a few hours before heading back. Tonight was going to be a really long night, so I just wanted to rest for a bit." He grimaced, a bit of color warming his cheekbones. "They must be drowning there tonight without me."

"We talked to Lia. She helped us find your home quickly. She's worried for you, so reach out to her when you can. What did you do when you found the letter?"

"I panicked for about a minute, then got myself under control. I had no reason to doubt whoever wrote the letter was telling the truth. Ever since the break-in last year, Katie had been extra careful about keeping the doors and windows locked, especially if I'm not home and it's just her and the kids. She didn't just let this happen."

"We know for a fact she didn't. Did you know the neighbor behind and one house to the north of you has security cameras around his house?

One of them covers the driveway area behind his home. In doing so, that feed captures the areas behind your house as well." She picked up her phone, flipped to another picture, and slid it across the table to him. "Do you recognize this vehicle?"

Kip stared down at the navy-blue panel van. "No."

"It's a Ford Transit windowless panel van. Doesn't ring a bell?"

"Not at all. But that's definitely my driveway."

"We have security footage of what appears to be a single man in a hood entering your house by forcing open the sliding door and walking in. Seven minutes later, your kids, then your wife, then the suspect come out. Your kids and wife get into the back of the van. The suspect closes the door, then gets into the front, and they drive away. So, let's begin with the basics. Where were you at 3:08 PM?"

"At the Flask."

"Can anyone attest to that?"

"Several can. Lia is one of them."

"Good, thank you."

"You thought I faked this? That I forced my own wife and kids into a van for show?" Kip's tone rose with appalled disbelief.

Gemma held up a placating hand. "I had to ask. We'll assume the suspect is a man for the sake of this discussion, but we never see his face in the video. He appears to be physically larger than you, but we'd need video analysis to confirm. I had to clear you, to make sure it wasn't all just an elaborate setup. We'll double-check your alibi, but I believe you."

Kip sagged into his chair like a balloon with a sudden leak.

"Even though we couldn't see one, we're assuming he held your family at gunpoint to get them to comply. He was in full view of your neighbors, so if he had a gun, he kept it camouflaged so no one could see he was forcing them into the van at gunpoint. On the video, from that distance, they looked calm, but that was the effect he wanted. They complied because they had to."

"Katie would do anything to protect the kids. If there was any threat to them, she'd do anything anyone asked of her. If she saw that note…

Well, I think it was clear he'd already killed. She would read the same into it. What would happen to all of them if they didn't go along with him."

"You're talking about when the note said the bartender for the party had been 'removed'?"

"Tell me that didn't mean he'd been killed."

"It did. Unfortunately, the man who was supposed to bartend was found dead this morning."

Kip curled in, his head down as if he'd taken a blow to the gut. "Oh my God. They're going to die."

"Not if we can help it." McFarland set down his phone where he'd just typed in a message. "We're getting close." His gaze flicked up to Cartwright. "Be ready to leave in five or six minutes."

"We're ready now." Cartwright's tone was flat. "Get us a confirmed location, and we're gone. The truck is outside; we can be immediately on the move. If we're not closest, I'll assign another unit."

"Kip." Gemma brought his attention back to her from where he'd turned in his chair to stare up at Cartwright. "We only have a few minutes. Leave your family to us. Tell us how you got onto the ship. About what happened there. Anything that might be useful for us to know."

Kip straightened a bit, as if boosted by the ability to help his family in any way. "After I got the letter, I grabbed my handgun and a box of ammo, stuffed it all in a knapsack, got changed into a typical black-and-white catering outfit, and drove to Chelsea Piers. Almost didn't make it because traffic was hell, then I had to find parking, then the boat, and I started off at the wrong end of the marina. By the time I ran there, I was so out of breath, I could hardly talk to the chief steward. Then she was pissy because her bartender didn't show and she was starting to panic, but didn't like me saying I was just following instructions and had been sent to fill a vacancy. She said everyone was supposed to be background checked and her boss wouldn't like a stranger coming on at the last minute."

"How did you convince her to let you on?"

"I asked if she knew what she'd make if she shook gin, lime juice, and simple syrup over ice. She had no idea and waved me on." He shrugged. "Saved by a gimlet. I got in there, got set up, and served for hours. I waited until there was a moment when the servers were clearing dishes after dessert where everyone was seated and most of the catering staff was still in the room, and then I pulled out my gun from my knapsack that I'd stashed behind the bar."

"How did you get everyone into the dining area?"

"I pointed the gun at Horner's head. He did the rest. Well, at least as far as demanding his staff come to join them." Anxiety streaked across his face. "He still hasn't paid. My family is going to die because Horner's a son of a bitch who doesn't care about anyone but himself. And his money. He loves his money. Other people's pain and desperation doesn't touch him. He doesn't care."

"We're handling that," said McFarland. "TARU is going to send out a fake email spoofing the beginning of a Bitcoin deposit to the wallet address included in the letter. They're just putting the finishing touches on it, but it's going to go out soon and should buy us some time." He glanced at the clock—11:54 PM. "In minutes. The goal is before midnight."

"You're going to make a Bitcoin transfer to the suspect?" Ramos asked.

"You can't fake that kind of transfer. Each transaction refers to the output of the previous transaction. There won't be any money going into his wallet address. But we don't need that. Horner's PA filled us in on which crypto exchange Horner uses. With that particular exchange, there's a series of emails the recipient receives for each transfer. The first is the pending deposit email. It will have all the information about the transaction—date, time, reference number, exchange, and deposit info. TARU is mocking up a matching email to look entirely legit. It won't hold water under close inspection, but it will buy us time. It could be up to an hour for the transaction to complete, so he won't be suspicious for a little while. We can string him along with a block confirmation email, but that's as far as we'll be able to go. By the time a real confirmation would have arrived, the money should be in his account. And it won't be."

"I don't think Horner would play ball if his own mother was being held hostage." Kip's tone was sour.

"Fortunately, we won't have to depend on Horner," said Gemma. "Let's get back into tonight. You were told one of the guests was wired and would be watching you. Did you know it was Sylvia Lansing?"

"No. I made the party guests toss all their purses and cell phones behind the bar, but I couldn't actually pat them down without getting too close or putting down my gun, so I had to believe the letter. I assumed the staff weren't carrying cell phones because they were on duty and no one seemed to have one when I told everyone to ditch them." He winced. "Missed the boat with the steward." Kip turned to his left to look up at Perez. "You're not the nephew, clearly."

"No. The nephew was belowdecks originally, but we got him into the RIB temporarily until the crisis was over. I stood in for him."

"I guess I should be grateful. If you hadn't stopped that woman, who knows what would have happened. To me. To the guests. I thought the steward was a major mistake on my part. It may have been a blessing in disguise."

McFarland's cell phone rang, and he picked it up. There was a flurry of activity as he opened cameras, finally landing on the image of a deserted street before opening Google Maps, typing in an address, and then pushing street view down the block. He froze the image of a pair of buildings, both covered with stucco, one three stories, one three and a half stories tall, both with large roll-down garage doors. "I see it. We're looking at 24 or 26 Commerce. I don't think it's 20. And 22 doesn't have a garage. Yeah, thanks, we'll need that. We'll be in motion shortly. See you there." He ended the call.

"What just happened?" Cartwright demanded.

"We have it."

A jolt of electricity shot through Gemma. "The van's location?"

"Yes. Using the DAS and DOT systems, we tracked the van from East Elmhurst all the way into and through Brooklyn. They're in an industrial area just past the Brooklyn Marine Terminal. But we got lucky. There's a DAS camera at the corner of Columbia and Commerce, and we watched it drive down the street and pull into one of the buildings, entirely disappearing from view."

"Allowing him to get the family out of the van unseen," Logan said.

Lights coming in from the harbor aimed directly at the pier pulled Gemma's attention toward the dark waters. "I think we have a Harbor Unit boat incoming. The rest of the team?"

"Would be good timing if it was." Cartwright pinned McFarland with a look. "What's the address?"

"Either 24 or 26 Commerce are our first possibilities. I saw the footage myself. The van turned into a building on the northeast side of the street and disappeared." He spun his laptop around to face the tactical officers. "Likely one of these two buildings, both of which have offices above with windows."

"What's on the other side of the street?" asked Logan.

McFarland spun the street view around. "Warehouses."

The images showed a three-story trio of warehouses, each with a long, peaked roof, and a pair of four-story warehouses with flat roofs.

Perez half leaned over Kip's left shoulder for a better view. "Could get up there. Might be the best view we'll have." His gaze flicked sideways to Logan. "Your M10's in the truck?"

"Yeah."

Gemma couldn't help but meet Logan's gaze across the span of the table. Logan's precision skill with a sniper rifle was what had put him six stories above the cemetery beside St. Patrick's Old Cathedral and had culminated in the death of John Boyle. It had been a masterful shot, taking Boyle down in a midair leap as he'd trained his weapon on Alex. If it came down to a shooter on the roof to take out the suspect because they had no other choice in defense of Kip's wife and young children, no one was better suited to the role than Logan.

They'd put St. Patrick's—and the betrayal she associated with it—behind them now. But putting Logan on a roof, putting that weapon into his hands, opened him to the trauma of killing. He would do the job that needed doing—especially if there were children involved—but would be forever marked by it. She hoped it wouldn't come down to that.

"I have you at nine minutes from here via I-478," said McFarland. "Any units closer?"

"Most of my units are dealing with the million people packed into Times Square. Nilsson, Cummings, and the rest of Unit 5 are still up in East Elmhurst. The rest are spread out. We're closest, so we'll take it, but I'll call Unit 5 in as well."

"We need to come with you." As Gemma spoke, Cartwright's expression closed. "We don't want in on the op, but we need to be there." She turned to where her father and Garcia stood at the head of the table. "We're likely moving from one negotiation to another. We don't need to be in the room with them, but we need to be closer." She could tell from Garcia's expression that he was already on board. She turned to McFarland. "TARU is sending a truck?"

"Yes, they're still narrowing down the actual address and are expecting us to meet them there." He turned to look up at Garcia. "Sir, we can set up in the TARU truck a block away. Two blocks away. Whatever you think is safest. But we need to be closer than this."

"Agreed, as is standard procedure," said Garcia. "Cartwright, my team won't be in your way. They just need a ride there. Then they'll stay in the background unless a bullhorn is their only option."

It wouldn't be the first time any of them had negotiated with a hostage taker locked in a location with no known communications. They'd fall back on practices used by the first hostage negotiators in the 1970s. It was communication at its most basic, but Gemma wondered if they'd have time for anything better than that. Maybe if the clock hadn't started ticking hours before, but as it stood now, they were running low on options.

Cartwright's gaze shifted to his chief for only a moment before moving to Garcia. "Your team needs to keep up."

"They will. Pack up what you need. TARU will provide communications. Leave the rest—I'll take care of it."

McFarland shot to his feet to pack his laptop.

Gemma stood, then paused, her eyes fixed on Kip.

"I have him," Tony said, reading her expression. "I'm not so far from my days on the streets that I can't hold and help transport a suspect. He's in good hands."

"I'm here, too," Garcia said. "We'll take him down to headquarters, get him into a holding cell, and will monitor the op from there."

At that moment, a staccato pattern of explosions sounded, and everyone whipped toward the picture window. Bright trails of silver exploded into brilliant streamers of red, green, blue, and gold, studded with silver stars. Gemma felt a heavy vibration deep in her sternum as the next screams of fireworks filled the sky.

The old year was over. The clock had tripped into the New Year.

Time was ticking away.

Gemma turned to look behind her to meet her father's gaze for a moment. He held it and then swept over the rest of the faces of his officers who had turned back into the room. "Good hunting. Now, let's bring the Slater family home to start the New Year right."

CHAPTER 19

THE A-TEAM TRUCK SPED NORTH on West Street with Wilson at the wheel and Cartwright in the passenger seat. Wilson only braked minutely, and then they were hurtling to the right. All four HNT members held on for dear life, while the A-Team officers looked like they barely noticed, their boots firmly planted but their upper bodies swaying lightly with the motion of the truck.

The team was fully realized once again, the rest of Unit 1 having joined them, jogging in from the breakwater where one of the larger Harbor Unit boats had dropped them off. They hadn't questioned what had happened but had simply fallen into step behind Cartwright and the rest of their team. As Cartwright explained their destination to Wilson, the rest of the team settled along one of the two hard benches running the length of the rear compartment.

The HNT filled the space opposite them. Gemma sat at the top of the bench, opposite Logan, with McFarland beside her, then Ramos and Chen. When they first got into the truck, McFarland had started to unzip his laptop bag, as if to work on the way there, but a pointed look and a headshake from Logan had stilled his hands. He dropped his laptop bag between his shoes, looped the strap over one arm so it didn't get away from him, and pulled his phone from his pocket.

Gemma met Logan's eyes as he sat across from her, his face thrown into shadow, the passing streetlight filtering in the windshield strobing briefly across his features. His expression was set, his gaze detached, actively getting into the zone for what was to come next.

She'd seen him do this on operations before and could relate. She, too, needed to prepare mentally for negotiations, needed to put aside the stress of the day—forgetting to set the timer on her coffeemaker the night before, so she was missing her morning cup of joe, traffic irritants on the way to work, unending reports or requests for information once she got there. More so than for her, he needed to get into the right headspace. The headspace where he could make the kind of snap decision that either saved a life or ended it in milliseconds.

Then the van sank into the darkness of the Brooklyn-Battery Tunnel, with only an otherworldly dull yellow glow coming from the front of the van. Gemma peered out the windshield to the two separated lanes moving to the southeast, the twin rows of lighting in the dark ceiling above, the silver railing to the left separating the narrow, raised emergency walkway, and the glossy white, yellow, and light-blue tiles lining both sides of the tunnel.

If traffic was moving well, it was approximately a four-minute drive from end to end, and though traffic was surprisingly busy for this time of night, they were flying through. When every second counted toward saving lives, the thought of being trapped in the tunnel was an absolute nightmare.

They hit a pothole, and the rear of the truck jumped, the equipment in the narrow open lockers on the outside walls thumping against their confines. Gemma clamped both hands on the edge of the bench, bumping McFarland's free hand as he tried to find purchase without dropping his phone. They both whipped their hands away at the contact, and then she grabbed at McFarland's arm when he started to tilt, anchoring them both with her left hand. With another sway, they stabilized, allowing Gemma to release him. When she looked up, she caught the edges of a smirk tilting Logan's lips in the shadows.

She gave him a pointed look, edged a little farther away from McFarland, and reestablished her grip on both sides of her thighs. She understood this was the easiest way to transport the team and their equipment for rapid deployment of large numbers of officers, but honestly, some sort of restraints for those who weren't used to this kind of travel wouldn't be amiss.

Looking up, she could practically hear Logan's words in her head simply based on the look in his eye. *You asked to come with us.*

He wasn't wrong.

She spent the rest of the time in the tunnel drawn by the bright light of McFarland's phone. He was on Google Maps again, perusing the area they were targeting, clearly looking for the best plan of attack for the tactical team.

After about four minutes in the tunnel, they drove back into the normal night sky and then angled off I-478 onto the Hamilton Street exit ramp.

Nearly there.

Two minutes later, they drove northwest on Delavan Street and pulled in behind a white van emblazoned with *NYPD TARU* next to a deserted lot, edged with a frost fence covered in green sheeting, its surface marred with multicolored spray paint. Wilson cut the engine.

Cartwright turned around in his seat. "HNT, this is where you get out. Unit 1, get ready to roll."

"Hang on a second." McFarland extended his phone to Cartwright. "You guys are moving fast and don't have the time to scope out the area as much as you'd like, so I tried to do some of that for you. Take a look."

Cartwright took the phone and moved the image around, studying it.

"They're not directly in front of the buildings we think are key, but the shorter warehouses across the road aren't going to be the best for visibility." His gaze cut to Logan. "You'd prefer an angle above for the best shot, I assume."

"Not always, but that usually gives the best line of sight, especially when using windows."

"Then the taller two warehouses, just to the south of the buildings in question, will work better for you. They transect the entire block, and there's a fence blocking off the area between the two buildings. From satellite shots, that area looks to be used for outdoor storage—or garbage, hard to say—but there's also a ladder for access to the rooftop there. Warehouse looks to be about four stories tall. If you scale the fence to get into that yard, you could get access to the roof that way. That will give you your bird's-eye view."

Cartwright extended the phone to Logan. "The ladder is closer to the Delavan Street side of the buildings. Hard to see if it extends all the way to the ground or whether you'd need a boost to get to it."

Logan used two fingers to zoom in to the area. "Can't tell. There's enough junk in this area—I'll be able to use something." He handed the phone back to McFarland. "Thanks."

"If you get into trouble, I'll be coordinating from here where I'll be able to give direction," said Cartwright. "But I could give you a hand if it's something you can't manage on your own. Johnson, I want you to check out the front of 26 Commerce; Perez and Turner, the front of 24 and 22. Sims, the lot beside 26—you'll likely have to go over the fence. Wilson, I want you to circle the buildings via Seabring Street to the north and watch from the parking lot behind those buildings. Logan, switch to the M10. Everyone suit up. We're moving out."

"Let's get out of your way." Gemma stood, the rest of the team following suit. "Everyone stay safe. We'll stay in contact via the radio."

Johnson opened the rear door to the darkness beyond and hopped down, then stepped back as Chen and then Ramos jumped down. McFarland bent to pick up his laptop bag, taking the time to hook the strap over his shoulder.

His pause gave Gemma a brief second to meet Logan's gaze.

Good luck making contact.

I know you'll make the right call.

Then, as McFarland turned away, she dropped her gaze and followed.

CHAPTER 20

HIS M10 SNIPER RIFLE HELD securely in both hands, Logan broke off from the rest of the team to jog down Delavan Street.

The industrial area was pitch black—not meant to be fully occupied at night, the city had opted to save money and only installed standard street lighting at the intersections, leaving the middle of the street extremely dark, especially as the warehouses had no external lighting. Only the illumination from the three-quarter moon gilded the sidewalk beneath his boots with a soft glow. Like his teammates, he wore night-vision optics mounted on his helmet; he currently had them flipped down to cover his eyes, converting the existing low ambient light—moonlight and bare traces of streetlight glow—and amplify it into a green wash, boosting the contrast on every shape, bringing the gloom into sharp focus.

His boots beat a steady staccato over the cracked and broken concrete sidewalk. He darted under bare overhanging branches, around an abandoned plastic cart full of construction trash, and then past colorful graffiti splashed across a redbrick building to his right that looked more like ghostly outlines in the dark than actual art.

Opposite the fenced gap between the two warehouses, he paused long enough to ensure the M10's safety lever was engaged inside the trigger guard, then he grasped the sling in both hands and tugged it down so the rifle lay against his back. He took one look at the eight-foot frost fence across the street, then cut across the deserted asphalt opposite. Halfway across, he poured on the steam and then launched himself at the fence, locking both gloved hands through the chain-link and getting the toe of one boot into a gap before finally finding purchase with the other. He quickly scaled the final three feet of the fence, swung one leg over, then the other, made sure the ground under him was clear, and let himself drop into a crouch on the far side.

Logan paused for a moment to scan the space. Bereft of any direct moonlight due to the height of the surrounding roofs, the goggles had to depend on reflected light and the general ambient glow of the five boroughs, leaving the long, fenced yard shrouded in gloom. He pulled his rifle around and flipped off the safety, letting his eyes adjust to the darkness. Slowly, dim items took shape—broken wooden skids, rusted metal bars, plastic-wrapped bundles of mystery materials, and the long length of a transport container against one wall. The bulk of more materials disappeared into darkness farther into the lot.

Highlighted better by scattered light, the side wall of the warehouse showed how age was wearing on the building. Jacketed with overlapping riveted sections of corrugated metal, the paint had disintegrated to reveal darker patches of rust and grime beneath, and the troughs were channels for long, dark stains of rusty rivulets.

Looking higher, he found a trio of windows, each window a cluster of three-by-six panes of glass. Some of the glass was dulled by smoke or fumes, making it nearly opaque. Some were splattered with dirt or showed evidence of rain. Some windows had been entirely replaced with sheets of metal to avoid future breakage. The metal window frames were rusted to near instability.

This place was in rough shape—he was in big trouble if the ladder was in a similar state. He swung the goggles to the left and finally caught the bottom of a ladder about twenty-five feet away.

Logan groaned. The ladder also didn't look like it was in great condition, but that was the least of his concerns. The first problem would be getting to it because the lowest rung had to be about ten feet off the ground.

Below the bottom rung were several pairs of metal bolt holders in the metal wall—clearly there was a section of ladder somewhere inside the warehouse that needed to be added to achieve the full length. It was no doubt missing to avoid someone doing what Logan was about to attempt—scale the side of the building to trespass onto the roof, or to prevent possible break-in to the building itself by thieves, vandals, or people looking for a place to crash for the night.

He studied the bottom of the ladder as he approached. This was going to be a challenge. The bottom rung of the ladder was likely so far off the ground to dissuade idiot kids from climbing the frost fence and then heading to the roof to drink or smoke weed. He was tall and had been blessed with long arms, but he would only be able to touch a little over seven and a half feet with his fingertips. With that gap, he needed a bit over two feet of lift to pull this off.

He was going to have to fall back on some old skills.

A memory filled his mind of him and Gemma standing in the sunny courtyard at Rikers immediately following the death of CO Garvey, as all her efforts for a peaceful resolution had shattered around her. Of plucking away the basketball she'd been dribbling and doing a neat free throw at the nearest basket. It hadn't been perfect—the ball had bounced off the rim—but it had gone through the net.

"Really?"

"High school varsity team. I'm a little rusty."

"That's hardly rusty. Did you come out here to get under my skin or just to show off?"

He'd been walking off stress from the crisis they'd been unable to avoid when he'd seen her doing the same. He hadn't truly meant to get under her skin or show off, but the moment had been an opening—they'd been able to sit at a deserted picnic table in the sun and help her work out her frustrations and feelings of helplessness.

His years on the high school varsity team were about to come in handy. He needed to not just touch the bottom bar; he needed to get both hands around it so he could lever himself up.

One more look around the assorted junk confirmed this was still the safest way to go, at least to start. If he couldn't make it work, he'd reconsider.

He flicked the M10's safety on and arranged the rifle at his back again, then flipped up and locked his night-vision goggles, greatly expanding his field of view. Giving himself another moment for his eyes to adjust to the darkness, he stepped away from the ladder, knowing he was going to need to take a running start, just like he would for a basketball jump shot.

Don't miss and hit the wall. You'll break your ribs for real if you do.

He hit the button for his microphone. "Logan to Cartwright."

"Go ahead."

"I'm inside the fence, about to tackle the ladder. It's ten feet up. Just have to get there. Will let you know when I'm on the roof."

"10-4."

He pulled back about twelve feet, dug the soles of his boots against the concrete pad, and pushed off, pounding toward the wall. He hit just below the ladder and went vertical, his arms stretched high over his head.

The rough, rusted metal rasped over the tips of his tactical gloves, just before he dropped down to the concrete.

"Damn it." He staggered sideways a few steps, the M10 bouncing against the armor plating in the back of his tactical vest, then got his balance.

Close, but not close enough. He needed about another three inches. That meant he needed more momentum carrying him upward.

He'd done the mental calculation using his own two hundred pounds. He hadn't taken into account all his equipment—loaded duty belt, the crucial odds and ends in the pockets of his cargo pants, body armor plates, a handgun, and a fully loaded rifle—when he was estimating the force needed to clear the two-plus feet he'd need. He needed to compensate for an additional seventy-five pounds.

He could almost hear Coach Lyford's voice in that moment, encouraging him as he worked his overhead reaching jump squats.

He could do this.

He gave himself an extra five feet of runway, fixed his eyes on the dim outline of the ladder in the gloom, counted down to three in his head, and exploded into a dead sprint before launching himself vertical just before the wall. Up into the air, his eyes still on the ladder, his arms and hands stretched out as far as humanly possible.

The rough metal of the rung hit his gloved palms, and he snapped his fists closed around it. He let himself hang for a few seconds, allowing his body to stop swinging with the effort it had taken to get him into contact with the ladder. Then he took a deep breath, gathered himself, and pulled himself up.

His pronated grip, with his palms facing the wall rather than himself, made it much harder, leaving his biceps mostly out of the action and relying on his lats and trapezius muscles, but he needed to be able to climb hand over hand up the outside of the ladder, so it was the only workable position.

Steadily, he hauled himself up until his chin was at the bar; then, holding position only long enough to draw in air, he clamped down on his right-hand hold, engaged his core, and, lightning fast, transferred the left to the next rung up. The uneven hold left him slightly twisted, but he quickly transferred his right hand up, then dragged himself to the next level.

Hand. Hand. Pull up.

His duty belt caught when he was moving from the second rung to the third, one of the front pouches on his left side becoming wedged, requiring him to hold position halfway through a pull-up to twist his lower body to the left and then continue the motion until his hips were past it. He swore under his breath—if it caught on the first rung, until he got his feet under him, it would likely happen again.

He kept methodically repeating the steps to himself, driving himself upward. *Hand. Hand. Pull up. Twist. Pull up.*

He was on the fourth rung when the ladder shifted, the right side pulling away from the wall by several inches, the metal under his grasp groaning under the stress.

Shit.

He froze, hardly daring to breathe, fearing the whole thing was about to give way. Staring just to the right of the ladder, trying to discern details in nothing but moonlight, he found that one of the bolts fixing the ladder to the metal structure near his right hand appeared loose. Not out of the wall but not holding tightly. About to come completely free? Or rusted in half and not holding at all? His pounding heart told him he couldn't be sure.

He couldn't stop—he had to keep going. The team, perhaps the Slater family, was depending on him. But the loose bolt meant he had to be even more controlled with his motions, ensuring he didn't inadvertently rip the ladder right out of the wall as he fought gravity to haul the weight of his own body and all his bulky equipment upward.

Nothing like cranking the physical difficulty level from eleven to thirty-five. Out of ten.

He was relieved at the next attachment point that the ladder felt solid again. But what went up must come down, and he was going to have to deal with that loose bolt again later that night.

Reports from his earpiece told him the other members of his unit were on the ground, checking out the buildings. So far, nothing conclusive, but they were moving as quickly as possible.

Time ticked on.

His arms were shaking by the time he got high enough to jam his left knee onto the bottom rung. His weight now braced on the bar under his knee, he gave himself five seconds of hard breathing and then managed to torque his hips out far enough to get his right boot onto the bar. By the next handhold, he had both boots on the bottom bar. He released a breath brimming with tension, gave his arms ten seconds to recover from the strain of pulling his equipment-loaded body up a half dozen rusty ladder rungs twenty feet in the air, then continued climbing the ladder normally the rest of the way.

He rolled off the ladder to sit on the edge of the roof, breathing hard and reminding himself of all those mornings when he would have given a few years of his life to stay in bed for another hour, *this* was why he went to the gym before the crack of dawn five mornings a week. Because sometimes there was simply no substitute on the fly for brute strength.

He took a deep breath, feeling a twinge on his left side, the last spot of discoloration to disappear after he'd been shot three weeks before. He'd considered himself healed, but apparently, that amount of muscular exertion brought home that he was still susceptible to overdoing it in extreme circumstances.

He rubbed a hand over the spot, then keyed his mic. "Logan to Cartwright. I'm on the roof, moving into position."

"10-4."

Logan slung the M10 around to his front and flipped his night-vision goggles down again. He scanned the rooftop, looking for any sign it was as worn and weathered as the outside of the building. But the roof was covered by a thick rubbery surface. It appeared intact, though the large puddle near the middle third of the roof gave him pause. Flat roofs were infamously less stable due to the damage done by a lack of drainage and high winds, not to mention how UV light had a way of breaking down materials.

If the roof gave way and he fell fifty or sixty feet to whatever lay below, it was game over. He'd stack the deck in his favor and stay toward the outside edge, where, hopefully, it would be reinforced. Not so close he'd risk slipping and toppling off, but close enough the slight sag he could see in the roof as it ran toward the middle hadn't done enough damage to lose its integrity.

He tested the section of the roof in front of him, slowly transferring his weight, but the substrate held. Then another step, then another. His confidence grew as the roof didn't seem to depress under his weight. It felt like there were multiple layers of decking secured to the frame of the building beneath.

He moved a little faster, cognizant as always that time was running out. Had Gemma figured out a way to contact the kidnapper? Had she essentially frozen the clock? If Cartwright knew, he wasn't saying. Then again, he needed his team to get into place as soon as possible, and slowing them down with details helped no one.

If Gemma had made contact, it might give them the opportunity to start from scratch. The opportunity to reset the—

The only clue to impending disaster was the slight groan beneath his right boot a millisecond before the support beneath him disappeared. Then he was falling as his boot punched through the surface of the roof.

He reacted instantaneously, letting go of the rifle with his left hand to reach out toward the edge of the roof where the rubber was edged with an inverted metal trough. He got his left hand over the trough, his fingers wrapped under the flat edge as he threw himself forward onto his left knee. He jammed the fore-end of the rifle against his shoulder, ensuring the end of the barrel was aimed at the night sky. He didn't have a spare finger for the trigger, but if he couldn't control the fall, there was still a chance the rifle could accidentally fire.

He hit the roof hard enough to squeeze all the air from his lungs, but he managed to get his left elbow braced so he didn't collapse down to the roof, keeping the rifle from striking any hard surface except his own body armor. For a few seconds he held, evaluating. His right boot dangled in the air, and the hard materials of the roof cut just over his right knee.

A single spot had collapsed under his weight, but the surrounding roof had held—he hadn't gone through to meet his maker in a fatal fall. Quick reflexes and the surrounding structure had saved him.

Logan muttered a curse and slowly straightened. The question now was could he pull himself free, or would he have to trust all his weight near the fault in the roof to pull himself out vertically?

Tilting forward, he tried to slide his leg out at an oblique angle, but the materials immediately below the roof caught at his tactical pants. Upright it was, then.

He flipped the safety on his rifle and reversed it to lie at his back, then released the edge of the roof to brace both hands on the rubbery surface. He tested the integrity with a couple of trial pushes with both hands. Satisfied, he pulled his knee far enough forward that he could get his left boot down on the roof and straightened his leg, pushing himself up and back. As he straightened and angled closer to the hole, the roof's grasp on his thigh shifted, freeing him. He leaned to his left—carefully, as the edge of the roof was only a foot away—and pulled his leg out, his boot only briefly catching on the top rubber lining.

He was free.

Let's not do that again. Might not get so lucky a second time around.

He scowled down at the roof as he scanned it again. The problem was likely puddling water and small cracks in the rubber surface leading to disintegrating supports below that weren't obvious until 275 pounds stepped on the fault line. Then it was a full-on collapse. How many other spots could there be on this roof, and how many might be big enough to swallow him whole?

Only one way to find out.

He forced himself to slow down, to test, even if only for a second, each step. It doubled his travel time across the roof, but slow was better than out of the equation permanently.

Finally, he reached the edge. It was a relief to sink down six feet from the drop, unclip his rifle from its sling, and commando crawl his way to the verge so he remained unseen from below. He definitely felt safer with his weight spread out over the roof as he lay on his belly.

The roof was edged with the same metal trough he'd used to save himself only minutes before, sitting four inches taller than the surface of the roof. Logan had seen a few of the drains used to keep the roof from flooding—small slotted baskets upside down over drainpipes to carry water but not debris into the gutter system—though clearly there was a flooding issue in certain spots on the roof. For tonight, it was too cold for water to move, and Logan was grateful for the lack of snow buildup, making his job of holding completely still, sometimes for long periods of time, more comfortable than it might be otherwise.

He eased carefully forward, studying the street below through his night-vision goggles. A line of buildings stood opposite, standing like individual Lego creations put together by a child—all different heights and architectural styles, and in a range of materials and color, from stucco to various colors of brick. At this end of the street, the buildings all had rolling garage doors; at the far end, the buildings were clearly used as offices. For now, the buildings were dark and there was no obvious trace of the navy van.

Movement flashed in his peripheral vision, and he turned to the left to see a figure dressed in black burst from behind a garbage dumpster in a crouched position, a rifle in their hands. The figure ran down the front of the last building, passing first the closed garage door, then a front entrance, to stand in the lee of the first and second buildings. The figure looked up at that moment, scanning the top of the warehouse looking for Logan. It was Johnson, but Logan wasn't sure he could see him from this angle.

He keyed his throat mic, then kept his voice low as he reported in. "Logan checking in. I'm in position on the northwest corner of the northwest warehouse. I have Johnson in clear view. Setting up now."

He pulled back ever so slightly from the edge to set up his sniper rifle, snapping out the bipod legs mounted on the bottom rail at the tip of the fore-end to support the barrel, and then hitting the button to deploy the monopod under the stock, giving the rifle tripod support, holding it above the short wall surrounding the roof. He'd need to brace a fist under the stock to change the angle as he was coming in from above, but he could change that on the fly when he had something to aim at. He flipped the end caps off his 4K digital scope, powered it on, switched it to night vision, and locked his goggles up and out of the way.

Lying flat against the roof, he pulled the recoil pad of the rear stock assembly in tight against his right shoulder and folded in his left arm, slipping his fist under the bottom of the pistol grip, then adjusted to give the rear end of the rifle some extra height, changing the angle. He pulled the rifle in a little tighter, the eyepiece of his scope falling into position at his dominant right eye. The world opened up before him, magnified.

He cycled through a slow inhale and exhale, feeling both his respiration and heart rate slowing, steadying his hands. The precision required to make a shot like this necessitated a stillness the normal workings of a human body could betray, but practice made sinking into the posture of the shot a well-worn habit.

The windows of the building across the street felt close enough to touch through the scope, but the space behind the glass of the farthest window of the end building was dark. He panned slowly across its four windows, then shifted to the next building.

All dark, all still.

Those were the two buildings most likely to have taken in the van, but, at least from his angle, there was no sign of life.

He knew from experience all that could change in a heartbeat. Knew Gemma and the HNT were trying to reach out and, if they could make contact, could turn the tide of this second negotiation.

He would wait, would stay still, stay ready. And be prepared to act at precisely the right millisecond.

CHAPTER 21

MCFARLAND KNOCKED TWICE ON THE side door of the TARU box truck, and it slid open seconds later. A man with blond hair and a complexion so pale Gemma doubted he ever saw the sun stood in the gap in beige cargo pants and a quarter-zip navy-blue NYPD sweatshirt.

"Brady, good to see you." McFarland's grin and tone spoke of familiarity. "I was afraid we were going to get stuck with Kershaw."

"Bad luck for you, then." A sarcastic female voice came from behind Brady.

McFarland simply laughed and climbed up into the truck like he owned the place.

Gemma suspected McFarland had done more work with TARU than he let on. "You been doing some moonlighting, McFarland?"

"Unofficially, now and then." He waved the group into the truck. "Come on up, and I'll make introductions."

Gemma stepped into a space very much like a smaller version of the mobile command center they'd used during the South Greenfield shooting. At the front of the cargo area of the truck were two built-in desks, each with an open laptop. Between them, a display monitor was mounted high on the wall, while underneath was all the computer equipment and hard drives needed for radio and satellite communication, to control and receive images from the roof-mounted cameras, and to manage all incoming data.

The rear of the truck held two built-in benches topped with data connection ports and power outlets under wall-mounted cabinets with dry-erase front surfaces, already covered with colorful drawings and notes. Flush against the rear wall hung a tabletop that could fold down for an additional workspace.

Kershaw stood from her workstation. As pale and bland as Brady was in all aspects, Kershaw was his polar opposite, though Gemma suspected if she didn't hold an entirely inward facing role, her commanding officer might have a word or two about her appearance. The NYPD tended heavily toward conservatism and only allowed a little variation from that classic look, and the brightness of the scarlet hair Kershaw had pulled into a ponytail—no way that was natural—and the makeup highlighting her vibrant green eyes was all a little too bright. But a good commanding officer knew making trouble with a solid detective over personal aspects that had nothing to do with the job itself could lose the force an exemplary officer. Basically, if no one complained, a good commander was happy to look the other way to keep the brain under that fun hair color in the department's corner. Personally, Gemma had no problem with it. The job was all that mattered.

"HNT, these are Detectives Tim Brady and Emily Kershaw. TARU, these are Detectives Gemma Capello, Ángela Ramos, and Jimmy Chen, some of the cream of the hostage negotiation crop. And me, of course, who needs no introduction."

"Sadly," intoned Kershaw dully, then ruined her response with a grin before turning to the newcomers. "Nice to meet you. Now, let's kick it into gear because the clock is ticking. Have a seat. McFarland, drop the table."

"You got it."

The team waited as McFarland set up the tabletop, then they slid into place around it. Gemma found herself bumping elbows with McFarland as he pulled out his laptop.

Kershaw pushed her rolling chair over with her laptop under her arm. She set it down on the corner near Ramos. "Sorry for the tight fit. The Winnebago's in the shop."

"Pity," Ramos quipped.

"Isn't it?" Kershaw opened the lid of her laptop as Brady came over with his own chair and laptop. He settled next to Gemma, balancing his laptop on his thighs.

"We enhanced the video feed as best we could," Kershaw said. "It clarified a few things. We were right about it being either 24 or 26. It looks like 22 converted its garage to a bigger front entrance, and 20 and 18 are too far down the street for what was recorded."

"Have you communicated that to Lieutenant Cartwright?" Gemma asked.

"You bet. He said he has five detectives on the ground and one on a rooftop somewhere. He'll let us know if they figure it out, and we'll do the same."

Crammed into the corner, McFarland spun his laptop around. An aerial view of Google Maps was on-screen, showing the row of buildings from the air. He pointed at the square building near the bottom of the screen. "This is 26. It's the smallest building on the block." He rotated the view so they could see the front of the building. "Bottom level is garage, front door, and a single high window. But if you look at this side"—he moved the view slightly down the street—"you can see the gated lot with a single exit door on the side. Both upper levels have four windows on the front." He spun the image to the back of the building. "Four on the back on both of those levels as well. A whole lot of junk in that yard, at least when this image was snapped, but no other ground-floor exits or windows."

"I have that address as the office space for L7L Designs, an interior design company," said Brady.

"That kind of business would use a van," Ramos reasoned. "Carrying sample boards for countertops or tile. Upholstery books. Toting around lamps or cushions or delivering smaller furniture."

"The building is owned by Robbertson Holdings, so L7L either is a subsidiary or they're renting," said Brady.

"Would be reasonable for a design company to use the upper levels as office space or storage or as a small showroom. The downstairs could be the back room for storing materials and loading for transportation." Ramos swung toward McFarland. "When was that aerial photo taken?"

"Date stamp says last year."

"So all that junk—the speedboat, the shipping containers, and all the rest of the crap piled up—may not be stored there anymore. Or they may not be renting the lot, just the building."

"I'm not seeing an obvious connection between someone at a design company and Horner. McFarland, you have the research on Horner. Any connections?"

"Nothing obvious. I found the contact page for L7L Designs. Small family business. Everyone working for the company has the same last name, but that name doesn't appear to have any connection with Horner or any of his business dealings."

"What about 24?"

"I had that one," said Kershaw, her eyes on her monitor. "And here's where it gets interesting. Two businesses are registered at that address. The building is owned by GEA Electrical."

"That's the name on the registration for the van license plates, isn't it?" Gemma asked.

"Coincidentally, it is," Kershaw said, in a tone that conveyed it wasn't a coincidence at all. "And if you needed extra proof, here's the company website." She turned her computer around. The header of the website showed a smiling man in a navy polo shirt with a bright-yellow logo on the left breast pocket. But it was the vehicle behind him that caught everyone's attention.

"That definitely looks like the van from the security footage," Gemma said.

"At least the same make, model, and color," said Kershaw. "The van is at the wrong angle in that photo to see the license plate."

"That van has a logo on it," Chen pointed out. "What we're looking for doesn't."

"But that's where the interesting part comes in." Kershaw turned the laptop to face herself, then used her touchpad to make some adjustments. "The second business registered at that location is Asher Millwright Services." She turned the laptop around again.

Gemma leaned in for a better look. "That's the same man. Different shirt but the same man. Same van, too. Same spot, even."

"Different logo on the van though." Ramos nudged the laptop a little closer. "It's magnetic signage. Same guy, same vehicle, two companies, probably shot at the same time. Change the shirt and the sign and, voilà, different purpose."

"Those are pretty different professions," McFarland said.

"I thought so, too," said Kershaw. "Then I looked into it a bit more. The most common dual ticket—that's the credential allowing you to work in a particular field—with electrical is millwright. Apparently, the two professions can work in tandem. Have a piece of industrial machinery that doesn't work? It could be electrical or mechanical. If you have someone who's dual ticketed, they cover both ends of the spectrum in fixing your machinery. It's on their About page—the CEO, Samuel Asher, is dual ticketed. But the two professions are also different enough that I can see why he didn't go under one umbrella, but two, simply so each company could be found by those looking for that particular service. And depending on what job he's doing, he can switch the van's signage to match."

"Remove all signage, and you have a nondescript van," Chen said.

"We need to reach out to those companies," Gemma said. "The websites list their phone numbers, but what are the chances they actually go through to a landline in there?"

"Maybe fifty-fifty?" Brady shrugged. "For a person, less than that, but some companies still depend on landlines. Especially if they have staff in the building answering phones. We could take the time to jump through hoops to figure out if it's a landline or cell, or we could cut to the chase and just call since time is of the essence." He stood, opened one of the overhead drawers, and pulled out a small black telecommunication unit. He handed the unit over to McFarland. "Plug it into the system."

McFarland connected the box to one of the jacks in the truck wall as Brady pulled several headsets from the cupboard. "How many are talking?"

"Just me." Gemma held out her hand and took the mic'd headset. "Thanks." She unraveled the cord and tossed McFarland the plug. "But first, time to get some boots-on-the-ground assistance." Gemma and McFarland both wore their throat mics but had left their earpieces out, knowing that if Cartwright had an update, he'd call them. Gemma tucked her earpiece into place and activated her throat mic. "Capello to Cartwright. We're about to reach out to the hostage taker via a potential phone in 24 Commerce. Do you have anyone on the ground near the building?"

"Affirmative. Johnson is in front of 26, and Perez is just on the other side of 24."

"We don't know if the number we have listed is for a cell phone or a landline, so we're kicking it old-school. It would be helpful to know if anyone hears a phone ring."

"Agreed. Perez, are you in place? Double mic click for affirmative."

Double mic click.

"Johnson?"

Double mic click.

"Go ahead, Capello. Perez and Johnson, report in if you hear a phone."

Gemma disconnected her throat mic and put on the headset, leaving the left earphone just behind her left ear so she could keep her radio earpiece in place, then adjusted her boom mic. One quick look at her watch said they needed to move. "We need to make contact in the next fifteen minutes or we're going to do it the old-fashioned way."

"What's that?" Kershaw asked.

"Standing on the sidewalk with the bullhorn in the A-Team truck. Not subtle, but we have two choices—make contact by phone or by bellowing at him through a window. Either way, he needs to know his original plan is finished. Knowing we have him cornered will hopefully stay his hand with Kip's family, at least in the short term. It's one thing to kill and leave your victim to be found days later after you've made your escape; it's another to know cops are outside your door, listening to you make the kill, and ready to arrest you immediately for the crime. It would hopefully make you change your mind when there's no chance of escape."

"The suspect may also not know we found Vann in the East River either, so he may think no death is associated with him," Ramos said. "He may think the hostage taking is the worst of it."

"If we're lucky. Kershaw, read out one of those two business numbers for 24 from their respective websites."

"Here's the millwright number." Kershaw read it out, and McFarland punched it in.

It rang four times and then flipped to voicemail. McFarland ended the call. He keyed his throat mic. "Perez and Johnson. Did anyone hear a phone ring?"

A single mic click, then two seconds later, another.

"10-4. We're going to try a second number." McFarland cut his throat mic. "The electrical number?"

McFarland entered it as Kershaw read it off. Four more rings, voicemail.

McFarland went back to his throat mic. "Perez and Johnson, did you hear the phone that time?"

A double mic click. Then a single.

"Perez, is that your double mic click?"

A double mic click.

"10-4. Thank you. We'll concentrate on that number. Cartwright, if that fails, we'll need the bullhorn."

"Affirmative," said Cartwright.

"McFarland out." His gaze swung to meet Gemma's. "We can't afford to give this much more time. We could call again and again and not get him to pick up in time to stop this. He would have no idea the NYPD was calling. He might think it's someone with an electrical emergency who's hoping he's calling someone's cell phone."

"Yeah, I know. Let's give it a little more time."

They called twice more, separated by two minutes, with no response.

Gemma sagged back against the bench. "We're going to have to use the bullhorn."

Across the table, Ramos nodded her agreement. "Not leaving us any choice if we can't communicate. Otherwise, we need to send the A-Team in, and who knows what could happen in the confusion. That family could die."

"We're not going to let that happen." She took off her headset and handed it to McFarland. "Take over. Keep trying. I'm going to talk to Cartwright."

"If you're going to armor up in A-Team gear so you can get close," said Kershaw, "we'll tap into your helmet cam feed and follow along."

McFarland took the headset in one hand and jabbed an index finger at Gemma with the other. "You make sure Garcia knows what's going on before you get close to that building. You get command approval."

He didn't say it out loud, but conveyed the rest of his thought through his stony expression. *No going rogue. Garcia approves this, or you don't do it. Not like last time.*

Last time—when Gemma had handed Garcia her badge and gun and walked out of the HNT headquarters to exchange herself for the seven remaining hostages in City Hall as per the hostage taker's request. Breaking the golden rule that no negotiator ever exchanged themselves for a hostage. They'd tried to find any other way to make it work, but in the end, Gemma had made the call herself and had walked away from her life in the NYPD.

"I don't know if you're the bravest person I know or the most foolhardy"—Logan's words to her that day after he followed at a jog to try to talk some sense into her.

"Don't do it again. There won't be any second chances"—her father's words as he handed back her badge after Garcia kept the secret of her resignation, as had Logan and Sanders.

Gemma met McFarland's gaze square on, so he was sure she heard his unspoken message. "Command approval, or it doesn't happen."

If any of the other team members noted the relieved shift of McFarland's shoulders, they didn't comment.

Gemma slid sideways on the bench and stood. "Keep your earpiece in. And while I'm gone, see if you as a group can figure out any connection between Horner and these businesses I can use in the negotiation."

"You got it. Be safe."

"Count on it."

Gemma opened the door of the truck, quickly scanned the area—the street remained deserted—and hopped down.

Squaring her shoulders, she marched toward the A-Team van and the next stage of the negotiation.

CHAPTER 22

GEMMA DIDN'T EVEN NEED TO knock on the van. Cartwright, still running the op from the passenger seat of the truck, was working the radio with the truck's mobile data terminal at his fingertips. His head snapped up as she jogged past his window, heading for the rear of the van.

Gemma could hear his boots inside the truck, then the door opened and she was looking up at him. "I'm going to need the bullhorn."

Cartwright stepped away, giving her space to climb up into the truck. "No luck with the phone?"

Gemma climbed inside and pulled the door shut behind her. "One of the two is ringing inside, but no one is picking up. And if they expect those are emergency calls coming through for the business, why would they? Which leaves us with two options—incursion number two for the night, or the bullhorn, so we can try to have a conversation." Cartwright opened his mouth to speak, and Gemma held up a hand. "I'm about to call Garcia. I'm not doing this without his approval. But if I get it, I'm going to need A-Team support." Her gaze slid to the shipment lockers lining the walls of the truck. "And a vest."

"And a helmet."

She hated the roughly five-pound weight of a loaded tactical helmet but recognized the necessity. Luckily, she didn't need to wear it often; in her case, not since the Rikers standoff when she'd hidden as a member of Logan's unit so she could get a look and a feel for the prisoner who was running the hostage situation. "Right. TARU also said they'd tap into my camera feed, so that, too. Bullhorn?"

"It's here." Cartwright jammed a thumb over his shoulder. "Garcia first."

"Yes, sir." Gemma pulled out her cell phone and speed-dialed Garcia.

"Capello. Progress?"

"Not really, sir. We've identified the company that owns the building we strongly suspect contains the hostage taker and Kip's family and have been able to call through. Detective Perez out front confirms he can hear the phone ringing inside, but it's not being picked up and we're running out of time. We need to announce our presence to keep him from killing Kip's family when the transfer doesn't actually go through." A thought occurred out of the blue. "Actually, you could help there, sir. Are you still with Kip?"

"We're already at One Police Plaza. He's being booked, but I can get to him."

"We're still connecting the dots and he may be able to help. Can you ask him if he knows either of these companies or anyone who works there? Asher Millwright Services or GEA Electrical."

"The van is at one of those companies?"

"Both, actually. Run by the same guy out of the same building, using a navy cargo van with magnetic signage that can be swapped out depending on what company is doing the work."

"Or removed altogether," Garcia said.

"Exactly."

"I'll ask him."

"Thank you. But as to why I called, I need command approval to suit up and have the A-Team get me closer to use a bullhorn. We can't get him to pick up the phone, and we're running out of time. We have to let him know we're here. It could keep him from killing Katie and the kids."

"You have Cartwright's approval to use his guys?"

"He's right here beside me." She held out the phone to Cartwright. "Garcia wants to know if I have your approval to work with Unit 1."

Cartwright took the phone. "I'll make sure she's armored up, and will give her two officers to keep her safe." The look in his eye as he stared down at her told her he was thinking back a few weeks to how she'd managed to keep herself alive long enough for Logan to find and save her as a killer dragged her through the depths of Grand Central Madison. The reticence he'd shown back at Rikers seemed to have vanished. "Not that she can't do that herself." He extended the phone to her. "I'll get you that equipment."

"Thanks." She put the phone to her ear. "Do I have command approval?"

"Approved," said Garcia.

"Thank you. I may have my hands full, so call McFarland if you figure anything out with Kip. He's working on it with the TARU techs. Anything they can give me could collectively give us a leg up."

"10-4 on that. Be safe."

"Thank you, sir. Will do." Gemma ended the call, put her phone on vibrate, and slipped it into the front pocket of her pants.

"Take off the long coat. Use one of our tactical jackets. If you have to run, that coat will be a disadvantage."

Leave it to Cartwright to see everything through a tactical lens. "Thanks." She quickly unbuttoned the coat, folded it in half, and tossed it over the end of one of the two benches.

"This is the smallest jacket and vest I have."

Gemma slipped into the black ESU jacket, then took the vest Cartwright handed her, remembering to hold on tight because the armor plating made the vest deceptively heavy. She slipped it on, the roughly twenty-five pounds settling onto her shoulders, wondering how heavy Logan's bigger vest was, especially as this one was empty and his was always loaded with magazines for his rifle and pistol, and the tools of his trade. Probably at least forty pounds, and he carried it around as standard equipment. She pulled the Velcro straps tight over the borrowed jacket, then made sure the Glock she wore in a belt holster on her right hip was still easily accessible, God forbid she needed it.

Cartwright eyed her critically, then turned away from her to select a helmet and a pair of binocular night-vision goggles. "Everyone on the ground is wearing monocular night vision so they can still view their rifle sights at the same time. No rifle for you, so we'll go with goggles." He quickly mounted the goggles on the helmet's front attachment, flipped them up, and locked them in place. She pulled the clip out of her hair, letting it fall to her shoulders as she tucked the clip into a pocket of her coat. She took the helmet in both hands, lifted it into place, and secured the chin strap. Cartwright fiddled with the camera mounted on the side of her helmet—likely turning it on—then extended a pair of safety glasses.

"I'm not planning on firing my weapon."

"No one ever does, but shit happens. Take them. Even just to put in one of the vest pockets. You're armed—you never know what will go down."

She pocketed the glasses.

Cartwright tapped his mic on. "Cartwright to Sims and Turner. Meet Capello on the south corner of Richards and Commerce Streets. You'll escort her to the northwest corner of 26, where she'll attempt to connect with the hostage taker via bullhorn."

"Acknowledged," said the two detectives, almost simultaneously.

Cartwright keyed off his mic and moved to one of the closed cabinets at the bottom of one of the equipment lockers. Squatting, he pulled out a large black bullhorn, with controls and the mic on the back of the speaker, a folded handle, and a thick wrist strap. "Used one of these before?"

"This isn't my first bullhorn negotiation. We try not to do it because it's simply too public, but sometimes there's no other choice." She took the bullhorn from him and tucked it under her left arm, leaving her right hand free in case she needed to access her weapon.

Cartwright stepped to the rear door, unlatching it. "Stay on your radio, and I'll continue to monitor from here. Unit 5 is nearly here, and I'll call in local backup to cordon off the area. Chances are good we're about to attract lookie-loos."

"Unfortunately. Thanks, that will help." Gemma jumped down, gave Cartwright a nod, and swung the door closed.

She crossed the empty street and jogged up Delavan to Richards. A single streetlight cast a watery glow down on the intersection, highlighting the cracked and crumbling asphalt, but didn't travel much farther. She circled the building on the corner, noting how each ground-floor window was covered with heavy metal security mesh, behind which light shone from some windows as Brooklynites continued to celebrate the New Year. The mostly industrial area apparently still had some pockets of apartments, which were about to get a rude awakening. She could keep the bullhorn volume down somewhat—the NYPD's high-wattage bullhorns were powerful and could be heard up to almost a mile away, overkill in this situation—but disruption or not, the message had to get through.

Her larger concern was that in falling back on such overt technology, the crisis was about to be blown into the open to anyone in the area, which could bring rubberneckers. No help for it, though. Time was ticking down on the lives of Kip's family, and not knowing who the hostage taker was, they had no direct way of contacting him.

Cartwright bringing in blue-and-whites to block off streets would help but would also add to the attraction. The area wasn't heavily populated, but the bullhorn would draw attention. Not to mention, anyone listening to the police band radio might come in to observe.

That included the media. The last thing she wanted was a standoff involving children under the watchful—and possibly filming—eye of New York City's story-hungry media.

She'd recently called a truce with what she had previously considered the worst of the worst—Greg Coulter from ABC7, one of the city's most dogged investigative reporters. If there was a story in the city, especially one centered around crime, Coulter would mobilize as soon as he heard about it. If she was lucky, he'd be somewhere up in Midtown, drowning in stories in Times Square, and she wouldn't have to deal with him.

She gave herself a mental wrist-slap. That was falling back on old habits. The man had literally saved her life only weeks before during the Grand Central Terminal crisis simply by recognizing her face and informing the NYPD that one of their own was inside. Small potatoes, perhaps, but it had started the cascade that had allowed Gemma to speak to her own team, to her brother Alex, and for Alex to decipher her coded messages, leading to the surrender of the bomber.

Granted, Gemma had returned the favor with a one-on-one sit-down in the ABC7 studios the week after the standoff, with Logan standing in the wings, having firmly refused to appear on camera. It had been the first reasonable interaction they'd had—Coulter had stowed his overflowing ego, she'd buried her resentment of past intrusions, and they'd tried to meet in the middle. It had gone surprisingly well.

Nonetheless, she didn't want to see him, or any of his ilk, tonight.

Gemma jogged down the street, past garbage dumpsters dribbling refuse onto the sidewalks, bare trees lining the road, more graffiti sprayed over painted walls, and building entrances installed with rolling doors as an extra security layer.

Two figures stood pressed against the building on the corner, lit by the streetlight on the far side, out of sight of anyone down Commerce Street. Gemma slowed to a fast walk as Sims and Turner stepped away from the wall.

Sims gave her a quick up and down, cataloging her equipment. "Ready?"

"Yes. Cartwright said you can get me one building away?"

"Yes. And keep you behind the front wall so someone would have to circle the building to shoot in your direction. Then Logan would have him." Sims tapped his mic. "Sims to Logan."

"Logan here."

"Turner and I are on the south corner of Commerce and Richards. We're going to cross to the far side, then proceed southeast to bring Capello to the far corner of 26. Keep an eye out for any response from the suspect from the front of the building that would put her at risk."

"10-4."

Sims pointed across the road. "We'll cross here to stay out of any line of fire from 24 and then move down the street. Let's go."

Turner took the lead, jogging across the road, rifle at the ready in case of trouble. Gemma followed, and Sims brought up the rear. Turner banked to the right, following the sidewalk past an auto parts depot, then their fenced lot, and then the fenced lot beside 26.

Turner slowed at the far end of the fencing, inset a full foot from the edge of the building, giving them a sheltered spot. Gemma tucked herself into the corner with her back to the fence, Turner and then Sims to her right. She slipped the bullhorn's strap over her left wrist and unfolded the handle, gripping it in her left fist.

She tapped her throat mic. "Capello to Cartwright. I'm in position."

"10-4. Unit 1, confirm positions."

"Logan, warehouse roof."

"Sims and Turner, with Capello."

"Johnson, between 26 and 24."

"Perez, behind the staircase leading up to 22."

"Wilson, behind 26 and 24, watching the second-floor windows."

"Capello, you're clear to begin negotiations." Cartwright again. "Unit 1, report in at any sign of movement. Officers are incoming to form a perimeter now negotiations are going public."

"Capello to Logan."

"Logan here."

"I'm about to start talking. You'll have the best view. Let me know if you see anything inside any building, especially in 24."

"10-4."

Gemma tapped off her throat mic. "Here we go, then." She powered on the bullhorn, the indicator light glowing red, adjusted the volume slider to only about one-quarter of full strength—she didn't need her voice to travel over Buttermilk Channel to Governors Island, three-quarters of a mile away; she only needed the sound to travel about forty feet and then penetrate through the windows and doors. It would have been better positioning opposite the building, but that would have left her an open target unless she'd spent all her time huddled behind the A-Team's ballistic shield. Not optimal either way.

One last check of the time—12:48 AM. Time to change the trajectory of the night for her suspect.

She raised the bullhorn to her mouth and angled it as far down the street as she could while staying behind the corner wall of 26. "This is Detective Gemma Capello of the NYPD's Hostage Negotiation Team. We have the building surrounded with tactical officers. We don't want to use force—we want to talk. We know you have Kip Slater's family. We want them released. I'd like to talk to you about it." She turned off the bullhorn, turned on her throat mic. "Capello to Logan. Volume check."

"Volume is good. Maybe even a little high, but until you know he can hear you, don't turn it down."

"10-4."

She disengaged her throat mic and then closed her eyes, straining to hear even the tiniest sound.

Nothing.

"How long will you wait?" Turner whispered.

"Not much longer." Gemma gave it another thirty seconds, then lifted the bullhorn. She released the locking lever on her night-vision goggles, lowered them into place, and then eased out around the corner just far enough to see all the way down the street. The goggles amplified the scant ambient light into a ghostly green glow, highlighting every detail around her with precision clarity. Gemma didn't wear night-vision goggles often in her line of work and always felt she needed a few seconds for her brain to make the jump to processing what she was seeing.

The street was mostly empty, minus one older vehicle she suspected had been there for weeks, if not longer, as it had a handful of tickets under a single windshield wiper. On this side of the road, a haphazard pile of wooden skids was stacked behind the rusty fire hydrant in front of 26. A small square planter with a scraggly bunch of greenery and a single red bow sat by the door to 24, the only sign of holiday spirit on the entire street. A garbage dumpster sat in front of 22, in the lee created by the back of the concrete steps marching up to a mid-level front entrance—this must be the staircase where Perez was hidden. The sidewalk cleared farther down the street, the buildings appearing neater and cleaner with no dumpsters in sight, but large planters containing winter-bare shrubs and yellowed grasses instead. Bare trees lined the edge of the sidewalk, their bases contained by short wooden fences.

The far side of the street was all industrial—bare sidewalks only broken by electrical poles, warehouses, cracked driveways, and fenced lots.

Nothing moved, but that meant she was safe to swing out a bit in an effort to make sure the sound was as efficient as possible.

She raised the bullhorn to her lips. "This is the NYPD! We know you have Kip Slater's wife and children. We don't want anyone hurt. We just want to talk to you. I don't want to send tactical in, or someone could get hurt. Please respond."

Silence again.

Then a distant voice behind her. "Shut up! Trying to sleep here!"

"Jesus." Disgust rode heavily in Sims's tone. "Read the room, jackass."

A siren sounded in the distance, the wail growing in volume from the northwest as the car got closer. Then a second coming from the east, even more distant but closing fast. As they grew in volume, the pressure would build inside 24 Commerce Street.

Gemma gave it another minute, waiting for the sirens to become extremely clear. A blue-and-white SUV with NYPD on the door pulled up into the intersection of Commerce and Richards behind her, blocking Commerce Street from the northwest. Parked on an angle, the SUV's headlights helped illuminate the dark street, but more than that, a hand came out of the driver's window and adjusted the spotlight positioned in front of the driver's side mirror, a beam of light lighting the scene.

Wincing from the sudden brightness of her field of vision, Gemma snapped her night-vision goggles up, locking them in the upright position. Sims and Turner did the same with their monocular goggle.

An officer in navy winter gear got out of the SUV and planted himself behind his car, staying covered in case of gunfire from down the street while watching the intersection in all directions. The officer had left his light bar on, washing the street in strobing white, red, and blue flashes.

"Unit 5 is en route." Cartwright's voice sounded in her ear. "ETA ten minutes."

More sirens, more lights. There could be no mistake for the man in 24 Commerce that he was in trouble.

Patience was one of the tools in her toolbox, and Gemma could wait the man out as long as there was no risk to the family inside. But that didn't mean she couldn't remind him of that fact, repeating the same message until he responded. Bullhorn back on. "I need to talk to you. I can assure your safety as long as you talk to me and as long as you don't hurt anyone inside. Otherwise, I have to step back and leave it to the tactical teams. Take my word for it, it would be easier to deal with me."

Gemma was holding the information about Sylvia Lansing to see if she could get the suspect's attention without it, but if he continued to ignore her, it would be time to add Sylvia to the mix. To let him know they were onto him and he needed to meet her halfway. She was drawing breath to speak again when she was interrupted.

"McFarland to Capello. I think we know who's in there. This information would help you, but it's a little complicated. Can you come back to the TARU truck for a few minutes? We can lay it out for you to use."

She turned off the bullhorn and keyed her throat mic. "Capello to McFarland. Affirmative. Be there in two minutes." Throat mic off, bullhorn on. "I'd really like to talk to you. Please consider my offer. I'll give you time to think. Ten minutes. Just remember, we have the technology to listen through window glass with laser microphones. If there's any hint you're hurting anyone from the Slater family, tactical will enter the building. Don't make us take that step."

It wasn't an actual lie—TARU had that technology. Though, in this case, because it would have to be on the warehouse roof to be at an effective angle to transmit, receive, or both, they couldn't actually use it in this situation.

Gemma turned off the bullhorn, pulled off the wrist strap, and extended the bullhorn to Turner. "You'll need to cover for me if he tries to reach out before I return. He hasn't heard me speak enough to nail down my voice. Any female voice will do in a pinch. Contact me, and I can run back in about ninety seconds."

"Will do." Turner took her left hand off her rifle and took the bullhorn.

"Be back ASAP." Gemma turned and sprinted down the sidewalk, arcing past the officer at the end of the street, now joined by two other cars and officers, and a growing crowd of spectators. Left on Richards, down to Delavan, another left, and then she was running past Cartwright talking on the radio in the A-Team truck.

Reaching the TARU truck, she grabbed the handle for the rear door and yanked it open. Five faces looked down at her.

"I'm here. Talk fast."

CHAPTER 23

BRADY SNAPPED HIS LAPTOP SHUT and hopped out of his chair as Gemma climbed into the truck. "Sit here where you can see."

"Thanks." Gemma unsnapped her helmet and set it down on the table before raking her fingers through her flattened curls. "What do you have?"

"I have Paul Asher." McFarland jumped in to take the lead. "Follow along. We know from looking up building records on the Automated City Register Information System that GEA Electrical owns the building at 24 Commerce Street. The CEO of GEA Electrical is Samuel Asher. His brother is Paul."

"The company has a connection to Horner?"

"Not the company, but Paul. Best I can see from some of their photos and social media posts, Paul did some side work for his brother Sam, so he'd be familiar with the building and its contents—including the van and where the keys are kept. It's likely that because of all that work and the close family relationship with his brother, Paul had a key to the building so he could waltz in and borrow the van. There's a note on the company website saying they're closed from December 24th to January 2nd for the holidays. Probably no one would have noticed the van being gone today, and chances are low his brother is going to walk in on him here tonight."

Gemma checked the time, felt the weight of the seconds crawling by. McFarland needed to speed this up. "But what's his connection to Horner?"

"Through a startup called Frütfl Inc. It was one of the smaller ones, so I didn't mention it before because it kind of never really got going. The point of Frütfl was it was an invention crowdsourcing company. Inventors registered a project they were working on, they'd get the hive mind involved, get it perfected, then the company would produce and market the product with glory and cash for all. Well, mostly to the company. The person with the idea got about ten percent of the free-and-clear profit once the product was made and sold."

"And the hive mind?"

"This was part of the problem. The hive mind thought it was fun at first, contributing to what could be some snazzy new products, but they figured out fast their skills and knowledge were being tapped for free, and some of the best minds dropped out to do their own thing, leaving them with a higher percentage of hacks."

"Paul was one of those inventors?"

"Yes. And I have to say, the guy could have had something incredible, but he was about five years ahead of his time. He wanted to crowdsource something he called Pocket EA—a pin with an associated app, something you wore day in and day out that recorded sound from everything you did, then translated it into a transcript. Want to prove you said something at some point during your day? Want to have exact notes from every meeting you went to? Here you go—a pocket executive assistant. Problem was, it was too much data with no way to efficiently sort through it all except for dumping the transcript into a word processor and looking for keywords."

"That doesn't sound like a great product."

"It is today. There are products just like that currently on the market, but they only work because of AI. Now, these products do the same thing but use AI to make summaries or determine priorities, create to-do lists, and input calendar entries. It will analyze the data and propose workflow and project improvements. You ask the associated app a question, and based on your own data collected through the hardware, it makes suggestions or offers insights. It's a personal assistant made for you specifically. But back then, it was none of those things. Paul's project got off the ground but wasn't well marketed, they only had limited distribution, they couldn't scale, and they sold…" McFarland's gaze slipped to his screen. "Thirty-four units."

"Ouch."

"The company went under a few years ago. Good idea in practice, but just not sustainable when it's up against big manufacturing and R&D."

"So Paul's pissed at Horner because his project failed?"

"Remember how Paul was before his time? Remember how those digital personal assistants work now because of AI? One of Horner's current companies is producing that exact item, with his SagAIcity AI integrated, and it's flying off the shelves. Horner is raking in the cash."

"And Paul is making ends meet working intermittently for his brother. The fifty million dollars is what he feels Horner swindled him out of when his product didn't become a smashing success."

McFarland drilled her with an index finger. "Best I can tell, Paul thinks he's getting his own back by doing this."

"He doesn't see that Horner has added value to the item by using AI to turn it into something truly useful. If it really is. All Paul is going to see is dollar signs. He's a victim. He has grievances. Someone needs to pay for those grievances. He was once in circles with Horner; he must still keep tabs on him enough that he knew about the New Year's Eve party."

"That's where Sylvia comes in."

"I knew she had to fit in here somewhere."

"She was a fellow angel investor, though truly small-time compared to Horner. This was before she divorced some big-time New York financial guy."

"Maybe there was a prenup," said Ramos. "Maybe times are tighter now. Back then, she had play money; now she's struggling."

"But trying not to look like she's struggling if she's at the fancy party," said Kershaw. "Still trying to look like a socialite, even if she's wearing gowns and jewelry bought years ago, and putting on appearances of keeping up and maintaining those old connections well enough to get invited to Horner's party. We can do a dive into her financials."

"I think that would help in the long run, thanks," said Gemma. "What's her connection to Paul?"

"Based on her recent social media posts, she and Paul are a couple," said McFarland. "I haven't had time to track back that far, but they may have met during the Frütfl days. What I can tell you is she refers to him as her 'inventor-genius.' But as far as I can see, he only made that one thing."

"But if he sees that as his identity, one stolen from him, then he may see that one failure as Horner stealing his future," said Chen.

"And this party was his shot at getting that future back," McFarland hypothesized. "Fifty million is enough to finance a number of new inventions."

"It may even be more than that," said Gemma. "What if Paul saw Frütfl as the first step in emulating Horner and his business acumen? Horner saw value in the company, in Paul's project, so what if Paul viewed his project as the first step toward his rightful success? But the project failed, which maybe sliced apart Paul's psyche and his plans for his successful life."

"If you and Chen are correct about how his identity and self-worth have been damaged, he might see pulling off this scheme as getting his life back. When Sylvia filled him in about the party itself, he started to make plans."

"Sylvia could have also filled in the blanks on the catering company," Ramos said. "It looks like Horner has a preference there, or at least his current PA does, because they use the same one on land or on the water when he's entertaining. They show up time and again in the background of these big party photos. If she's in his circle, she'd know them. From there, Paul could target the staff of that company, namely Jerome Vann." Ramos drummed her fingers on the table a few times, her lips pursed.

"What?" Gemma asked.

"I'm thinking about what Sylvia said to Horner." Ramos turned to Chen. "Do you have the exact wording?"

"Of course." Chen picked up the yellow pad he'd brought with him and flipped to near the end of his notes, scanning the page. "She said, 'You're responsible for much more than that. He should have had it all. *We* should have had it all. But you ruined it. You stole from us. We're just getting our own back.'" He set the pad down on the table. "She thinks

Horner ruined her life as well. Had Frütfl done well, maybe she wouldn't be struggling."

"Or maybe she'd be with a man who wasn't struggling," suggested Gemma. "But the interesting thing is that while she played a part, he did the heavy lifting. Did she push him into that? Is Paul having such a crisis of confidence that she's calling the shots from behind the scenes?"

"You're saying Sylvia is Lady Macbeth?" Kershaw asked.

Gemma snapped her fingers and pointed at Kershaw. "Exactly like that. He might not even be aware of how much he's being manipulated. I wonder if the whole idea was hers versus his. She's feeding him information. She'll keep Kip on the straight and narrow on the boat, but he's killing and kidnapping, possibly with her encouragement."

"If so," Chen interjected, "when it's clear this whole thing has fallen apart on Paul, he may not feel he has anything left. If his identity is wrapped up in his persona of inventor, when he finds out he's surrounded and has no hope of freedom or a fortune in Bitcoin, he might be a danger to that family."

"And to himself," Gemma finished. "This is going to be a delicate juggling act. I need to keep him feeling in control while wresting it from him. This is all making sense now, but there's still one hole—what's the connection between Paul and Kip, allowing him to get someone on that yacht?"

"We confirmed this with Lia at The Wandering Flask. We sent her his DMV photo, and she recognized Paul as a regular. A kind of quiet guy, he used to sit down at the same end of the bar with a buddy. The buddy's a talker and chatted with Kip during quiet moments. Kip was friendly, and over time they got familiar with each other and Kip shared part of his life with the buddy. Like how his house was robbed last year. And how he was worried someday the same thing might happen again, but this time when his wife and kids were home, so he bought a gun to keep in his bedside table. In a gun safe, so it wasn't a threat to his kids."

"And Paul was there, just soaking it all in. But not being so in-your-face about it to ring alarm bells for Kip."

"Exactly. A bit more from Lia. She said Paul appeared to be unemployed from the amount of time he spent at The Wandering Flask. And they cut him off more than once because he'd had too much. She thought he was teetering on the edge of alcoholism."

"It sounds like Paul was hitting rock bottom, so he may have seen the party as an opportunity to break out of a cycle. But he thought it through. He had to know it was a risky move being so isolated out on the harbor. On the other hand, it worked in Paul's favor to keep Horner isolated—it didn't allow him to call for help or easily signal for it in any way—but it also meant whoever did the hostage taking was also at risk of being trapped and surrounded. He wanted it to happen, but didn't want to be the one taking that risk, so he found another way. In fact, I wonder if he kind of considered Kip dispensable. If Kip didn't work out, Horner was still there for the taking—he'd just have to plan another incident."

Ramos shook her head. "That's cold."

"He did all of his work in the background, killing Vann so there was an open spot and then kidnapping Kip's family to force a damned good bartender into the spot in a way that no one on board would be suspicious about the late substitution."

"He chose a ransom that can be hard to trace and can happen essentially without corporate approval, so he could then sit in the shadows and wait for the money to roll in. It was actually a solid plan. If it hadn't been for Noah, I'm not sure how this would have resolved."

"With at least one death on top of Vann," said Chen. "Kip would have started to kill or Sylvia Lansing would have. And she would have played it off as self-defense. If she had any legal troubles, Horner might even have footed the bill in gratitude for having 'saved'"—Chen made air quotes around the word—"them all."

Gemma slid her helmet on and secured the chin strap. "Anything else I need to know?"

"There are more details, but that's the important stuff. That's the stuff you'll need to reach out to Paul."

Gemma stood. "Good work, team. I think you've given us, as well as Kip's family, a fighting chance." She stepped to the door.

"Good luck!" McFarland called. "We'll keep working it and will monitor the radio and your helmet cam. We'll jump in if there's anything important we missed."

"Thanks. Gotta run. Literally. I have less than two minutes to get back in place."

Then she was gone, sprinting down the dark streets to return to a family in crisis.

CHAPTER 24

GEMMA DROPPED TO A JOG and then a walk just down the sidewalk from Turner and Sims. "All quiet?"

"Affirmative." Sims didn't take his eyes off the street from where he stood angled toward the cruisers blocking the far end. "You're right on time. Was it worth it?"

"Yes. I may be able to get him to stand down with what I have. I'm certainly going to try." She held out her hand for the bullhorn. "Thanks for being ready to jump in."

Turner handed it back. "Happy to help."

Gemma powered on the bullhorn and swung it up to her mouth as she positioned herself just out from the corner of the building. "Paul Asher, this is Gemma Capello again. I want to talk to you about your relationship with Lucas Horner. About his theft of your idea. And about Sylvia." She paused for a slow count of ten, letting that lightning bolt sink in.

Each aspect of his situation was turning into yet another bar on the cage surrounding Paul—the officers around his building, the cars blocking the street, her knowledge of his identity, the details about his motivation. The walls were closing in.

She was careful to couch her knowledge in sympathy. She needed to connect—*quickly*—needed to get him on her side. She could accuse him of extortion, but that would just put his back up. He clearly felt victimized, so she'd play into that to soften her role. She had to offer him an out before he took out his rage or fear on the family in his grasp.

"Paul, I want to work this out with you. You have the Slater family in there with you. You have nothing to gain and everything to lose by hurting them. Talk to me, please. I've heard things about you, but maybe they aren't true. You should be able to speak in your own defense."

She lowered the bullhorn. Time to give him a moment to think this through. If she kept talking, he'd never have a chance to get a word in edgewise. Now, the question was, exactly how would he talk to her?

Her earpiece buzzed to life. "Logan here. The house was dark before, but there's light now in the upper level, like one of the back lights has been turned on."

"Wilson here. Can confirm lights now visible through the back window of 24 Commerce. Not bright enough to be in the room, but somewhere on the second floor."

It sounded like Paul was on the move. Unless he was going to crack open the front door, which would leave him vulnerable to law enforcement stationed on the sidewalk, there was no easy way for him to talk to her from the ground floor, so he was moving to the upper floor, where he had the option of windows. But was he alone, or was he forcing Katie and the kids with him?

"I can see movement at the leftmost front window." Logan again. "The sash is rising, but there's no one directly behind the window."

Paul knew the house was surrounded—she'd told him herself. Whether he thought anyone was positioned on the surrounding rooftops or not, he'd be a target from the street simply by standing directly in front of the window, so he'd somehow managed to raise the window from the side. Bottom line, he'd found a way to communicate. Hopefully, she'd be able to confirm his identity quickly. Only Paul Asher would have the answers to specific questions.

Time to open the door for him. "Paul? Let's talk. Let me know you can hear me."

"I can hear you." A man's voice at a half shout sounded.

"Paul, I'm Gemma." Silence followed that statement, and she didn't let it last. "Are Katie and the two kids all right?"

"Who?"

"I know you have Katie, Olivia, and Riley Slater. I know you sent Kip Slater onto the *Salacia* to get money from Horner. I know you're working with Sylvia Lansing. I know why you did it. So I ask again—are Katie and both kids unharmed?"

Long moments passed, and a chill of foreboding snaked down Gemma's spine as the silence stretched.

"Yes."

Some of the radiating tension across her shoulders softened, but not all. That had been too long a pause. "Let's make sure we keep it that way. What will it take to release Katie and the kids?"

"I just want my money."

Gemma noted he wanted his money, but not the woman who had possibly pushed him into this situation. Was he trying to cut his losses at this point to concentrate only on the money? He had the transaction email but not the deposit confirmation. But even once he had it, then what? He'd committed murder, forced an extortion, and taken hostages. Did he think he'd just be able to take his money and walk?

It was crucial at this point he not realize the transaction email was a fraud, or he could be pushed toward violence when he found out every risk he'd taken tonight had all been for nothing. She needed to move this along before he became suspicious. The pressure was on—Gemma had to have a resolution in minutes. She'd never had to come up with a win in so little time.

"That's a little above my pay grade, that kind of money. What can we do for you?"

"I don't want you coming in here. I don't want you busting up the shop."

Doesn't want his brother to pay for what he's done.

"I can ask the tactical officers to stay out. How about a sign of good faith? You don't need children involved in this. They're not responsible for the actions of adults. They must be scared."

A memory flitted through her mind. *A small girl huddled against her mother, her eyes fixed on the terrifying dark muzzle of the gun as it waved past the group of hostages. If it went off, pointed at her, she wouldn't even have time to scream—*

She pushed the memory away.

This negotiation could move forward in steps, even slow ones, but her first priority was to get those kids out. They'd already be scarred for life—as she could attest—but at least they'd have a life to live.

"They're maybe even making your life difficult," she continued. "Why don't you send them out, and I'll tell the tactical officers to give you some space? Then, when they're out, we can keep talking."

"I don't want this hassle!" Paul's voice was growing strained. "I want my goddamned money."

"Then let's minimize the hassle. Send out the kids, Paul, then let's work on what you need. All you need to do is send them out the front door."

"Leaving me exposed and then dead when you shoot me through the open door?"

"That won't happen. You have my word on it. Send the kids out and you won't be touched."

"And when you lie and I'm dead?"

"I promise I won't lie to you. Our officers will not shoot at a doorway with children coming out. They simply won't. You'll be safe. Then come back upstairs, and we'll talk more."

"And if I don't?"

"I'm going to be totally honest with you, Paul. You're surrounded by a number of tactical officers. The only way you're going to get out of this situation intact is to negotiate with me. I'm holding them off. Otherwise, they might be tempted to think deadly force is their only option."

Silence stretched.

Come on, come on. Work with me.

"Fine. Tell your guys to back off, or it doesn't happen."

Gemma knew the A-Team officers could hear every word, but it was the performance that mattered. She keyed her throat mic and dropped the bullhorn slightly but still kept it close enough her voice could be magnified for Paul. "Capello to Units 1 and 5. Pull back. I repeat, pull back. Juvenile hostages will be released from 24 Commerce."

"Cartwright to Units 1 and 5. Pull back. We don't want to risk anyone being in sight when the door opens."

The sound of jogging footsteps heralded Johnson as he retreated, then tucked in behind Turner to stand in the lee of 26, out of sight of 24. Perez must have pulled back in the other direction to avoid passing in front of 24 and potentially in range of any fire coming from within.

Gemma gave it a full minute more before picking up the bullhorn again. "We're clear out here, Paul. Please proceed with releasing the children."

Two minutes passed with nothing happening, then Logan spoke. "The front door is opening. One kid is through." Then there was a pause. "Door is closing."

Gemma didn't wait for confirmation, but stepped out from the corner of the building to find the boy, Riley, dressed in dirty jeans and a long-sleeved red sweatshirt, standing on the sidewalk. He stood stiffly, his eyes wide, his head on a swivel, trying to figure out where to go now he was free.

"Riley." Gemma waved him closer, and the boy took off at a trot. "Capello to Logan. No Olivia?"

"Negative. The door is closed again."

One out of the two children free wasn't a bad thing, but that wasn't what she'd aimed for. She wanted them both free.

Riley came closer, and she held out her hand for him. He put his in hers without hesitation, and she drew him into the shelter of 26.

She squatted down to get to his level, and his eyes went wide at the sight of her helmet and goggles. But Gemma, though not a mother herself, had a lot of experience with children in her role as an aunt and pulled his attention back to her as he took in the armored officers behind Gemma, took in their rifles, and inched back a step involuntarily. "Riley, I'm Gemma. Look at me." She took both his hands, pulling him into their safe space.

Riley bit his bottom lip and inhaled shakily, but his gaze dropped to focus on Gemma.

"I don't want you to be scared of these officers. They're here to help you, to keep you safe, just like I am." She ran a thumb over his tear-streaked cheek. "Don't be scared."

"My mom...Olivia..."

Riley's voice was thin, timid, but Gemma could see he was trying to be brave, trying in his own small way to push for their rescue. She gave him a reassuring smile. "I was hoping Olivia would come out with you."

A frantic headshake from Riley.

"He sent you downstairs on your own?"

Another headshake.

"He went down?"

"Olivia."

"Olivia let you out but then went back?"

"He said if she didn't come back, he'd...he'd..." Riley's voice shook as tears filled his eyes. "He'd kill Mom. She told me to go. To leave her."

Anger burned hot in Gemma's gut. *Didn't trust us not to shoot him through the door, so he sent a disposable child in his place, threatening her mother if she didn't do exactly as he commanded.*

Gemma kept her voice light and hoped the smile she attempted didn't look overly false. "You did exactly right. Your mom and sister will be so glad you're safe. And now we have one less person to rescue and can concentrate on them. And we will, Riley. We'll do everything to get them free. Now, let's get you safe." She looked up, considered the detectives around her, deciding the tall intimidating men would work against her, and mentally apologized to Turner for calculating her gender would be more comforting in Riley's eyes. "Detective Turner, would you mind taking Riley down to the officers?"

The expression in Turner's eyes said she understood Gemma's strategy. She bent slightly and held out a hand to Riley. "Come with me, Riley. Let's get you to where you can wait for your sister and mom." They walked down the sidewalk, staying well to the side nearest the fence, headed for the patrol officers at the intersection.

When they'd moved far enough away that Gemma wouldn't be heard, she activated her mic. "Capello to Cartwright. Riley is on his way with Turner to meet the officers at Commerce and Richards. It would be best if we can get someone in a patrol uniform with no body armor, preferably a female officer, to meet him. He's extremely shaken."

"10-4," replied Cartwright over the radio.

She turned her back to the small child walking away from her and pushed away any residual anger. Emotions like anger and disgust were not allowed free rein during a negotiation, not unless the negotiator wanted to blow the whole thing sky-high. She'd wanted both children free, but if it had to be only one, she was glad he'd sent out the younger of the two.

Leaving a child inside who wasn't much younger than she'd been herself in a very similar situation.

She raised the bullhorn. "Thank you, Paul, for sending out Riley. I thought Olivia was coming as well."

"One is good."

"What do you need to send out Olivia?"

"My money." Paul's tone was flat, unyielding.

"Logan here." His voice slid into her ear. "Asher just closed the window most of the way."

They had a problem, starting with the fact she really didn't like Paul's tone. Gemma powered down the bullhorn and pulled back, activating her throat mic. "Capello to McFarland. When should he expect confirmation of the deposit?"

"Sometime in the past half hour."

They were in trouble. They'd tried to manage this crisis as fast as possible, but they were running out of options.

"Is there any way he could find out the transfer email is fraudulent?"

"Affirmative. If he logs into his crypto exchange, he'll find out they were never contacted about an outgoing transfer. He'll know that not only is it not deposited, it's not coming, period. It bought us time, but we may have just run out."

"Options from TARU or HNT?"

"10-6." *Stand by.*

Two full minutes ticked by. Gemma exchanged a tense look with Sims, whose flat-lipped, hard-eyed expression told her exactly what he thought their chances were at this point.

"McFarland to Capello. We have a few options, but none are good."

"Give them to me."

"Because of the secure nature of cryptocurrency, TARU says their hands are pretty much tied. Their only suggestion is to ditch the crypto payment and tell him we're working with Horner on making a wire transaction, but if he knows anything about wire transactions, he'll know that can be traced through a Federal Reference number and there will likely be limits on the max transfer. HNT suggests bringing in his brother, Sam, to see if he can talk Paul down. He seems to hold him in regard, which might help us." McFarland paused, and Gemma could hear his defeat. "But you know how dicey it can be, bringing in family."

"I do, but we may not have any choice. Start working on those two suggestions, and I'll try to buy us time. Capello out."

She didn't even have time to draw a breath before Cartwright was on the radio. "Cartwright to Units 1 and 5. Move into offensive position."

Johnson didn't look her way, just jogged past her, staying close to the wall, heading back to where he'd been stationed between 26 and 24.

The unsaid message was clear—*prepare for incursion before someone dies.*

She wasn't done trying. She raised the bullhorn. "Paul! Paul, I need to talk to you. We can't sort this out unless you talk to me. We understand you've received word the transaction is in progress. We need to wait for it to go through." *We need to buy time.* "Paul?"

She waited for several tense seconds, but there was no reply.

"I don't like this," she whispered to Sims.

"Ditto."

She let another thirty seconds slip past. "Paul, it's Gemma. You remember what I said? You need to keep talking to me. I'll keep them out as long as we keep talking. Please respond."

"Cartwright to Capello. You have one minute for a response. Otherwise, we're going in."

It didn't make her happy, but they were running out of options. "10-4."

She checked her watch, noting the exact seconds. If she had sixty, she was going to use every one of them. "Paul—"

The dull bang of a door slamming sounded, followed by a muffled scream, a sound of sheer terror shredded with panic.

"Things are going sideways in there." Gemma activated her throat mic. "Capello to Logan. Can you see anything?"

"Nothing." Logan's response came quickly. "They're too far inside the building."

A single gunshot cracked.

"Cartwright to Units 1 and 5, you are cleared for incursion. Cummings, get that door open with the ram."

"I have activity at the rear window on the second floor." Wilson's voice over the radio. "The window is opening. Someone's coming out… No, wait! It's the kid. He's forcing the girl out onto the roof."

An ESU officer ran down the street, headed straight for number 24, carrying the short black battering ram with a wide impact disk on the front and two hinged handles for easy swinging.

Sims, Turner, and Gemma sprinted toward the doorway to GEA Electrical. Johnson, already at the door, waited for the ram.

Cummings pounded up behind them just as Perez joined them from down the street. "Look out!" Bracing himself in front of the door, Cummings swung the heavy rod away and then smashed it into the door directly behind the handle. The door bucked and started to cave at that spot. "Solid locks," Cummings grunted, swinging the ram out and then letting it crash home again. He breached the door on the third hit, the panel slamming against the inside wall, just as three more Unit 5 officers joined them.

Sims went through the door, bellowing, "NYPD! Get your hands in the air!"

Gemma pulled her Glock, only able to hold it in one hand, as she still held the bullhorn. A two-handed grip would be better, but she'd be prepared to drop the bullhorn if she needed both hands. Better to have the bullhorn with her in case she needed to negotiate from the rooftop at a distance. She followed the A-Team officers through the door.

They found themselves in a small reception area, and they moved in farther from there, splitting up to clear the space one room at a time. The high-roofed garage was beside the reception room, containing the navy-blue van that had led them here. They pushed farther into the building, with Johnson, Cummings, and the Unit 5 detectives going through to what looked like a giant storage room. As she followed Sims up a staircase, Gemma caught a glimpse of piled cable reels wound with heavy-gauge wire, coils of metal conduit, scattered tools, drawers of fasteners, and boxes of plugs and light switches.

They pounded to the top of an extended flight of steps, Turner and Perez right behind her. The upper floors were only half the length of the ground floor, and as Sims cut to the right at the upper landing, Gemma found the open window immediately in front of them.

"He's dragging her across the roof," Wilson reported. "Heading southeast toward Columbia Street."

"Wilson, do you have the shot?" Cartwright asked.

"Negative. Terrible angle, and it's behind the tree line for me. With the night vision, they're popping in and out of view through branches."

"Logan?"

"Negative. They're down below the upper roofline from my angle."

Gemma had heard enough. "We need to go after them. We can't leave Olivia out there with him. I need a chance to talk him down."

"Go. I'm right behind you. Perez and Turner, search the rest of the building. Find the mom. Get her out or get her medical help if she needs it." The look on Sims's face said he was focused on the single gunshot. "Call in support if she doesn't."

Gemma set the bullhorn down on the floor, holstered her Glock, braced both hands on the windowsill, and jumped. She wedged her left knee onto the sill, then tipped sideways enough to bring her right boot up and through to push off and hop down.

"Wait for me." Sims passed her the bullhorn and then squeezed his much larger body through the gap with considerably more difficulty.

Gemma flipped down her night-vision goggles, then pulled her Glock again.

The goggles lit up the roof, which would let them travel faster than Paul and Olivia in the dark, but they provided clarity, not magnification, and the two were nowhere in sight.

Sims took the lead, jogging down the roof along the higher wall of 22 Commerce, then paused at the corner of its lower section of roofing. All clear, and they were on the move again.

"Sims and Capello running southeast. Over 22 or 20 Commerce." Sims kept a readout going so other members of the team could follow their progress in the dark and hidden by the bulk of the front sections of the buildings.

A cry came from in front of them, signaling to Gemma it was safe to pour on a little more speed. There remained some distance between them, but they were gaining. Over the combined roof of the lower sections of 22 and 20; then there was a ladder leading them up a level at the next building. Sims cleared them, then she followed.

"We have Katie Slater." Turner's voice this time. "She's unharmed. The gunshot was a blind shot through the door to keep her from following when Asher took Olivia. It came close to hitting her, but luckily missed."

The next few buildings were less deep, with huge old trees in their backyards, their bare branches spreading wide over the rooftops.

"I think I see them," Gemma called between heavy breaths. "They're headed for the end of the block."

The end of the block. Where the tallest building—a five-story redbrick residential structure—was located.

Gemma knew in her gut that was where Paul was headed. To the highest drop in the area. Where he could end it all if he wasn't granted a way out. His last source of leverage.

Safety or death.

And he clearly planned on taking Olivia with him.

CHAPTER 25

LYING FLAT ON THE ROOF, frustration flooded Logan. His role was crucial, could be the linchpin of the operation in some circumstances, but there were times when his position as the team's top sniper left him out of the action.

This felt like one of those times.

His teammates had left their radio mics engaged so they could communicate on the fly. Gemma and Sims were racing over rooftops across from him, but even as they called out their positions on the roof so they could be tracked, they were invisible to Logan. They were simply too far back and possibly down as much as a story behind the front facade of the buildings facing the street.

That didn't mean he couldn't track Asher and Olivia. But this simply wasn't the best spot to do that now.

He flipped the safety on his rifle and jumped to his feet, then pulled down his night-vision goggles. The world opened wide before him, green and softly shimmering.

Time to tackle the roof again. He could track down to the end of the street from his spot on the northmost front corner of the building, but it was the far corner on the front face of the building that would now suit him better based on the suspect's change in position. That new location would present a much wider field of view, as he could shift to the southeast wall of the building, if needed.

Now to get there in one piece.

Logan moved quickly, though not as fast as if he'd entirely thrown caution to the wind and jogged across the roof. Fortunately for him, this time the footing under every step felt firm, and he covered the distance in less than sixty seconds.

Back down, prone on the roof, this time not using the bipod to support the fore-end, but the metal trough that lined the roof, allowing him an easier pivot if he needed to entirely change direction.

He flipped up his night-vision goggles, and one look down the scope told him he needed to go back to regular optics. The light of a single streetlight at the intersection combined with the four or five cruisers parked at that end, all with flashing lights and spotlights, lit up the building, even to roof level, and overpowered the optics.

He keyed his mic. "Logan here. I've changed position, now on the southmost front corner of the warehouse. Better visuals on the southeast corner of the street. Present approximate position of the suspect?"

"Suspect still in front of us heading for the end of the street." Sims's throat mic picked up his heavy respiration as a rasp. "Don't know the exact address, but we're on the roof of a building with big trees behind it. Light roof, skylight near southeast end."

Logan panned down the rooftops with his scope, quickly finding the contrast of two dark figures running over the light roof. Sims was in the lead, both hands holding his rifle angled securely against his chest. Gemma ran behind him with her Glock in her right fist.

He swept the scope farther to the right, over another roof, then over a short wall, to a cluster of patio furniture arranged under a canopy.

All was still.

He swung the scope farther to the right. *Bullseye at about eighty yards.* "I have them. He's forcing Olivia up an emergency ladder, up to the roof of the last building on the block."

"Do you have the shot?" Cartwright demanded.

"Negative. He's forcing her up by being practically on top of her. If I fire, I could hit them both."

"He's cornered, so he's trying to find a way out. He's going to threaten to throw her off the roof," Gemma panted. "He could have left her and gone down one of the trees we just passed. He's intentionally keeping her with him as leverage." She sucked in a breath. "He's going higher to increase the danger to her. Is he still armed?"

"Not that I can see. He needs both hands to climb and to hold on, as she's fighting him."

"He'll still have the gun on him. We have to be careful."

Logan's gut told him Gemma was reading Asher's plan correctly. He followed their movements under the magnified power of his scope, zooming in a bit further as they reached the roof. Asher wasn't a tall man, but he was stocky and solid in his jeans and plaid shirt, and while he appeared to be in his thirties, he already sported a bald spot on the crown of his head. Olivia wore her long brown hair down over her shoulders and had on a rainbow-striped sweater, black leggings, and white sneakers. Neither wore winter garb—testifying to the spur-of-the-moment decision that pushed them out onto the roof—and the girl was visibly shivering. But was that from the cold or terror?

Asher dragged Olivia toward the edge of the building overlooking Commerce Street, an edge that led to a full five-story drop. But the girl was not going willingly, instead trying to dig in with her feet, while struggling to slip from his overpowering grip.

Even at only nine years of age, it was clear this kid had spunk and had made the calculation that if she was about to die—whether she fought him or was tossed off a roof—she'd fight to the end. She might try even harder if she knew help was right behind her.

"Logan to Capello and Sims. She's fighting him. Make sure she knows you're there if you're out of Asher's line of sight."

"Olivia! We're coming! Don't give up!" Gemma must have turned off her mic to avoid blowing out everyone's ears when she yelled loud enough that he could hear her clearly a half block away.

Not daring to take his sights off the man and girl on the roof, Logan wasn't sure how close she and Sims were at this point.

Up on the roof, Asher froze momentarily, recognizing the voice floating up from below, but Olivia took advantage of his momentary distraction to elbow Asher in the face with all her strength. She might have had him, too, but her smaller stature meant she missed hitting him with full force, her elbow only glancing off his jaw.

Still, it snapped his head back, and approval surged through Logan for the gutsy attempt. She had nothing to lose at this point, and Logan couldn't find fault in anyone who went down fighting.

Asher wrapped his arms around the girl and lifted her off her feet, stumbling slightly as Olivia exploded into panicked motion, struggling to free herself. But Asher held on, dropping her feet to the ground and dragging her sideways toward the edge.

"He's moving toward the edge with her," Logan reported. "They're still too close together for me to take a shot."

Pounding feet sounded on the road below combined with yelling from the officers at the corner, forcing back the growing crowd. The crisis had moved closer, and now none of them were safe.

They hadn't anticipated a rooftop chase moving the incident nearly a full block from where it started. They hadn't known they'd need a bigger perimeter. They'd been applying pressure, keeping the cruisers close, a show of force to shut things down quickly, but it had backfired on them. Now they were scrambling to catch up. Even if Asher had only a handgun, he had a 320-degree vantage point on the roof to shoot down into the growing crowd and hit—perhaps kill—someone.

They needed to contain this before anyone in the crowd was hurt. Before Olivia was hurt.

Sims stepped into his field of view as he hit the top of the ladder and moved straight ahead, his rifle fixed on Asher and Olivia. Gemma stepped onto the roof and moved to the right, forming a triangle between herself, Sims, and Asher. She must have holstered her Glock and left the bullhorn behind to make the climb safely and quickly, because the hands she held up on either side of her head were empty.

"Paul, don't do this." She'd activated her throat mic again so the team around her could follow along. They'd only be able to hear her end of the conversation, but it was better than nothing.

Logan could see Asher's lips moving through his scope. Anger twisted his face, his words clearly delivered at a shout.

"That's not true. That's not the point of hostage negotiation. My job is to bring everyone out of the situation safely. *Everyone*. That includes you."

Logan studied Asher's stance. His back was to the edge of the building, about four feet away. He held Olivia in front of him like a human shield, his arms wrapped around her as he hunched slightly over her, keeping his head close to hers. That stance meant that both he and Sims were at the wrong angle to take the shot.

Asher started screaming something at Gemma and Sims.

"And if we do that," Gemma said. "If we put down our weapons, will you release Olivia? Then we can talk."

More words from Asher, more backward movement.

Gemma snapped out both hands. "Fine, fine. We'll do it. Detective… your rifle. Put it down." She pulled her Glock from its holster, keeping it pointed down. She slowly crouched to set it on the roof, then stepped away from it, putting her hands up on either side of her head.

Across the roof, Sims did the same.

Asher said something to Sims, who unsnapped his thigh holster, pulled his Glock, and set it on the roof next to his rifle. Asher waved him backward. Sims took a step. Asher's next words came with more force. Sims stepped back even farther.

Sims was a big man, made bigger by his gear, and Asher was insisting on space between them so he couldn't be suddenly rushed and tackled. Gemma must have felt like less of a threat—female, smaller, still dressed in body armor, but hadn't brought a rifle and wasn't loaded down with extra equipment.

Logan now held the only firearm capable of reaching Asher in a split second if he tried to toss Olivia off the roof.

He'd be ready. He settled into his well-practiced stance—propped on his right elbow, his cheek pressed to the rest on the stock, his left arm folded in front of him, his left fist propping the stock to exactly the right height, his eye comfortably in line with the scope. He dialed up the magnification, bringing Asher and the girl closer, every expression, every twitch crystal clear through the scope's optics. His breathing slowed, his heart rate sinking with it, and he slipped his index finger into the trigger guard, resting his finger pad just barely against it. The M10 had a two-stage trigger, but he wouldn't even breach the first stage until he was truly ready to shoot. For now, he was prepared, but the opportunity wasn't there yet.

Add to that, he'd shot before when Gemma was negotiating face-to-face and it had caused a catastrophic breach between them. He wasn't going to make that mistake again. He trusted her to make the call.

"Logan to Capello. I need a sign from you. You keep both hands in the air, or put both down if he tells you to, but if you drop a single hand, that's my signal you can't reach Asher anymore. If you agree, make a fist with one hand, then release."

Gemma's right hand curled into a fist, then spread wide.

"Message received."

Logan could have sworn Gemma's shoulders relaxed ever so slightly. *She had the same thought and was worried it would be Boyle all over again.*

Never again. They were in lockstep like they hadn't been before. Logan had trusted Kip wouldn't fire on him during the incursion because Gemma had said he'd be safe. She trusted him to wait for her to try to save the hostage taker if she could.

"Paul, the weapons are on the ground." As Gemma talked, she took a small step closer to Asher, closing the distance. "Now let's talk about releasing Olivia." Gemma took another step forward.

Straight into Logan's line of sight. "Logan to Capello. I need you to step a full foot to your left. If you're going to approach Asher, stay in that plane."

Gemma didn't say anything but nonchalantly took a step to her left like she was resettling her weight. After a few more seconds, she did it again.

"Logan to Capello. Perfect. Stay in that line. Do *not* step farther to your right."

Her next step took her even slightly more to the left, relieving a little of Logan's stress. He didn't even want to imagine the nightmare situation where he accidentally shot her when she stepped in front of his speeding bullet.

"Paul, let's talk about Olivia. What do you need to let her go?" A pause. "I'm focused on her because she has nothing to do with this situation. Whatever relationship you had with her father, that's none of her doing. She's a child, trapped in a violent situation because she was in the wrong place at the wrong time."

The wrong place at the wrong time.

It hit home for Logan in that moment that Gemma would have made an instant connection with this child, something the other hostage negotiators might not necessarily have been able to pull off. But not Gemma, the woman who carried the memories of a child who had the misfortune to be standing in a Brooklyn bank when gunmen walked in. She'd only been a year older than Olivia. She knew the terror the girl was feeling right now. Viscerally. That wasn't something you forgot.

He knew in his gut Gemma would be willing to take bigger chances for this child. To not leave her to the fate Gemma herself had only barely avoided. Logan needed to keep that in mind.

Now it wasn't just about protecting Olivia. It was also about protecting Gemma.

Asher glanced over his shoulder, but when he looked back at Gemma, there was an expression of resignation Logan *really* didn't like.

It was the look of a man with no options.

He'd seen the crowd of cops below, seen the throng of rubbernecking onlookers. He was *entertainment*. More than that, he had to realize at that point there was no escape. No fifty million dollars. No guarantee of leaving New York City, of a life of ease and pleasure, of freedom. No dream of never having to work again because he'd finally gotten what he believed he justly deserved.

All that was now gone. And the look in his eye said he was prepared to burn it all down.

If he could see it, so could Gemma.

But she didn't have time to question Asher as he lurched backward toward the edge. Olivia seemed stunned, as if overcome by terror that this was the end, and stumbled along with him.

The rooftop was edged with a short wall—maybe a foot tall from Logan's best estimate at this distance. No real deterrent from tumbling into thin air. It might even be a deadly trip hazard.

Gemma shot her palms forward in unison—she wasn't done yet—as she took another step forward. "Paul, don't do it. You don't want to do this. Think of Sam. Would he want that? Think of Sylvia. You don't want to leave her behind."

Logan had no idea who Sam was, but the name hit home for Asher, his face tightening with grief. He screamed something at Gemma, and while Logan could hear the voice, the words were indistinct.

Goddammit. He wished he could hear the whole conversation. He trusted Gemma, knew she'd give the signal when there were no more options, but being this disconnected didn't sit comfortably with him. He was used to making his own call in a situation like this. He trusted Gemma, but he would have preferred if the decision wasn't mostly in her hands.

"That's not it at all," Gemma pleaded. "Your life has worth; your skills and ingenuity have worth. You don't need to end the life of a child simply so you'll be remembered for something. People love you. Think of your brother. Don't do this to him. Don't do this to Olivia, to her family."

Asher took another step and Olivia snapped out of her daze—possibly prodded by Gemma's words about the end of her life—and started to struggle again, as if recognizing this was her last shot at survival.

This was it. Either Gemma was going to get control of the situation, or it was over.

Logan blew out a slow breath, holding on the end of the exhale, and pulled through the first stage of the trigger, the smooth motion stopping after a fraction of an inch as it hit the "wall," the resistance he met every time, as if the trigger was asking him to make sure it was the correct choice to take the shot.

Death was never the right choice, but sometimes it was the necessary choice.

Through the scope, Asher was nearly at the short wall, Olivia trying to pry his right arm from around her throat; the hold hooked under her chin would be a death sentence if he used it to lever her over the wall. Then it would only be a few short seconds of terror in the air before it all went dark. Forever.

It wasn't the shot he'd prefer—center mass was always better—but only Asher's right shoulder was a clear target as he held Olivia with her head on his left shoulder, her shorter form engulfed from behind by his larger body. A shoulder shot would be enough to disable at the very least. But he was unhappy about how close everyone was positioned on the roof from his perspective—Asher in the middle, Olivia pressed against him to Logan's right, with Gemma to his left. Gemma, who, in an effort to maintain a shot clear for him, was blocking Sims from leaping directly into the fray.

A scream reached his ears, a sound of fear and fury. Olivia making a last stand as best she could, considering her smaller size and strength. Then Asher's roar joined hers as Olivia got enough of her chin behind his forearm to sink her teeth deep into his fleshy forearm.

Asher's surprise had him jerking his arm free, stumbling backward to hit the wall.

Gemma's left hand dropped a fraction of a second before she dove for Olivia's knees.

Logan squeezed the trigger, the rifle's kick punching the recoil pad into his shoulder. A tenth of a second later, the impact from the .308 Winchester spun Asher, his arms snapping wide to windmill, instinctively trying to catch himself as his body was propelled toward the nothingness of space behind him.

Gemma hit Olivia hard, wrapping both arms around the girl's legs, the impact pushing Olivia free of Asher's flailing arms, driving her sideways on the roof, falling just inside the wall and taking Gemma with her.

Asher's scream as he fell five stories to the concrete below cut off abruptly a second and a half later.

Out of the habit of long practice, Logan automatically lifted the bolt handle, snapping it back and then seating the bolt home again after loading a new bullet, hearing the *ping* as the empty cartridge hit the roof to his right. But he already knew he wouldn't need to make a second shot. His shot wouldn't have been fatal. But the impact of the bullet had been enough to drive Asher over the edge. The screams coming from the end of the street confirmed Asher's gruesome ending.

The bodies lying motionless on the roof hollowed out the pit of Logan's stomach. "Logan to Capello. Report."

A low groan sounded, then, "Nice shot, Detective. I'm not sure I could have held on to her if you hadn't offset Paul's balance. He might have taken her with him otherwise. Maybe both of us." Gemma rolled to her back as Sims sprinted over and dropped to his knees beside Olivia, helping her sit up.

The girl buried her face in her hands and, from the jerking of her shoulders, had burst into tears. Gemma sat up and pulled her into her arms, rubbing a hand up and down her back, telling her it was all going to be okay and her mother and brother were safe and waiting for her below.

Logan let himself study them for a minute longer, woman and girl, both physically fine, the overwhelming relief that his precisely placed shot had hit only its target dispelling his body's chill.

It had been entirely too close.

CHAPTER 26

GEMMA SPOTTED LOGAN STRIDING DOWN the street toward where she stood with McFarland, Ramos, and Chen, waiting for the all clear that they were no longer needed. She'd left the tactical gear in the A-Team truck and was now more comfortably wrapped in her long coat with her hair tucked up again.

Logan had disarmed, leaving both his Glock and his rifle in the A-Team truck. He'd likely also had a chat with Cartwright and had his marching orders—an officer-involved shooting required an investigation by the New York State Attorney's Office of Special Investigation. Over the next few days, Logan would be debriefed regarding the incident several times to ensure his actions had been justified. It was an open-and-shut case with multiple witnesses and would clear quickly—still, proper procedure must be followed.

She hoped there was no doubt in Logan's mind he'd had to act. There was no doubt in hers that his precisely placed shot had saved Olivia's life.

Logan had ditched his Kevlar vest and helmet and was now wearing only his ESU uniform and winter gear. His short blond hair was in disarray and damp with sweat after hours under a helmet.

"Logan." McFarland gave him a guy nod of approval. "Nice shot."

"Thanks. Good job of figuring out who he was and his motivation so quickly. Cartwright caught me up on the details."

Logan's clipped initial response told Gemma that even if he felt at peace about his participation in Paul's demise, he didn't want to discuss it. That he changed the subject only substantiated it.

"Credit where credit is due, TARU played a big part in that. They have the chops to be digital bloodhounds. They helped get us here, then helped close it down." He rolled his eyes. "Kershaw will never let me forget it, either. But we had the easy job." His gaze cut to the roof of the warehouse. "How hard was it to get up there?"

"A ladder tried to kill me in two directions and the roof gave way at one point. Other than that, a walk in the park." Logan turned to Gemma. "Did the Slater family get back together?"

Gemma turned and pointed to an ambulance facing the intersection near the end of the street. A woman sat on the back bumper, flanked by her son and daughter, each wrapped in a blanket. A paramedic was wrapping the girl's arm in a white bandage. "I slammed into her hard, and then she was under me when we hit the roof. Skinned her arm pretty good when the sleeve pushed up. Minor abrasions, but I'm glad she's getting medical care."

"How is she otherwise?"

"Shaken. She held when it counted up there but understandably fell apart afterward, which was definitely justified. She's one hell of a gutsy kid. The whole family is amazing, actually. And I heard from Garcia—he thinks Kip will be released in the next day or so without charges considering the circumstances, after they jump through all the official hoops. The family should be together soon."

"I hope they're going to look at family counseling," Ramos said, her eyes fixed on the rear of the ambulance. "They've all experienced a trauma, but if they work on it, they may come out of it as a stronger family unit."

A yell came from the end of the street, drawing Logan's attention. A smaller crowd still remained, pushed back up the opposite cross street. "I assume there was nothing to be done for Asher."

Gemma hadn't gotten close but had taken one quick look from the roof of the building as Sims led Olivia toward the ladder. Paul's body lay sprawled on the concrete below, one leg at an impossible angle, a red halo oozing over the sidewalk around his head. "No." She met his gaze, held it, needing him to hear her. "Your shot didn't kill him."

"Technically, no." His brows drew together. "Is someone calling you?"

"I don't think so—" Gemma cut off as she turned to face the end of the street. A good hundred feet away, she caught dual spotlights, like the kind on a shoulder-mounted camera. Under the camera was a flash of electric blue.

She groaned.

"What?" asked McFarland.

"It's the ABC7 news crew."

McFarland echoed her groan. "Has to be Coulter if your name is being called."

"Must be. I was hoping he was jammed up in Midtown somewhere with the revelers, not listening to his police band radio, looking for the next crisis."

"Everyone is covering New Year's Eve," Chen stated. "He's always on the lookout for something unique on a night like this."

"Of course he would be." Gemma blew out a frustrated breath.

"You can always walk away from him," Logan suggested.

"Yeah." She didn't take her eyes off the end of the street. "But then I have to be prepared for what he reports about me. About us." She looked toward Olivia, now slumped sideways with her mother's arm around her shoulders. "About what happened up there."

"How much do you think Coulter saw?"

"I'm about to find out."

"You sure?" McFarland asked.

"Yeah. After a night like this, I'd be happy to walk away from him, but I want to make sure he doesn't take advantage of Olivia in any way. I'll be right back."

Logan fell into step with her as she started down the street, and she gave him a sideways glance. "You don't have to come along. I know you're not his biggest fan."

"Neither are you."

"Do you want him asking you questions about your role tonight?"

"I didn't say I'd talk to him. I'm just stretching my legs."

"Uh-huh."

As they got closer to the crowd, Gemma confirmed it was Coulter—who could mistake that perfectly styled hair or the shine of his teeth from twenty feet away—and one of his cameramen. She gave him a thumb jerk toward a quieter area up Columbia Street.

"Capello." Coulter's tone was magnanimous, as if she should be lucky he'd tracked her down.

She held up a hand. "Don't. Not tonight. It's been a long night."

"You didn't come here for an interview?"

"Definitely not." She waved a hand toward the cameraman, squinting under the bright lights. "Turn that off."

Coulter studied her with a nonplussed expression for a moment, then turned to his cameraman. "It's okay, Don. Why don't you go wait over there. I'll join you shortly."

The cameraman shrugged and wandered toward the crowd as it started to disperse.

"Why did you come?" Coulter asked. "You'd know I'd want an interview."

"I know. I just wanted to make sure you left the people involved tonight alone."

"You mean the girl on the roof?"

"Especially her."

"It's her I'd really like to interview." Excitement edged Coulter's tone, as if he could already see himself leading the newscast tomorrow with his major scoop. "The hellcat who fought her way off the roof, saving her own life. Everyone would want to hear about how she—"

"*No.*" Gemma's temper rose hot and fast, and she had to battle it down. She would not lose her temper in front of this man. Apparently, their truce hadn't entirely minimized his ability to get under her skin. She took a breath, calmed herself, and changed tack, going for a personal appeal. "Greg, I want you to think about what you just saw. A *child* nearly died. She just survived a horrific experience she may never recover from. She's not your headline. Be kind and leave her in peace. Please."

"You want me to ignore this story?"

"Of course not. It's the news. Reporting the news is what you do. Just think about what the spotlight would mean for her. No peace, no recovery. Don't glorify what happened here tonight."

"Just the facts, ma'am?"

"Yes. The Office of the Deputy Commissioner, Public Information will release the public media points on this case later today. Please don't hound this family."

Coulter's eyes narrowed on her. "Is this personal experience talking?"

Gemma should have known Coulter would make the connection. The loss of her mother and her involvement at a similar age in a hostage situation was certainly no secret. "Maybe."

"Can I talk to you, then?"

"Not tonight." Gemma turned away from him to walk away, Logan following her lead. Then she paused to spin back. "I'll give you one tip, though. Take a long look at Lucas Horner. I'd certainly like to see an exposé on the kind of man who would let others die to protect his obscene wealth."

Coulter's eyebrows winged skyward. "Really?"

"Really. As far as I'm concerned, Horner is fair game. Have at it. But if you write anything about that girl or her family besides the facts, you'll never get another word from me."

A sly smile curved Coulter's lips. "And if I follow your rules?"

Gemma turned and walked away from Coulter. "Call me and we'll discuss."

"Later today?" he called after her.

She threw him the bird over her head and didn't look back, but his rolling laugh followed her.

"A leopard doesn't change his spots," Logan commented casually.

"No kidding." She shrugged. "I shouldn't be surprised." They walked a little farther before she looked up at him. "So…heading home after this?"

"That was the plan since it's well past one in the morning. Unless you have a better offer once we're cleared?"

Gemma halted, grasping his forearm so he stopped with her, then sliding her hand down to intertwine her fingers with his. "Actually, yes, I do."

One eyebrow arched. "Really? What's that?"

"I know we said we'd wait until we both agreed it's time to move forward." She met his gaze. "I'm ready. I think we've done what we wanted to do in waiting." He remained silent for a moment, and unease started to creep up her spine. "Unless you're not. In which case, I can wait."

"Hell no. I was just trying to figure out a way to answer without seeming overly desperate."

That drew a laugh from her. "Desperate?"

"I've been ready for a little while now, but I didn't want to rush you. I wanted to hear you say it."

"I'm saying it. Come home with me tonight."

He grinned. "I'm starved. Got any of those amazing Genovesi cookies at home?"

Gemma's laugh bubbled up, breaking the seriousness of the moment. "You mean my Genovesi Ericine Sicilian cookies?"

"Yeah, those."

"It just so happens I do." She gave him a pointed look. "You know, sometimes I think you're with me just for my baking."

"Definitely not, but it sure sweetens the deal." Logan slipped an arm around her waist and tugged her up against his side. "Let's make sure everything is clear; then let's get the hell out of here. We have somewhere more important to be."

EPILOGUE

GEMMA CLOSED THE DOOR TO her apartment and leaned back against it with a relieved sigh. Home, finally.

What a night.

Time to lift the spirits and bring on the ambiance.

She clapped her hands twice, and the Christmas tree in the corner of her dark living room lit up, its colored lights, shining balls, and bright decorations giving her an instant lift.

Logan was one step in front of her and stopped dead. "You actually installed it?"

Gemma looked over at her tree, picturing the small device plugged into the wall that now powered the lights. It had been a joke gift from Alex at Christmas—a Clapper plug because Alex knew it was the closest his sister would come to a true smart device in her home because of the hacking risk of Internet of Things devices.

"I did. Works pretty well, too. I've turned the tree off from as far away as the kitchen. Little did Alex know it would be such a festive accessory." She unbuttoned her coat and slipped it off, hanging it in the front hall closet, then reached for his jacket. She pulled her clip from her hair, tossed it onto the ladderback chair by the door, and ran a hand through her curls, shaking them down over her shoulders as she let out a deep sigh.

"You okay?"

She looked up to find him standing close, his eyes midnight blue in the low light. "Just glad to finally be home. The bigger question is—are you? We haven't talked about it tonight, but I know it has to be weighing on you." She searched his face for any of the misery she dreaded finding there.

"Actually, not this time."

"Really? I know what taking that kind of action can do to you. To anyone in that position, even if forced into it."

He looked off to the side, blew out a breath, then paused as if considering before meeting her eyes. "I'm really okay. Does it bother me to take a life? Of course. Did I have a choice tonight? No. Would I do it again to save the life of a child? *Yes.* So…I'm okay. Olivia Slater is going to have some healing to do, but she'll have the best of allies in her father, a man who would do anything for her, even risking his life. She'll also have allies in the rest of her family. It's going to take some time, but she'll make it. They'll all make it. And someday, Paul Asher will be a footnote in her life she'll close the book on."

"You know, it might do her some good to meet you someday. The man who saved her life."

His head cocked slightly to one side, his expression reluctantly hopeful. "You think so?"

Gemma knew the work required to come back from tragedy, but family bonds could strengthen, could sustain when you didn't have the wherewithal all on your own. "I do. Sometimes it's good for people to know there are real heroes out there, doing the job that needs doing, even at risk of harm to themselves. She met the monster in person; it would be good to meet the hero of her story. For now, though, she needs the love and support of her family. And has it. *Grazie a Dio.*"

She thought back to the evening, to the negotiation that had started with her questioning her readiness. She'd answered that question definitively tonight. She'd been ready. More than that, *they'd* been ready. "You know, I think we made our case tonight."

"In what way?"

"In showing the powers that be we can successfully work an incident together. If Garcia or Cartwright had any hesitation about us being able to pull it off, I think we convinced them we work even better as a team now. They won't think twice the next time." She ran her hands up his chest, then went up on tiptoe to wrap her arms around his neck. "But let's not think about the next time. Let's think about now. It's our first New Year together. Happy New Year."

The warmth in his eyes flashed over to heat as he moved in closer. "Happy New Year. It's well past midnight, but let's start the year over, you and me. Start it off right."

Then, as he pressed her up against the door, she let him take her under.

ACKNOWLEDGMENTS

The planning of *Countdown* was truly a family affair. I had the concept and setting laid out, but it was a round-robin family discussion that really cemented the idea and proposed the story's major twist. Many thanks to Shane Vandevalk, Jordan Vandevalk, Jess Newton, and Rick Newton for their contributions in bringing *Countdown* to life. Shane, despite your concerns that you make my life more difficult with your tendency to play devil's advocate, it consistently makes the writing stronger. Always a good thing!

Thanks to Shane as well for his continuing advice on weapons, tactical protocols, gun selection, and strategies around night-vision goggles and scopes. You graciously humored me in an hour-long phone call when I was in a time crunch, and made sure I had everything I needed for Kip's personal firearm as well as clarifying the world of dual ticketing to nail down aspects of Asher's modus operandi. As always, you make the story better and more realistic.

Congratulations to Jordan—this time you won the title competition with an excellent suggestion. Let the marital title scorekeeping begin!

Huge thanks to James Abbate for his help on this one. James doesn't just edit but covers every aspect of each book from concept to finishing touches. *Countdown* was no exception, and he had a hand in each stage, helping to make the book shine. As always, James, I'm endlessly appreciative of your flexibility, congeniality, and availability, even if it's in the small hours of the morning. Thank you!

So much appreciation to my critique team of Jess Newton, Rick Newton, Jenny Rarden, and Sharon Taylor for their usual quick and complete edits, with amazing insight into incomplete plot aspects and how to round out the characters for a more robust story. I'm not exaggerating when I say I couldn't do this without you!

My agent, Nicole Resciniti, is always in my corner, working behind the scenes to ensure I can concentrate on my writing while she makes sure the business end of my career runs smoothly. Many thanks to you and the agency for all you do!

And finally, the team at Kensington is one of the best in the business. From cover design to production to publicity and marketing, I'm fortunate for their skilled and enthusiastic assistance. To the Kensington team—Alexandra Nicolajsen, Madeleine Brown, Renee Rocco, Susanna Gruninger, Vida Engstrand, Kait Johnson, Kristin McLaughlin, Andi Paris, and Catherine Kenny—many thanks for helping to make all my books the best they can be!